Shadow Lance: Operation Firelight

Shadow Lance: Operation Firelight

By
Angel Giacomo

**1st Battalion
Publishing**

Copyright ©

First publication in 2025 by 1st Battalion Publishing
1stbattalionpublishing@gmail.com

ISBN 979-8-9874744-6-4

Library of Congress Control Number: 2025914221

Printed in the United States of America

First Edition: 2025

DEDICATION

This book is dedicated to all who have served in every branch of the military. I write it with extreme humility. It is intended to honor the veterans of the United States who have fought in our conflicts—past, present, and future.

"It is not the critic who counts; not the man who points out how the strong man stumbles, or where the doer of deeds could have done them better. The credit belongs to the man who is actually in the arena, whose face is marred by dust and sweat and blood." – President Theodore Roosevelt

"Courage is not having the strength to go on; it is going on when you don't have the strength." – President Theodore Roosevelt

"Whenever you are asked if you can do a job, tell 'em, 'Certainly, I can!' Then get busy and find out how to do it." – President Theodore Roosevelt

"Courage isn't the absence of fear, it's the choice that something else is greater than that fear." – President Theodore Roosevelt

"We can have no '50-50' allegiance in this country. Either a man is an American and nothing else, or he is not an American at all." – President Theodore Roosevelt

ACKNOWLEDGMENT

Thank you to those who believed in me.

A special thank you to:
Dr. Russell W. Ramsey, Lt. Colonel (1935-2023) - U.S. Army (retired) USMA 1957 - 8th Regiment, 1st Cavalry Division – Vietnam – 1965-66. Thank you for being my friend. Hooah! I will miss you always. Go Army! Beat Navy!

Robert A. Soles – Specialist 4th Class, U.S. Army, 14th Inventory Control Company – Vietnam, March 1966-67.

YN2 Paul C. Giacomo (1940-2017), U.S. Navy – U.S.S. Valley Forge (LPH 8) – Vietnam (U.S. Navy - 1959-1970, SSGT, 445th MP Company, Oklahoma National Guard 1976-1992).

CHAPTER 1

0335 Hours
May 8, 1970
Near the Krâchéh Province Border
3 km South of the Snuol Pocket
Eastern Cambodia

The jungle wrapped around him like a living thing—wet, hot, dense, and utterly indifferent to the agony crawling through Colonel Theodore "Teddy" Roosevelt IV's body.

Teddy moved forward inch by inch. Not out of discipline or stealth, but because it was the only speed left to him. His left leg dragged behind him at an awkward angle, jungle boot twisted halfway off, ankle swollen beneath the torn green canvas upper, resembling a rotting melon. Not just a hairline fracture. Broken. A tremendous crack he heard, not just felt, as it snapped through bone and nerves when the blast threw him off the rock ledge, causing him to land wrong with his left leg twisted under him after the first mortar burst.

He could still feel the fiery burn of shrapnel where it had ripped across his left hip. Blood had clotted along his ribs and dried sticky beneath the green-black tiger-striped fabric of his cotton ripstop fatigues. Something hot slammed into his left shoulder during the hasty withdrawal—he hadn't had time to check if it went clean through or a chunk of metal was still buried inside him. Didn't matter. Not now.

In his right hand—his good one—he clutched the remnants of their PRC-77 radio pack. The antenna had snapped off, the housing was cracked, and its ceramic circuit board was half-exposed to the elements. Useless at first glance. But Teddy wasn't a tourist. He'd worked long enough with communication gear as a member of SOG teams to know what mattered. Power, tone, and modulation. The rest was fluff.

He rewired it using a burned capacitor from the PRC-25 radio pack his dead radio man had carried. Half a roll of rigger's tape now held it together. The tape was thin yet strong, designed for splicing and securing ropes, and water-resistant, even maintaining its adhesive properties when wet, a necessity in Vietnam's ever-present humidity. An aluminum radio housing would be a breeze. He'd scavenged a length of wire from a pouch on an AK chest rig worn by a dead NVA soldier, stripped it, looped it over the branch of a tree, and used it as a vertical antenna. Not optimal. But he only needed one transmission. Just one.

The brush around him smelled like wet, decaying vegetation and burnt cordite. The rain hadn't started yet, but the humid jungle air was thick, viscous, almost drinkable. Visibility was limited to no more than ten meters in any direction. The trees here were dense—massive Dipterocarp trunks with moss-covered roots, lush ferns, and thick "wait a minute" vines choking out the light filtering through the dense canopy overhead. The dark undergrowth had closed in tight around him after he'd limped two klicks east from the last overrun position.

That position hadn't even had a name. Just a map grid on the CIA's blackboard and a red circle around it labeled *SHATTERHORN*.

Teddy lay now in a shallow ditch beneath a fallen log, camouflaged by nature and the dead. One of the Montagnards on his team—Chin—had died shielding him from the mortar round. Teddy hadn't moved the body far. He couldn't. But he'd buried Chin's body, dog tags, weapon, and combat gear in a shallow grave and whispered the only words he knew in Jarai—*Nda'k têh*—*Rest in peace* in English.

Now he reached for the small handset—jury-rigged—the cord taped into the mic cable hole of the cracked radio set—and keyed it open to transmit.

"Mayday! Mayday! Mayday! This is Rough Rider One," he said, his voice gravelly over broken glass, speaking between gasps. "Grid sector Bravo Romeo zero-four-zero-seven-niner. Repeat, Bravo Romeo zero-four-zero-seven-niner. One survivor. Friendly. Authentication Whiskey-Foxtrot-Lima-Eight-Zulu. Request immediate extraction, over."

No reply came through the shattered, nearly non-existent speaker. Static whispered back like distant voices in a tin can.

He adjusted the tuning knob to a secondary frequency, his fingers covered in blood and mud, and tried again.

"This is Rough Rider One. Operation Shatterhorn compromised. Confirm last man standing. Zero-four-zero-seven-niner. Request immediate extraction. Over!"

He repeated it twice, then stopped. Breathing hurt. His side throbbed with every shallow breath, ribs bruised or cracked. Pain rippled up his spine every time he shifted his weight on the slick mud. His right jungle boot was soaked with sweat and rancid water. The left leg was a dead weight. He was sure the tibia was snapped—maybe the fibula too, somewhere near the ankle. He'd used two strips of bamboo, a canvas strap ripped off a rucksack, and the remains of an M16 cleaning rod to rig a makeshift splint, but it wasn't holding anymore. The bones ground together when he moved, sending searing pain up into his brain. And he still had to move. To remain still was to die.

A successful extraction meant one thing—survival until the rescue chopper arrived. And that assumed someone was listening and heard his broadcast.

Somewhere high above, he heard the faint rotary whup-whup-whup of helicopter blades moving southward. Fast moving. Maybe Cobras, slicks from the 1st Cav, or maybe one of the few NVA gunships hunting for wounded Americans. That would be a problem if the U.S. Army helicopter had to use a jungle penetrator—a specialized rescue device attached to a cable that safely extracts individuals from dense jungle or hazardous environments. He'd be exposed to enemy fire. And if he fell from a great height, he'd end up a big, dead, messy splat in the muddy jungle. Since this was a covert operation inside a sovereign nation without permission, recovery of his body by the JPRC was slim to none.

Teddy slumped against the fallen log and leaned his head back against it. The dense canopy above was a shadow-soaked mess of green-black leaves and spiderweb-covered branches, sending his imagination into overdrive. Sweat dripped into his eyes, causing them to sting. He blinked away the pain.

And then a tinny voice came over his improvised radio.

"Rough Rider One, this is Outpost Copperhead, say again your position, over."

He jerked the mic up to his lips. "Copperhead, Rough Rider One. Grid Bravo Romeo zero-four-zero-seven-niner. Authentication Whiskey Foxtrot Romeo Eight Zulu. Solo survivor. Need a chopper. Danger close. NVA hunting. I've got less than an hour."

"Copy Rough Rider One. Standby. We're vectoring in a Huey from Firebase Berchtesgaden. Fifteen minutes out. Pop smoke when visual. Green if you're mobile. Yellow if not. Red if under fire."

Teddy closed his eyes, exhaled through gritted teeth, and lowered the handset. His hands trembled from shock—not fear. Blood loss. Too much. Infection was already setting into his wounds in this nasty, germ-filled environment. He'd treated what he could with the last bandage in his field medical kit. Chin had carried two morphine syrettes in his pack. Teddy had used one of them hours ago and rationed the second until now. He reached down, cracked it open, and jammed the needle into his left thigh.

A warm fog started sliding over the pain. Not gone, but distant enough for him to function.

He looked at his broken left leg, now purple and swollen, straining against the boot leather. A lump just above the ankle where the bone pressed against the skin. He wasn't going to walk far.

But maybe he wouldn't have to.

He crawled, inching forward, dragging himself hand over hand to the small clearing fifty yards to the east. The jungle had been blasted open there from an earlier B-52 airstrike—fragments of bodies, blood, gear, weapons, and twisted jungle brush still marked the soil. He dug out the three colored smoke grenades from the pouch he'd stripped from Chin's body—green, yellow, red.

He lined them in a row and waited.

Minutes passed by without a sound other than the small animals and insects in the underbrush. He started to think no one was coming.

Then the feel of the jungle changed.

A low-pitched, rolling thunder spread across the sky. The sharp snap of rotor wash cracking above the trees.

The UH-1 emerged from the canopy like a mythical ghost rising from the ground—olive drab, tail-flag whipping in the wind, its side gunners already locked in with their M60s, sweeping them back and forth, searching for ground targets. The chopper banked once and started its descent.

Teddy grabbed the yellow smoke grenade, pulled the pin, and threw it ten yards in front of him.

The jungle burst into a sulfurous, swirling yellow cloud as the smoke grenade hissed in the underbrush. The Huey circled the clearing, flared, and slammed into a hover.

Teddy lifted his head, grateful to be found.

He'd made it.

Barely.

0408 Hours
May 8, 1970
Extraction Zone
3 km South of Snuol
Eastern Cambodia

The Huey swooped in fast and low, rotor blades cutting through the treetops, the thump-thump-thump of its approach echoing across the jungle floor like distant artillery. Hot wind tore through the clearing, ripping leaves and charred ash from the underbrush, sending yellow smoke churning in violent spirals that clung to the damp air like mustard gas.

Teddy felt the artificial wind blast through the jungle as the rotors screamed overhead, scattering leaves and branches. Dirt peppered his face. He raised his right hand to protect his eyes.

The tail boom swung wide as the helicopter approached at maximum velocity, dropping into the clearing like a rock falling from the sky, the rotor wash kicking up a spray of mud. The door gunners stayed alert, their M60 barrels sweeping the tree line as if expecting the NVA or Viet Cong to emerge from the brush at any moment.

Teddy raised his good hand—just enough for them to see him—and dropped it again. That was all he could manage. His entire body throbbed with the dull ache of shock and morphine. The helicopter banked sharply to starboard and flared, side door already open, the crew chief crouched with an M16 aimed into the tree line.

The skids touched down with a bone-jarring crunch, and two shadows dropped from the door—crewmen in tiger-striped flight suits, goggles, and combat web gear. One of them hit the ground running, already unrolling a nylon collapsible litter from his pack, probably a medic. The other raised a CAR-15 and swept the perimeter in tight arcs, finger steady on the trigger.

"Sir, we've got you," the medic shouted, dropping to one knee beside Teddy.

Teddy didn't answer. He couldn't—his jaw clenched against the fire in his left leg where the bones no longer aligned, just a swollen mess of fractured bone, shredded tissue, and soggy boot leather. The morphine had faded to background noise. His vision pulsed, alternating between white and gray, making everything appear blurry like an out-of-focus camera.

"Jesus," the medic yelled over the rotor wash, eyeing the twisted ankle and the blood-soaked field dressing wrapped high on Teddy's left side. "You're held together by spit and stubborn."

The second man dropped beside him and shoved the litter open.

Teddy didn't resist when they rolled him onto his back. The jolt sent a hot knife of agony straight through his leg, but he gritted his teeth and let them work. The first man checked his wounds in the yellow haze—one to the shoulder, mostly superficial, and another slice along the ribs where shrapnel had peeled his side open like a razor-sharp fruit knife through an orange peel. The real issue was his leg.

"Compound fracture, left tib-fib," the medic shouted. "Litter evac now!"

They pulled him onto the litter and tightened the web straps across his chest and thighs. One of the straps across his ribcage pulled against the wound in his side. He choked back a groan.

All the jostling knocked loose another wave of pain from his shoulder where shrapnel had torn a jagged crescent across the surface. Pain flared white-hot behind his eyes, but he said nothing. Couldn't. Every breath rattled like wet gravel in his lungs.

They lifted him and sprinted across the twenty yards to the Huey. The helicopter never shut down, the rotors spinning at idle. The skids bounced once under their weight, and the deck vibrated beneath the turbine engine's whine as they hauled him inside and clipped the litter to the overhead hooks with practiced speed. One of the gunners gave a thumbs up, and the helicopter lifted off. The pilot took them straight up into the canopy.

Teddy lay flat, staring at the dark green ceiling of the cabin, sweat running into his ears, muffling the constant hammering of the rotors and the rattle of brass in the M60's feed trays.

The medic leaned over and shouted, "We'll get you to Berchtesgaden! Closest firebase with an aid station—hang on!"

Teddy nodded. His mouth was too dry to answer.

Inside the Huey, a roar of noise, oil, sweat, and adrenaline filled the air. The crew chief shouted something he couldn't hear over the blades. The pilot tapped the stick twice, and the bird screeched, nose down, climbing over the jungle canopy.

Teddy's vision blurred as the floor tilted. Blood dripped from the torn fabric of his sleeve, pooling on the deck.

He felt the first stick of an IV slide into his forearm—a large-bore needle hastily taped in place by a trembling hand. Fluid flowed through the tubing into his vein. Lactated Ringer's, if they had it. Saline if they didn't. All standard issue and already warm from the cabin heat. The morphine fog thickened, sending him into a blissful euphoria, making the pain feel distant and unimportant.

The medic—probably trained at a stateside hospital and learning trauma on the fly—checked the flow with a quick glance and moved on to examine the leg. His hands were already covered with dirt and blood.

"Traction's holding," the medic shouted. "No distal pulse. Might be the swelling. We'll get it elevated when we land."

A headset earcup was pressed to Teddy's left ear.

"Colonel Roosevelt," someone said—voice crackling with static. "This is Outpost Copperhead. Hold on tight. ETA six minutes to Firebase Berchtesgaden."

Teddy tried to speak. Nothing came out. He turned his head toward the open door. The jungle slipped past in waves of green shadows and ground fog, trees fading into the darkness where artillery fire had rumbled hours earlier. He blinked twice. That was enough.

The pilot stayed low, flying the Huey nap-of-the-earth, hugging the terrain like a serpent in motion. Teddy could just make out the faint amber flicker of tracers in the distance—another skirmish line, VC, or maybe a Khmer Rouge splinter group taking shots at the chopper. No one cared anymore who the bullets belonged to. They just wanted to avoid them.

CHAPTER 2

0421 Hours
May 8, 1970
Firebase Berchtesgaden
Landing Zone Charlie
Republic of Vietnam

The jungle parted to reveal the smoldering outline of Firebase Berchtesgaden—a hastily built MACV-SOG forward fire base carved into a small ridge east of the Mekong River, less than twenty klicks from the Cambodian border.

The firebase barely earned a name. It was little more than a perimeter of sandbags and concertina wire surrounding artillery pits, radar dishes, green-painted steel CONEX boxes, and a gutted bamboo and thatch hooch used as a Tactical Operations Center (TOC). Claymore warning signs hung from every angle on the wire. A stack of 105mm and 155mm shells leaned precariously against an ammo trailer. Half the firebase was still blacked out to avoid drawing NVA artillery fire. There was no airstrip—just a hard-packed landing zone large enough for two slicks and a hovering Loach. The makeshift LZ had been marked with a white strobe light.

The Huey flared and dropped like a stone, coming in fast to avoid enemy fire, touching down amid a cloud of dust and noise. They hit the ground hard—skids bouncing once before settling. Rotor wash flattened the tall elephant grass surrounding the pad as ground crews rushed forward, ducking low under the slowing blades—already moving before the chopper even stopped vibrating.

A pair of field medics in faded olive-drab jungle fatigues and battered helmets with hanging chinstraps met them at the edge of the LZ. They grabbed the litter, shouted something Teddy didn't catch, and sprinted down the muddy gravel path lined with sandbags toward a Quonset-style green canvas triage tent pitched near the commo shack.

The night sky was still starless and low with broken gray clouds, but the LZ glowed orange from the smoldering fire barrels, flashlights, and generator-powered floodlights. Somewhere behind the wire, an M2 .50 caliber machine gun fired off an automatic burst into the darkness. Nothing was incoming—just nerves, maybe.

"Sir, hang in there—we've got you," one of the medics said, ducking through the canvas flap. "You're at Berchtesgaden. We're going to stabilize you and get you on the next dust off to Tay Ninh or Firebase Buttons."

Inside the tent, the temperature dropped about ten degrees. Not enough to be called cool, but enough to feel like air. It smelled of sweat, bleach, and diesel fuel. Bright floodlights bathed the tent in cold white light. Unfolded cots lined one wall—half were occupied by men moaning beneath silver heat blankets. Blood stained every square inch of the canvas floor.

Two medics dressed in sweat-soaked green t-shirts met them. One was a black man, barrel-chested with a silver cross necklace bouncing on his chest over the outline of his dog tags. The other appeared barely out of high school, peach fuzz instead of stubble on his face.

"Get him on table two!" the black man yelled, waving them to a metal field cot lined with a poncho, a wool blanket, and a thin pillow at one end.

They laid Teddy on the cot, and he saw the light above him—a bare bulb swaying back and forth on a thin wire—then the ceiling blurred into wavy, distorted lines. He couldn't rub his eyes—someone was holding his arm.

"Colonel Roosevelt," the black medic said, moving to his head, "Can you hear me?"

Teddy grunted. His mouth wouldn't form any words to reply.

"Name's Sergeant Pittman. I'm gonna check you over, but I'm not cutting anything until I know you're with me."

Teddy forced out a whisper. "You cut off the boot, you better save it."

Pittman smiled. "Roger that, sir."

Teddy felt them cut away his boot, sock, then the splint. He heard a low whistle from one of the medics.

"Jesus…there's no pulse in his foot. We've got arterial compromise," the young medic exclaimed.

"Get two IVs in—start a bolus of saline," Pittman ordered. "Start a unit of O-neg and Lactated Ringer's, wide open. He's in early shock."

Teddy opened his mouth to speak and vomited the meager contents of his stomach onto his shoulder. Someone cleaned it up before he could feel ashamed.

"We're going to cut those pants off and check that leg, sir," Pittman said. "Don't try to help."

Cold scissors slid under the remaining fabric. Teddy craned his head up to look. His leg was exposed, mottled and purple-black from the ankle up.

The skin was taut, and the foot was pale and pulseless. He dropped his head back to the litter. This wasn't good. A bad feeling grew in his chest.

The next ten minutes blurred together—scissors, gauze, Betadine stinging on raw flesh. They cleaned the wounds with canteen water and saline flushes, redressed the shrapnel tear across his shoulder and hip, and wrapped his ribs with compression bandages.

The leg was worse—deep bruising, swelling, and crepitus when they manipulated the ankle joint.

"Check the dorsalis pedis," someone said.

"No pulse. We're losing that foot," Pittman replied.

"I'm not losing a goddamn thing," Teddy rasped. His voice was shredded, but the medic looked up, surprised to hear anything at all.

"Copy that, Colonel Roosevelt," Pittman said. "Let's fix it. Hang on for a few more minutes."

They set up the traction bar. Teddy felt the weight and tug as they realigned the tibia with a mechanical click, like reloading a broken rifle. He screamed in pain, digging his fingers into the canvas cot.

"We'll hold you here for the dust off to Tay Ninh," Pittman said. "They've got surgical staff and a full evac unit. We're just a patch-up station."

"I've been worse," Teddy muttered.

"Not from where I'm sitting, sir. You're lucky your radio kludge worked. Not many get out of Cambodia alive with half a radio and a broken leg."

Teddy didn't answer. He stared at the ceiling, his heart pounding in his chest, hoping the pain would stop soon.

The door flap opened behind them, and a young second lieutenant stepped inside. He looked out of place—wearing a clean fatigue shirt and trousers, shined boots, and a clipboard with a map attached tucked under his arm. Probably a recent ROTC graduate—new in country and didn't know any better than to broadcast his rank to the enemy.

"Colonel Roosevelt?" the lieutenant asked.

Teddy turned his head to acknowledge the lieutenant's presence.

"We've notified Tay Ninh and confirmed the airlift in thirty. Is there anything you want recorded or logged before transport?"

Teddy stared at him. "Yeah. Operation Shatterhorn was a setup. Black bag operation, no oversight. We were cut loose before we crossed the border. My team was used as bait. I want a recorder when I wake up."

The lieutenant didn't head for the door to follow the order. "That's not really something I can do...sir."

"Then make a note of it in the records!" Teddy ordered. "Because someone higher up in the chain of command is going to pretend they never heard of it."

The tent fell quiet except for the rattle of the IV stand.

"Yes, sir." The lieutenant nodded and backed out.

Pittman leaned over and tightened one of the straps on Teddy's splint. "You're going to sleep now, Colonel Roosevelt."

"No! Gotta stay awake long enough to forget all their names. I can't live with this shit."

"You'll forget the pain before that," Pittman said.

Teddy doubted it.

"And it wasn't a suggestion...sir. You're going to sleep."

Teddy closed his eyes—but not to sleep. Just to wait. Welcome to the part of the war that no one wanted to admit exists.

Then Pittman injected something into Teddy's IV line, and a warm sensation spread up his arm. For a few seconds, he struggled against it, forcing his eyes open and trying to stay awake, but he lost the fight, and the room went black.

CHAPTER 3

0551 Hours
May 8, 1970
45th Surgical Hospital
Tay Ninh
Republic of Vietnam

The UH-1 circled once above the perimeter of Tay Ninh before sharply banking and descending toward the illuminated pad behind the main hospital compound. The sun had not yet risen, but the pre-dawn light revealed the pale gray haze hanging low over the red earth like a ghost refusing to clear the area. The Dângrêk Mountains of Cambodia loomed distant in the west—silent, dark sentinels against the breaking pinkish sky of sunrise.

The pilot eased the helicopter to the ground. Teddy barely registered the touchdown. An improvised field splint kept his leg immobilized, the morphine fading into static, and his blood pressure was low enough that he could feel each heartbeat behind his eyes. The litter rocked as the crew transferred him to a waiting pair of medics in faded green fatigues who moved with practiced efficiency but not panic—experienced hands, Army surgical techs assigned to the nearest Evac Hospital. They spoke without urgency, the way men do when a chaotic situation is normal.

"Roosevelt IV, Theodore. Colonel. 5th Special Forces Group," one of them read from a clipboard as they moved through a long aluminum-sided corridor. "Sustained multiple injuries during a cross-border recon operation. Shrapnel wounds to the left shoulder, lateral torso, and hip, blunt force trauma to the right ribs. Suspected pulmonary contusion. Left leg—open fracture of tibia and fibula with suspected arterial impingement. Last morphine dose," the medic checked his watch, "was one hour ago. He's borderline hypotensive."

The hallway reeked of carbolic acid and diesel fumes coming from the generators. Fluorescent lights hummed overhead. A nurse stepped aside to let them pass, her fatigues streaked with dried blood and her eyes sunken, likely from a long overnight shift. The cot wheels squeaked over the uneven floor as they moved through a set of swinging doors marked—*TRIAGE – S2*.

The trauma area was better lit—four curtained bays, surgical carts lining the walls, and one stainless steel prep table covered in gauze, hemostats, clamps, scalpels, and a well-used suction rig. Above the noise, a portable radio played Nancy Sinatra's *These Boots Are Made for Walkin'*, barely audible over the chatter of medics, techs, and nurses.

A tall, slender doctor in green surgical scrubs and a scrub cap pulled tight over his graying hair stepped into view.

"Get the splint off. What's he got?" the doctor asked, pulling on surgical gloves.

"Left tib-fib open fracture with significant swelling. No distal pulse upon stabilization. Possible arterial compression or possible thrombosis. He's tachycardic and borderline shocky," the medic replied.

The doctor nodded and leaned over the litter, peeling back the dressings from Teddy's leg. "Colonel Roosevelt, I'm Captain Mathers, orthopedic surgeon. You've been through hell, but you're at Tay Ninh now. We're going to get you sorted out."

Teddy didn't respond. He drifted in and out, aware of the voices but unable to follow them with any certainty in a morphine-induced haze. He felt the sting of alcohol wipes, the cool touch of a stethoscope against his chest, then the pressure of a blood pressure cuff squeezing his arm.

Mathers glanced at the readings and nodded. "BP's 88 over 50. He needs blood."

"Already typed and cross-matched for O positive," said a nurse as she hung the first unit of whole blood on an IV pole.

"Good. Let's get him to OR three. We'll clean the leg, reduce the fracture, and check for vascular patency. If we can restore circulation, we save the limb. If not..." He didn't finish the sentence. He didn't need to. Teddy understood what was at stake—whether he kept his leg or faced amputation.

They wheeled Teddy out of the trauma bay and turned down another corridor. A second team joined them—orderlies and techs in clean green surgical scrubs carrying instrument packs. OR three was already prepped with the surgical lights casting harsh reflections off the polished tile floor. A pair of assistants moved like a well-oiled machine, securing the overhead stirrups and loading trays with bone saws, clamps, and external fixation gear.

"Anesthesia's ready to go," one of them said.

"Ketamine protocol. No gas," Mathers ordered. "He's hypovolemic—we're not risking hypotension. 50 mg IV push to start, followed by a drip. Let's keep him light but out."

The anesthesiologist administered the injection.

Teddy felt the burn in his arm, then everything narrowed. For a moment, his mind filled with jungle shadows and the smell of burning bamboo, then everything faded into a pain-free silence.

0703 Hours
May 8, 1970
Operating Room Three
45th Surgical Hospital
Tay Ninh
Republic of Vietnam

The operating theater was illuminated with a harsh white light that washed out the surgical drapes, giving them a sterile blue-gray hue. Captain Mathers stood at the head of the table, gloved hands hovering above the open surgical field of Colonel Roosevelt's lower leg while the suction hissed at the pooled blood and a steady drip of saline from an overhead bag washed the area around the fracture. The smell of antiseptic mixed with the sharp iron scent of exposed tissue. A clatter of instruments echoed as a technician passed a rongeur to him across the sterile field.

The open fracture tore through the skin along the medial line from just above the ankle to the mid-calf, exposing a twisted, displaced tibia and a splintered fibula pointing toward the muscle like a dagger. The bone ends were visible under the surgical light, ragged and gray-white, pushed through bruised muscle and connective tissue already swollen with inflammation. No major bleeding occurred, but the compartment was tight—close to failing.

"Bone's in decent shape, considering," Mathers said, peering into the exposed length of Teddy's left lower leg. "No major comminution. Spiral fracture across both shafts, but we can stabilize it with rods. No exit wound."

Dr. Mathers sliced the skin open from just above the ankle to mid-calf and pinned it back with retractors. Blood welled from the deep tissue as the vascular technician traced the posterior tibial artery with a gloved finger.

Mathers leaned in and motioned with his chin. "We'll start with a full debridement. He's got necrotic margins along the lateral side. Get the bone curette and clean it down to healthy tissue."

The assistant responded by pressing the instrument into the wound and scraping along the damaged edge of the bone. Each pass uncovered new layers of reddish-pink muscle and periosteum, dotted with tiny deposits of dirt and blackened tissue from where Roosevelt had likely dragged himself through the mud for hours before extraction.

"He's been down for a while," the vascular tech, Sergeant Zeigler, said. "There's some hypoperfusion. No pulse distally at triage, but no thrombosis visible on Doppler now. The artery's compressed—kinked, not severed."

Mathers nodded. "Good. Then we have a chance. If we relieve the pressure and restore blood flow, he keeps the leg."

They moved as a team, anticipating each other's needs as Dr. Mathers cut along the fascial planes to relieve the compartment pressure, using spreaders to separate the muscle bundles without damaging the remaining vascular structures. Blood flow gradually returned to the lower leg, confirmed by the appearance of a weak but steady pulse in the posterior tibial artery.

The tech checked it again, lips pressed together, then gave a quiet confirmation. "Pulse is holding."

They flushed the wound with warm saline from a squeeze bulb, suctioning out blood, dirt, and bone fragments.

"Prep the intramedullary nail," Mathers said. "I'm not screwing around with external traction or pins on this one. He's going to evac in a few days, and I want this stabilized before transport."

Another technician handed over the long titanium rod—already pre-sized for Colonel Roosevelt's height of six feet two inches—and Mathers began the reduction. A temporary tourniquet kept the field dry while they realigned the fracture with a pair of orthopedic clamps.

Using fluoroscopy guidance from a ceiling-mounted unit, he aligned the tibial shaft with steady, precise adjustments and advanced the nail through the bone canal in increments. The impact driver was manual, not pneumatic—this wasn't Japan or Germany—but it was effective. Each tap echoed dull and solid in the room.

The fibula was non-weight-bearing and didn't require full fixation. They aligned it by adjusting the foot and ankle into a neutral position, then stabilized both bones with side bracing and a half-cast wrap that would later become a long-leg cast. For now, the main focus was on infection control and vascular salvage.

"Good purchase," Mathers confirmed. "Vascular integrity?"

"Pulse is back. Faint, but steady," Martins said.

"Then we saved his foot. Let's close the fascia with interrupted sutures. He's going to be lucky if he walks straight again."

While the orthopedic team worked, a second surgeon focused on the shrapnel wound across Colonel Roosevelt's shoulder. The laceration extended in a crescent from his upper scapula to the midpoint of his clavicle. Though the bleeding had been slowed at triage, it was deep, barely missing the brachial artery by less than half an inch. The jagged edge of the metal had cut through the muscle layers and embedded itself just beneath the acromion process. The assistant stabilized the shoulder while the surgeon used a pair of Kelly forceps to extract the shrapnel in one slow, steady movement.

"Metal's intact," the assistant said. "No fragmentation."

"Flush it thoroughly," the surgeon replied. "No irrigation shortcuts. I want Betadine and triple saline until the field runs clean. The gash on his ribs and hip is minor. Same procedure. We'll leave them open for now and close them later today."

They worked in silence for several minutes, cleaning the area and packing the wounds with fresh gauze.

There was bruising along the chest wall—deep, visible contusions across the right sixth and seventh ribs—but no flail segment or sign of hemothorax.

Mathers examined the portable X-ray film on the lightboard and verified the findings. "Contusion only. It required no intervention, just wrapping, observation, and continuous pulse oximetry monitoring. Keep him on a monitor post-op. If his O2 level drops or he spikes a fever, chest tube him."

The shoulder wound was closed with layered interrupted sutures. The leg incision was packed with medicated gauze and left open, covered with a sterile wet-to-dry dressing to allow for drainage and inspection within 24 hours. No primary closure was performed on a field wound like this— sepsis was the greater concern now.

Mathers stripped off his gloves, sweat sticking the collar of his scrub top to his neck. He looked down at the unmoving form of Colonel Theodore Roosevelt IV.

"You got lucky, Colonel Roosevelt," he said. "One more hour on the ground and we'd be amputating below the knee."

"He'll be out for hours," Zeigler said. "Do you want to update his chain of command?"

Mathers re-examined the name on the chart. "No. He's got no listed contact. Just a note that he was on detached status from his unit—verbal orders only." He set the chart down and turned away. "That means someone high up doesn't want him found."

1735 Hours
May 8, 1970
Post-Op Recovery Ward
45th Surgical Hospital
Tay Ninh
Republic of Vietnam

Teddy woke up feeling the softness of clean sheets. He was lying on a steel-framed recovery bed wearing a thin hospital gown tied awkwardly around him. An IV line was in one arm, a blood pressure cuff on the other, and a pulse oximeter clipped to his index finger. His leg was elevated in traction, wrapped from the knee to the toes in clean cotton and white bandages with a plastic drainage tube leading out to a small reservoir by the bed.

His left shoulder was wrapped in gauze bandages, and a row of sutures ran along his ribs where the bruising had turned purplish-black. His side ached. His shoulder burned. His leg, well, it was still there. But he was alive.

The recovery room looked more like a wide, semi-cooled barracks than a typical hospital ward, with canvas dividers separating the olive drab cots and screened windows. The walls were constructed from concrete cinder blocks, painted in dull Army sea green, and the smell of antiseptic and floor wax lingered in the humid air like a second skin. Overhead, the rotating fans clicked rhythmically as they moved the sluggish, humid air around. Someone had hung a voluptuous USO pinup girl calendar next to the ice machine.

A nurse—a petite, red-haired woman with wiry arms and the piercing gaze of someone who'd been in country too long—checked his chart and jotted a note on the clipboard at the foot of the bed.

"He's coming around," she whispered to the medic standing nearby.

Teddy blinked. His mouth was dry, and his tongue felt like leather. Every part of his body ached with a kind of clarity he hadn't known was possible. He tried to move but failed, unable to even lift his head.

"Easy," the nurse said, stepping closer. "You're out of surgery. You're safe. Don't try to sit up—your leg's braced, and you have two deep wounds they had to debride thoroughly."

"What's the damage?" he croaked.

She handed him a cup with a bent straw and waited as he took a long sip, then she placed the cup on the bedside table.

"You've got more stitches than a football and an intramedullary rod stabilizing your tibia. Ligaments around your ankle are mostly intact but will need time to heal and months of rehab. Your shoulder was cleaned and closed. You've lost about a unit and a half of blood overall, but we've stabilized you. Your ribs are bruised but not broken. We'll keep you under observation for pulmonary complications," she said.

He nodded. "How many sutures?"

Twenty-eight in the leg, eighteen in the shoulder, ten in your side and hip. You'll see them before we take them out. The surgeon left notes—he was impressed you made it to Firebase Berchtesgaden in that condition.

Teddy leaned his head back on the pillow. "What about the rest of my team?"

"You were the only one they brought in." The nurse paused. "Someone from intelligence is coming by later. Said they want to debrief you."

Teddy didn't respond, looking up at the ceiling as the fans kept spinning endlessly.

Then he made a decision. One that might bury him. "Then start the recorder. There's a story someone needs to hear."

Outside, the world kept moving—the sound of a chopper lifting off from the LZ, the distant automatic crack of an M16 at the perimeter. But here, in the green-painted quiet of the ward, Colonel Theodore Roosevelt IV lay still, surrounded by the sterile scent of survival—and the silence of betrayal not yet spoken aloud.

CHAPTER 4

1905 Hours
May 9, 1970
Post-Op Recovery Room
45th Surgical Hospital
Tay Ninh
Republic of Vietnam

The morphine had worn off just enough for the discomfort to start speaking the language of pain again. Teddy lay in a dim corner of the 45th Surgical Hospital at Tay Ninh, one bed among many in the corrugated steel shelter, warmed by the day's heat and the sour breath of open wounds.

His side was stiff, taped down with gauze covering a deep line of sutures stretching from his hip to the edge of his ribcage. His ankle—what remained of it—was immobilized in thick surgical cotton and pressure bandages. The white sheets beneath him were already stained with blood in four spots due to leakage from the bandages.

Teddy hadn't said much. He didn't feel the need to engage anyone in conversation…yet.

Even the nurses knew better than to stand too close to his bed for very long. He was a senior officer, and something about him—about the way he stared through the slatted air vent when no one spoke—made them move more quietly.

The curtain rustled.

Teddy shifted his gaze but didn't move his body. The man who entered wasn't wearing standard jungle fatigues, a name tape, or insignia to identify his rank or organization. He wore pressed plain olive-green slacks, a simple tan shirt with the sleeves rolled up to his elbows, and a black watch that didn't tick with the second hand frozen in place, which was strange. Why would anyone wear a broken watch? Of course, the man could be a morphine-induced hallucination.

The man pulled the curtain all the way shut and sat in the metal chair next to the bed as if he'd done it many times before.

"You won't be returning stateside," he said, not as a question.

Teddy didn't answer, still wondering if the man was real.

"Your CO thinks you'll be on a C-130 by morning," the man continued. "Orders were cut three hours ago. Stamped and routed through official channels. But you won't be on it."

"Then where am I going?" Teddy asked, his throat sore from the breathing tube during surgery.

"That depends."

"On what?"

"Whether you're done making a difference."

Teddy turned his head, reaching out to touch the chair and feel its warmth. Maybe he was real. "I was told I was being rotated home to recover."

"You were told what someone thought you needed to hear to make it through the night. The truth's much more flexible out here."

"Flexible? How? And who in the hell are you?"

The man's ghoulish smile made the hairs on Teddy's arms stand up. "Nobody. But I work for people who need someone like you. People who don't operate inside MACV, the Army, the CIA, or under Congressional oversight. The kind of people who saw what you did on the Ho Chi Minh Trail. And saw what happened in Cambodia."

Teddy clenched his jaw. "That operation was never approved. That much I know. Even though the orders were signed by a general at the Pentagon."

The man leaned forward, a sickly sweet smile on his lips. "Exactly." He reached into his breast pocket and pulled out a folded manila card. Not paper. Not military issue. He didn't hand it over—just held it up.

On the back was a handwritten string of letters and numbers Teddy didn't recognize—*OP/SEG-9 — VST-714-AZ9/OR5*. Below that, one phrase—*ROUGH RIDER INITIATED*.

Teddy stared at it. "That's not an operational name."

"No. It's a designation...a call sign. You don't get one unless someone upstairs already signed off on it. You're not being invited to join, Colonel Roosevelt. You're being activated."

Teddy closed his eyes for a moment, trying to fight the nausea curling under the pain, threatening to empty his stomach contents all over his unexpected visitor. "Activated for what? Where's the NDA? I didn't sign anything."

"You don't have to. You already said *yes*. You said it when you went into Cambodia without backup or confirmation of the orders. You said it when you extracted through enemy territory, dragging two wounded South Vietnamese soldiers, a half-dead ARVN interpreter, and leaving them behind. You said it when you refused to write your own after-action report because you knew it wouldn't be read anyway."

"Fuck you. How am I supposed to write an after-action report while unconscious during surgery or doped up on morphine?"

"That's your problem. But that is what's been documented in your service record. Refusal to follow the regulations." The man rose from his chair, arrogance extruding from every pore. "You're being moved to a forward compound near Biên Hòa. You'll have a week, maybe two, to finish your recovery. Then we'll start giving you real targets."

"Two weeks? How in the hell do I recover from a broken leg in two weeks? I was told it would take six to eight weeks before I can even start walking without crutches.

"Again, that is your problem. Figure it out."

"And if I say *no*?" Teddy asked, angry at being told to *figure it out*. What did they expect him to do, hop on one leg in the jungle wearing full combat gear?

The man glanced at the curtain. "Then you'll be listed as KIA from complications during surgery. Internal bleeding, maybe. Very tragic. Closed casket. No viewing recommended for your grieving mother, Margaret Roosevelt." He turned back to face Teddy. "But I don't think you'll say *no*. You still believe this war can be won."

Teddy remained still at the mention of his mother's name. He didn't really believe they had any chance of leaving Vietnam with a victory. The politicians in Washington, D.C. would never let them win.

The man paused by the curtain. "You're not alone in that belief, Colonel Roosevelt," he said, as if reading Teddy's thoughts. He left, and the curtain whispered closed behind him. No name. No file. No proof he had ever been there.

Teddy lay back in the dark and stared at the ceiling, the morphine drip ticking in a slow rhythm beside him.

And somewhere deep in his gut, he knew that he'd already said *yes* but hoped he imagined the whole conversation in a drug-induced haze.

2337 Hours
May 9, 1970
Post-Op Recovery Room
45th Surgical Hospital
Tay Ninh
Republic of Vietnam

The morphine drip was still running but at a lower dosage now. The haze had faded enough for his thoughts to sting. Teddy lay there, jaw clenched, staring at the ceiling slats glowing with the reflection of distant parachute flares lighting up the perimeter to guard against enemy infiltration over the wire.

His ribs ached. His ankle throbbed with every heartbeat. And that damned curtain kept rustling every time someone passed by. The noise made it impossible for him to sleep.

He knew the man would come back. Men like that didn't walk away. Not when they had someone like him already on the hook or thought they did.

Sure enough, just after 2330 hours, the curtain parted again. The same man returned wearing the same clothing. A presence Teddy had hoped would leave him alone. Unfortunately, that wish did not come to pass.

Teddy refused to look at him. "I didn't give you an answer."

The man didn't sit this time. He stood beside the cot and looked down at him, using his height to his advantage, like a foot crushing a bug. "Didn't need one. But I respect your reluctance, Colonel Roosevelt. Most good men hesitate when faced with this kind of decision."

"Is that what I am to you? A good man who's too tired to argue?"

"No. You're a man who still thinks the system can fix itself." The man's voice was calm, steady, and convincing. "You're still fighting the war you believed we were sent here to win. That's why you're valuable to us."

"I've seen your kind before," Teddy muttered. "Langley types. CIA. Ghosts in khaki shirts with black hearts and no compassion. Always with a sales pitch. 'The real war's behind the curtain.' Save it for someone who cares."

The man sat in the folding chair, crossing one leg over the other. "What if I told you the curtain fell a long time ago? That what's left is shadows holding up a façade because the alternative is total collapse?"

Teddy looked into his eyes. "Then I'd say maybe that collapse is overdue."

22

The man held up six fingers, his way of rubbing salt into an open wound. "You lost six good men during Operation Shatterhorn. Not because they weren't ready. Not because you weren't a good enough leader. But because someone in a clean office in a nice, safe place made a call based on politics instead of intelligence."

Teddy remained silent and let his unwelcome visitor do all the talking because he needed information.

"You know it wasn't a sanctioned op," the man continued. "The CIA floated that mission to prove a lie. And when it started going sideways, they pulled the ladder from under you and denied there was ever a roof. Your team was bait. The footage they recorded was edited to show a completely different outcome. The aftermath was pinned on a village you didn't even enter."

"I buried my men," Teddy said, his voice hoarse. "I buried them in silence. No one will ever know their sacrifice."

"I know," the man said. "That's why I'm here." He leaned in, not in a threatening manner—just closer. "You believe in the Constitution. So do I. But what happens when the enemy isn't outside the wire anymore, but inside, sleeping beside you? What happens when it's men in your own chain of command who sell out operations and the men conducting them for policy and profit? What happens when the people pulling strings in Saigon or Washington aren't accountable to anyone, and someone needs to stop them?"

"And you're telling me I'd be that someone?"

"No. I'm telling you that without men like you—the ones who still believe in duty—the people who profit from war and bloodshed will win every time. There's a Black Sabbath song that calls them *War Pigs*."

Teddy's fingers twitched on the edge of the sheet. He knew that song and agreed with the lyrics. His ankle throbbed, but the words hit harder than the pain.

"You won't wear a uniform for this," the man continued. "You'll never get a medal—not that you're that type of soldier but exactly the opposite. You hate the accolades. If you're lucky, someone in a room you never see will clear your name after you're dead and inscribe awards on your headstone or carve a star in a wall. But you will save lives. You will stop things no one else even knows are happening. You'll be the reason some kid in a Montagnard village doesn't vanish for body parts." He reached into his shirt pocket and placed a photo on the tray next to Teddy's bed.

A man in South Vietnamese ranger fatigues. Tortured. Mutilated. Hung from a tree. Left as a warning to others near the Laotian border.

"That was one of ours. Interrogated for days," the man said. "They got nothing from him—but they still made an example out of him to discourage others from following in his footsteps. We didn't get to him in time."

Teddy glanced at it then looked away, his tender stomach wanting to give up its contents.

"There are names," the man said. "There are facilities. Targets. You won't be killing civilians. You'll be cleaning up the mess the sanctioned channels ignore as irrelevant."

"And when I get burned? Because it will happen."

"You'll be erased. That's the deal." The visitor stood again. "But at least this time, you'll know why." He turned and paused at the curtain. "Think about it, Colonel Roosevelt. You already know too much to walk away clean. The only way anyone ever leaves covert ops is in a body bag."

The curtain whispered closed. Again.

This time Teddy stared at the photo long after the man had left. He didn't move it out of his view, but he also didn't ask anyone to take it away either. He really hoped this nightmare was just a dream and not reality.

CHAPTER 5

```
0450 Hours
May 10, 1970
Post-Op Recovery Ward
45th Surgical Hospital
Tay Ninh
Republic of Vietnam
```

The ceiling above him was made from repurposed wood planks, painted in faded olive drab, its surface cracked like old tree bark with dark shadows flickering like Halloween ghouls in the twilight mist before sunrise. A single fluorescent light buzzed overhead, its glow dimmed by a folded strip of mosquito netting draped over the cot. The ward smelled of iodine, rubbing alcohol, damp canvas, and sweat—a field hospital's signature blend. Somewhere near the far end of the room, a medic whispered something to a nurse, their voices blending with the rhythmic creaking of steel bedframes as men moved restlessly in pain.

Teddy lay still, cocooned in heat and gauze. The heavy dosage morphine fog had lifted hours earlier, replaced by a throbbing clarity that reminded him of every inch of bone and tendon that had been cut, drilled, or sutured. His left leg was encased in fluffy surgical cotton, wrapped in a pressure bandage extending from mid-thigh to his toes, and propped up on several pillows. An Ace bandage looped around his chest beneath the hospital-issue light blue pajama shirt, and a thick dressing covered the wound in his left shoulder where shrapnel had torn away a hand's width of flesh.

The morphine dulled the pain but couldn't bury it completely. Not with wounds this deep and severe.

He turned his head, looking behind him. A clipboard hung on the wall with his triage sheet attached to it.

Roosevelt IV, Theodore O72684, OR 3 – 8 May 1970 – 0703 HRS – Debridement/ORIF – Tib/Fib Fracture, Lacerations, Compartment Syndrome Evaluation.

Someone had underlined *No nerve damage* in red ink.
Small mercy.

A nurse approached the bed wearing faded OD-green jungle fatigues—a young, blond-haired American with a name tag stitched over her right shirt pocket—*BURNS.*

"You're lucky, Colonel Roosevelt," she said. "Clean tib-fib fracture, no vascular compromise found. The surgeons did a good job saving your leg. You'll be leaving here in a day or two. Transport to the 93rd Evacuation Hospital at Long Binh for additional treatment."

Teddy blinked once. "Am I still in country?" With the cocktail of different drugs coursing through his system, he wasn't sure of anything except being in a hospital. Did a guy really threaten to erase him? Or did he imagine that?

She nodded. "Tay Ninh. It's normal to be disoriented after injuries this severe. You came in on a dust off about forty-eight hours ago. You coded once in pre-op. Lost a liter and a half of blood, but we got you back."

"Shatterhorn?" he murmured.

"I don't know what that is, sir," she replied, shrugging her shoulders. "We don't get briefed on current operations. Just patients."

She checked the IV line, adjusting the drip rate. "Dr. Mathers said you should try sitting up today. It'll help with your circulation and prevent blood clots. You up for it?"

Teddy felt a surge of apprehension as a knot formed in his stomach. Was he? Given the alternative, remaining on his back, bored with nothing to do, he nodded. "Yes."

A few minutes later, she returned, accompanied by a Specialist Fifth Class—mid-twenties, square jaw, broad shoulders, and sunburned skin beneath his fatigues, sleeves rolled above his elbows, and a faded 101st Airborne Screaming Eagle tattoo on his forearm. There had to be a good story behind that particular tattoo. Maybe he lost a bet? He wore the subdued patch of the 44th Medical Brigade on his left shoulder and carried himself like someone who had seen too much war without ever firing a shot.

"Sir," he said, offering a polite nod. "Name's Dempsey. I'll do the heavy lifting, if that's all right."

Teddy didn't respond but glanced at the nurse. She nodded, and Dempsey moved into position.

"On three, we're going to pivot you up slowly," Dempsey said. "No hero shit. If the pain's too much, you tell me."

Teddy grunted. "Been hurt before."

"Not like this," Dempsey whispered, placing his hand behind Teddy's shoulder blades.

They lifted him together—levering him upright, an inch at a time. Muscles screamed along Teddy's side as the pressure shifted off his back and into his core. The pain crested somewhere behind his eyes like a turbulent ocean wave ready to break. His broken ankle pulsed like a heartbeat inside the bandages, hot and wrong, but he didn't cry out. Just clenched his teeth and kept going.

"Easy, sir," Dempsey said. "Just breathe through it."

By the time they had him sitting upright, leaning against the two pillows behind his back, Teddy's sweaty pajama shirt stuck to his chest and shoulders despite the overhead fan. Sweat trickled down his face, and the slight tremor in his fingers revealed his condition, but his breathing remained steady.

"That's good," Burns said, checking his pulse and adjusting the IV tubing. "Color's coming back. You took that like a champ."

"Feels like I got hit by a jeep," Teddy rasped.

"Better than not feeling it at all," she said, offering him a plastic cup with a bent straw. "Dehydration won't help."

He drank the lukewarm water with a metallic aftertaste, but it helped—removing the dry, cotton-like feeling in his mouth. His thoughts grew heavier and harder to follow. Did she increase the morphine again, or was it the strain of sitting up?

"When's my ride?" Teddy asked.

"Tomorrow morning," she said. "C-7 to Long Binh. They'll finish the paperwork there."

Teddy didn't answer, watching the tent wall flutter in the breeze from a nearby fan, the shadows it cast flickering like silhouettes of men moving through jungle brush.

He saw faces that weren't there.

Six men. His men. All dead. He tried to tell himself, *It don't mean nothing.*

It didn't work. The faces remained.

1532 Hours
May 10, 1970
Operations Tent
VIP Quarters
45th Surgical Hospital
Tay Ninh
Republic of Vietnam

The air inside the VIP tent was thick and heavy, filled with the smell of mildewed canvas, rotted jungle stench, and heat. Dust stuck to every surface—the folding table, the cot in the corner, even the worn field maps pinned to the side wall. The fan mounted near the ceiling barely stirred the humid air. The tent flap was tied open, and a breeze carried the distant thump of rotor blades from the nearby flight line. Overhead, the shadows of circling birds flew across the sun-bleached fabric.

Teddy sat in a standard-issue folding metal chair, his injured leg elevated on a plastic milk crate stacked with sandbags and wrapped in a foam pad. The surgical dressing on his shoulder was still fresh, but the pain was manageable—dulled by a morphine drip in his IV, the saline bag hanging from the pole beside him. He wore a loose hospital pajama shirt and fatigue pants with the left leg slit open to accommodate the thick bandages. His boots were gone, one foot bare, the other encased in a brace and surgical padding.

Across the table sat a lean, angular major wearing a starched set of new-looking olive drab ripstop jungle fatigues with his sleeves rolled up to the elbows. Way too neat to spend any time in the field. No name tag was sewn over the right pocket or a unit patch on the left shoulder. Just a plain gold oak leaf on the right collar, crossed infantry rifles on the left, no combat or skill badges, and a clipboard resting on the corner of a Manila folder labeled—*ROOSEVELT IV, THEODORE - O72684*.

The folder was thin.

Too thin.

His U.S. Army service record went back fifteen years, not counting his four years as a cadet at West Point.

"Colonel Roosevelt," the major said, glancing at the top sheet, "I appreciate your willingness to meet with me under less than ideal circumstances. I know you've been through a lot."

Teddy didn't respond. Instead, he studied the man—his haircut, a simple crew cut within current Army regulations, dull and plain, similar to a recruit. He had no visible sidearm on the web belt around his waist,

28

clean, manicured fingernails, and pale, uncalloused hands. The kind of officer who pushed paper instead of leading soldiers. But his combat boots were scuffed at the toes, clearly well-worn and unpolished, and a faint line was visible on his left ring finger where a wedding band had been removed. Not a career soldier. Maybe not even a real soldier. An alias, perhaps? A fake? Someone brought in for top-secret, compartmented work.

"You're not G-2 or CID," Teddy said, running his hand over his head, reminded that he needed a haircut. He'd ask the nurse to send the barber to his bed to trim his hair in his normal high fade.

The major gave a faint, polite smile. "Correct."

"What's your name?"

"Need to know, and you don't have the clearance level. My tasking here is provisional. Temporary attachment through MACV-SOG debrief channels. You're on the books as an over-the-border recovery."

"Over-the-border?" Teddy asked, his voice low. "My team was assigned to Operation Shatterhorn. Grid sector Bravo Romeo zero-four-zero-seven-niner. Covert surveillance of Chinese material and weapons flowing into southern Laos to supply the Pathet Lao."

The major didn't blink. "Your file shows you rotated out of the 5th Group thirty days ago."

"I never left the country."

"Your commanding officer at the 5th believes otherwise."

Teddy shifted in his seat. A sharp twinge shot through his thigh as he moved his left leg. He let it pass before leaning forward, trying to look the man square in the eye. "I was pulled under verbal orders. No papers. No chain of command. Just a name, a date, and a rendezvous at Ben Het with a CIA forward area handler named Paul Hofstetter."

The major wrote nothing on his clipboard, remaining impassive and still, clearly not impressed by Teddy's explanation.

"There is no record of that meeting in either MACV or CIA records," he said. "Hofstetter is not currently attached to any active MACV-SOG unit. His last confirmed assignment was six weeks ago in Cambodia. He has since been declared non-operational."

Non-operational was a polite way of saying missing or dead. Teddy clenched his jaw. "He was my handler and approved the team's insertion. I had six men on that ridge. None of them made it out."

"Do you have the team roster?" the major asked.

"You already know I don't. All copies were sealed at Firebase Ripcord by Hofstetter. I burned my own field notes when the fallback point was compromised. That is standard procedure to prevent them from being used as enemy propaganda."

"Convenient."

"Necessary," Teddy corrected. "Our safehouse near Bavet was stripped clean. Intel told me it was secure. We were compromised within hours. Every move we made was tracked. The fallback position near the Cardamom Mountains was under attack before we even crossed the Sre Ambel River. That's not a coincidence. That's exposure. Someone leaked our position to the NVA and the Royal Cambodian Armed Forces."

The major folded his hands. "Colonel Roosevelt, I am not here to accuse you of anything. I am tasked with collecting a statement from a wounded officer recovered under unclear operational circumstances. But I do need you to understand—no one has confirmed your mission. There are no surviving team members. There are no logs. And the commanding officer of the last unit you were assigned to believes you're back in CONUS."

He sure as hell wasn't in the United States. "What? Then someone made sure it looked that way."

The major tilted his head. "Would you care to speculate who?"

Teddy didn't answer. In truth, he didn't know and could only guess about the person's identity. He glanced toward the open tent flap. Outside, he saw a group of enlisted men walking past, their uniforms dust-covered, rifles slung low. The war dragged on. "Not at this point in time. I want a secure line. I need to speak with Colonel Thomas Fowler at Fort Bragg. He'll know which teams are deployed on the current rotation. I also want the duty roster from Long Thanh North for April."

"I'm not authorized to grant that request."

Teddy slammed his hand on the table. "Then who is?"

The major stood, smoothing the wrinkles out of his pants, a useless gesture in Vietnam. "Colonel Roosevelt, this is just the initial stage of your processing. You'll be medevac'd to Saigon in forty-eight hours. From there, your orders and status will be reevaluated. Until then, you're to remain under observation here at the hospital. Do not attempt to contact external channels through MARS or discuss this with anyone." He reached for the folder and tapped the cover once. "For what it's worth...I believe you," he added almost as an afterthought.

Teddy looked up. "Is that supposed to mean something?"

"It means," the major said, "if you're telling the truth, someone went through a lot of trouble to erase you. That's not typical. It's deliberate. And the kind of people who do that...don't lose track of their targets. I'll arrange for an orderly to return with a wheelchair to take you back to the hospital." He stepped away, leaving the folder on the table.

It was still almost empty.

Teddy leaned back, feeling the pain in his leg intensifying as the numbness from the morphine wore off. Sweat stuck to his skin. He reached out and opened the folder. Inside was a one-page incident summary—partially redacted with some dates missing—all related to Operation Shatterhorn. At the bottom was a single phrase typed in black ink.

Operational recovery pending further assessment. Subject claims assignment under non-verified orders. Recommendation: Hold for reassessment and additional security review.

He closed the file.
Someone had buried him alive.
And he'd just started clawing back to the surface.

1735 Hours
May 10, 1970
Recovery Ward
45th Surgical Hospital
Tay Ninh
Republic of Vietnam

The painted ceiling above him was stained with heat ripples and discolored tape where a sticky fly strip had once hung. The fluorescent lights flickered in irregular intervals, humming just loud enough to irritate the back of his skull. Teddy lay half-reclined on a cot pushed against the far wall of the recovery ward, a khaki privacy curtain half-drawn at his side. He hated playing musical hospital beds.

His chest still burned from the shrapnel they'd extracted from his shoulder. His ankle—encased in surgical cotton and pressure bandages and elevated by folded blankets—throbbed dully beneath the lightest pressure. Stout painkillers, namely morphine, took the edge off, but not the underlying intense pain.

Teddy heard the boots before the voice. Steady, deliberate. A man who didn't rush unless rushing mattered.

"Teddy," the gruff voice said.

He blinked, trying to clear the haze. A familiar silhouette appeared at the edge of the curtain, the sunlight from the ward's single louvered ventilation window slicing across the officer's chest like a half-formed grid.

"Vince," Teddy rasped. "You look like shit."

Lieutenant Colonel Vincent Cross cracked the faintest smile and stepped into view, his pressed khaki summer uniform already damp with sweat under the weight of Tay Ninh's humidity. He tucked his cap under one arm, eyes scanning the array of IV poles, handwritten vitals taped to the bedframe, and the thick bandages encasing Teddy's leg.

"Nice of you to pick a quiet place to nearly get yourself killed...Cambodia of all places," Cross said. "You always did have a flair for understatement." He tapped his lips. "Or is it the overly dramatic?"

"Good to see you too." Teddy laughed, pushing himself up with his good arm to sit straighter. Pain gripped his ribs. He winced and sank back into the pillows.

Cross pulled the one steel folding chair into position beside the bed. "You weren't listed on the rotation. I had to check the casualty manifest by hand to find your name."

"I'm not supposed to be listed anywhere," Teddy said. How did word get out? Was there a leak?

Cross's jaw tightened. He didn't ask why—not yet. "I know. Your CO thinks you rotated back to CONUS. Your name surfaced during a humanitarian reconnaissance operation into Cambodia. But no routing logs. No asset IDs. No evac manifest. No orders on file or a roster. The bandages on your leg are the only real thing I've seen."

Teddy stared at the ventilation window where jungle heat shimmered outside the mesh screen dotted with dead ants and decaying flies. "You're the second person today to tell me I'm not supposed to be in country. The mission wasn't recon."

"I figured that."

"You won't find a name for it anywhere. Burned out of existence and almost took me with it."

Cross leaned forward, elbows resting on his knees. "Do you still have a team?"

Teddy closed his eyes for a moment. "No...they didn't make it out." Those words weighed heavily on his heart.

Silence filled the space between them. Outside, the familiar low thump-thump-thump of Huey rotors circled west, fading toward Cambodia.

Cross stood, straightening his shirt. "They'll transfer you out of here within the next forty-eight hours. Word on the grapevine is Long Binh. A quieter place to recover. Someone made sure your paperwork arrived there before your body."

"Not me," Teddy muttered. "I haven't seen anything official since I got here."

"I know. Neither has anyone else." Cross pulled a cigarette from his breast pocket and placed it, unlit, on the small table next to the cot. "For later…when the nurses aren't looking. I don't know what in the hell's going on, but if you need me…"

Teddy looked at him. "Yeah, I know. You'll be in the wind like the rest of them. Something's not right around here. Don't take any chances."

Cross shook his head. "No. You're one of the few people I still trust. And I remember what you did in Kontum. You saved my life. Don't think I forgot about it." He placed his cap back on his head. "You watch your six, Bull."

Teddy smiled, pointing his finger at his friend. "You too, Iron Vince."

And just like that, the curtain closed on both the visit and possibly their lives if whoever burned him suspected Vince was involved or knew something. Only time would tell if they would make it out of this mess alive.

CHAPTER 6

0819 Hours
May 12, 1970
C-7A Caribou
En route from Tay Ninh to Long Binh
Republic of Vietnam

The C-7A Caribou shuddered as it flew through the morning thermals over III Corps. The noise inside the fuselage was a constant roar from the twin propellers and turboshaft engines—too loud for conversation, which suited Teddy just fine. He sat strapped into a canvas sling seat along the bulkhead with his braced leg elevated on a footlocker padded with his own flak vest.

The rough stitching of the elastic pressure bandages itched beneath his knee, and every bump jarred the fracture deep in the bone, serving as a reminder of just how much of him had been broken into pieces but not buried deep in the Cambodian jungle.

He kept his eyes on the open ramp at the rear of the plane, watching the green smear of jungle and rice paddies far below pass in a blur. Somewhere down there in the vast expanse of jungle lay the bodies of six good men— his men, his friends—left to rot for the buzzards under the dense tree canopy or to be swallowed by the river mud, devoured by bugs and scavengers. Operation Shatterhorn—unsupported, unauthorized, and now effectively disavowed by everyone, including the CIA and Pentagon—the people who signed off on it. Sanctioned it. Ordered him into the Cambodian jungle. Ordered men to die and left them forgotten.

The medical orderly sitting across from him checked his watch and tapped the oxygen regulator mounted on the aircraft's interior frame. The tank wasn't connected to anything, but the man appeared to be going through the motions anyway. Optics, Teddy thought grimly. Nothing in Vietnam was ever what it seemed. Everything was a ruse to fool both allies and enemies.

By 0845, the Caribou banked into a long descending turn over the wide concrete expanse of Cu Chi. The base came into view—corrugated steel Quonset huts, perimeter concertina wire, tall steel radio masts reaching skyward like skeleton fingers. Rows of green-painted warehouses lined the grid-marked roads as a few cranes moved at the logistical docks that served as the staging area for U.S. forces in southern Vietnam.

As the rubber tires screeched on the hot tarmac, Teddy braced for the jolt, his leg flaring red with heat from the sudden impact. The aircraft taxied for a few seconds before coming to a complete stop.

A waiting jeep stood nearby, manned by two MPs and an officer dressed in plain OD-green jungle fatigues with no visible unit insignia or rank. The man stepped forward with a clipboard but didn't salute. Not unusual. Most U.S. soldiers in combat didn't salute. It tipped off the Viet Cong by identifying the officers and senior enlisted soldiers, making them vulnerable to sniper attacks.

"Colonel Roosevelt," he yelled above the whine of the slowing props, "you'll be coming with us."

Teddy reached for the crutches the orderly had secured beneath the seat. They were lightweight aluminum—standard hospital issue—with dull rubber grips worn from use. It took him a while to swing himself down the ramp, keeping his left leg elevated above the ground, every jolt sending a sharp shock up his spine from the still-sensitive fracture. His injured shoulder screamed in protest as he placed his full weight on the crutches, clenching his jaw against the rising wave of pain. He didn't let it show. Weakness in any form in the unknown was the enemy, even when supposedly among friendly allies.

0924 Hours
May 12, 1970
Secure Intelligence Compound
Long Binh
Republic of Vietnam

The compound wasn't listed in the base directory. Located behind a motor pool and next to a communications switchyard, it resembled a standard administration building—flat roof, concrete walls, nothing to set it apart from hundreds of others.

Inside, however, the walls were lined with sandbags, and the hallway was patrolled by uniformed MPs wearing black armbands without shoulder patches or unit insignia. Each door had a simple number stenciled in black paint. No attached name plaques identified who occupied the offices.

Each step felt like a struggle. The hall seemed to stretch longer than it should have, and by the time he reached Room 3 with his armed escort, sweat had begun to collect beneath the collar of Teddy's fatigue shirt. The effort of balancing on one good leg, keeping weight off the other while compensating for the pull in his bandaged shoulder was starting to tire him out. He probably should have stayed in the hospital. Why do this now? Surely it could wait a few days for him to recover from surgery. Why the rush to throw him back into service?

The room contained a standard military metal desk, two chairs, and a wall-mounted oscillating fan stirring the humidity-laden air. A silver thermos and two tin cups sat on the table, already sweating from the temperature difference between the cool water and the warmth of the room. Behind the desk stood a man in his early fifties, an Airborne tab over his MACV shoulder patch and a gold oak leaf on his right collar— Lieutenant Colonel Harry Desmond—according to the clipboard in his hand.

"Colonel Roosevelt," Desmond said, offering him a seat. "I appreciate you making the trip. I understand the medevac was rough on you."

Teddy leaned his crutches against the side of the desk. He steadied himself with his good hand before lowering himself onto the metal folding chair, using the desk for support to avoid jarring his leg extended in front of him. His casted foot thumped once on the floor as he searched for a position that wouldn't light his nerves on fire. There wasn't one. The pain had settled into a dull, pulsing ache, but it was still there—constant and unmistakable. It would keep him alert during the meeting.

"I wasn't given much choice," Teddy said behind a grimace. "It felt like a direct order." And since they already said he refused to follow regulations by not writing an after-action report, which he did at Tay Ninh, why make the situation worse? Who knew if it had even been received by headquarters in Saigon? It could have been thrown in a burn pile. He provided a detailed report on what happened, naming every person involved in the chain of command.

Desmond nodded. "Fair enough. What I'm about to show you is highly classified, well beyond MACV-SOG channels and clearance levels. You're being read into a provisional, compartmentalized operation. Eyes only. This meeting does not appear in any operational record. You will not be listed as being here."

Teddy's expression didn't change. "So we're done pretending."

Desmond placed a thin file on the desk. It bore the marking—*SUBNET-ECHO, ALPHA/BLACK*. The label was a clear indication that it was something beyond the reach of Congressional oversight.

"That's not MACV or anything associated with it," Teddy said. "That's compartmented intelligence beyond my clearance level."

Desmond didn't reply. Instead, he opened the file. "That clearance level is about to change, and your operation designation and assignment along with it. You were pulled from the 5th Special Forces Group under a fabricated operational reallocation. We confirmed the information this morning. Your commanding officer believed you were on a stateside rotation. Your unit file was closed out two weeks before Operation Shatterhorn ever launched, timed to coincide with Nixon's invasion of Cambodia."

"Who authorized the transfer?" Teddy asked.

"We don't know," Desmond replied. "The routing code on your personnel packet dead-ends at a black world facility outside Clark Air Force Base called the Covert Operations Directorate. Anything beyond that is need-to-know."

He pulled a page from the folder and slid it across the table. Teddy looked down at a single word printed across the top in red—*LEGACY.*

"I'm not activated," Teddy said after a long pause.

"No. You're not. Yet."

"Then why show me this?"

Desmond leaned across the desk. "Because someone who's been burned at the highest intelligence levels shouldn't have survived. Someone tried to erase you, Colonel Roosevelt. Not kill you in the field, but completely erase you from existence. That means one of two things. Either you stumbled onto something you weren't supposed to see…or you're part of something that isn't supposed to exist."

Teddy looked down again at the word—*LEGACY.* It wasn't a protocol he recognized, but he'd heard rumors—nothing concrete or verifiable, nothing actionable. Just a phrase slipped across poker tables in Saigon safehouses or in code between CIA and SOG handlers—*delta-one-niner-black.*

"The Legacy Protocol is a top-layer recovery framework," Desmond said. "If triggered, it overrides all active chains of command and initiates what we call Directive Seven-Two. That's not something I'm authorized to brief you on...yet. That time may come soon. But I'll tell you this—once you're on that list, you're either the last line of defense…or the evidence someone needs destroyed."

Teddy leaned back in his chair. The pain in his leg flared up again, but he pushed through it. He needed clarity, not more morphine to dull his reactions. "And you brought me here to do what—warn me?"

Desmond shook his head. "No, Colonel Roosevelt. I brought you here because someone above both our pay grades wants you reassigned to something so secret that only a select few have the clearance level to know the full details of the missions. No paperwork. No files. No oversight. You'll receive target packages and mission parameters verbally through cutouts. You'll report to no one and expect no backup. Your existence from this point forward will be need-to-know. And most people, including the Pentagon, Congress, and even the President at times, don't need to know."

Teddy didn't blink. "And if I say *no?*"

Desmond didn't move except for raising a single eyebrow. "Then I have orders to put you on a transport back to the States. But I'd advise against that. Because the people who buried you once? They don't like unfinished business. And you being alive and talking is unfinished business. It's unlikely you'd survive the trip."

Teddy closed the folder and pushed it aside. "So what's the job?"

Desmond smiled. "Asset retrieval and termination of those deemed a threat to national security when needed, outside conventional jurisdiction. There's a team being formed. You'll pick your own people. We'll give you names as informed suggestions. Start with this one—Captain Jack Stratton. Intelligence officer. Currently assigned as a MACV-SOG liaison officer. Speaks five languages fluently. Already in theater. Trained by East German defectors in the art of blending into the environment and noticing what others don't. The man is a ghost when released into a populated setting. He gathers intel and no one even notices, even in East Berlin under the strict watchfulness of the Stasi, where he slips in and out like smoke."

Teddy gave a slow nod. "Who else?"

Desmond stood, smoothing out the wrinkles in his pants. "You'll meet him soon. But be ready. There's a mission brewing—something about arms trafficking by the Chinese along the Cambodian border. We'll be in touch." He opened the door without saluting. "Rest while you can, Colonel Roosevelt. Your war's just getting started."

CHAPTER 7

1425 Hours
May 12, 1970
MACV Liaison Compound
Long Binh
Republic of Vietnam

The corner-mounted oscillating fan did nothing except move hot, humid air from one corner of the room to another. It clacked in a tired metallic rhythm that matched the ache in Teddy's ankle every time he shifted his weight. He stood in the doorway of the makeshift MACV liaison office, leaning heavily on a pair of dull aluminum crutches. The flight from Tay Ninh had been rough—a C-7 Caribou with failing hydraulics—and the landing hadn't done his contused ribcage any favors.

The room was plain—sandbags lined the walls, and blackout curtains covered the windows, shielding the space from both sunlight and wandering eyes. Two desks sat in the center—green metal, dented, typical government issue. One was empty with the chair pushed in under the desk. The other had a man sitting behind it.

The man didn't look up at first, flipping through a dog-eared file folder as his eyes darted back and forth across the pages. He was lean, probably in his late twenties, with blue eyes, dark blond hair a little too long for regulation, and a quiet stillness about him that didn't match the worn intensity of the compound. He wore no rank or branch insignia—just jungle fatigues and a red, gold, and white MACV patch stitched to the left shoulder. No sidearm. No jungle boots. Just rubber sandals, a sharpened pencil behind one ear, and an M1911A1 Colt .45 caliber pistol field-stripped on the desk in front of him next to an open Vietnamese phrasebook.

"You Roosevelt?" he asked without looking up, setting the folder aside and meticulously wiping the pistol barrel clean with a rag.

Teddy took one slow crutch-length forward and nodded. "Colonel Theodore Roosevelt IV."

That caught the man's attention. He looked up, set the barrel on the desk, his eyes sharp, intelligent, and assessing. Not the type of man who overlooks details.

"Captain Jack Stratton," he said, standing now and offering a hand. "MACV liaison officer for off-book asset reassignment, or whatever they're calling it this week."

Teddy shook his hand. Firm grip. Dry palm. The man didn't flinch at the bandages, the crutches, or the shadowed pain lines under Teddy's eyes.

"Let me guess," Teddy said. "You're the one they send when they don't want things written down."

Stratton smiled. "Only when they want it remembered correctly. I have an eidetic memory. Call it an occupational necessity." He gestured at a folding chair. "Sit. Please. Carefully."

Teddy lowered himself, fighting back a wince as he hand-levered his bandaged leg onto a second chair, grateful for the support as he settled into a more comfortable position.

"I've read your service jacket," Stratton said, moving behind the desk again. "West Point graduate. Fourth-generation soldier. Four combat tours. Numerous awards for bravery. Related to President Teddy Roosevelt. Fifth Group battalion commander. And now Cambodia."

"Operation Shatterhorn," Teddy said.

Stratton nodded, his face unreadable. "Not in the file. Not officially. Only what I heard through the grapevine."

"Nothing about the six men who didn't make it out?"

"Not even your dust off shows up in the movement logs. All the radar recordings of that area during the specified timeframe have been erased."

Teddy clenched his jaw. "So what am I doing here, Captain Stratton?"

Stratton picked up a new folder—this one slimmer—and slid it across the desk. "The people who sent you into Cambodia without orders are afraid you're still breathing. That makes you inconvenient and expendable. But someone higher up in the chain of command—someone with influence and a lot of clout in Washington—filed a verbal override on your transfer back home. You're being reassigned."

"Covert operations?"

"No official designation yet. No record. Not affiliated with MACV or the CIA. You'll report to a cell structure known only to six people in this theater called the Covert Operations Directorate. No flag or banner. No command-level staff officers. Just names and targets."

Teddy opened the folder. Inside, there were three sheets of paper—a map of Laos, a heavily redacted operational order marked *Firelight*, and a photo of a burned-out village. The faces in the image had been blacked out with ink.

"You'll be the point man for a team they're calling Shadow Lance. It's not official. Hell, it's not even acknowledged by anyone in the Pentagon. You'll recruit, manage, and carry out the missions—surveillance, interdiction, asset recovery, and intelligence gathering. In and out without leaving a trace." Stratton smiled. "Only whispers and shadows in the dark."

Teddy didn't speak, continuing to look at the photo. Something about it set his nerves and instincts on edge.

"They say you're great at working without a net—that you don't ask too many questions," Stratton said.

"Who are *they*?"

Stratton's stone-faced expression flickered just a little. "Major General Dorsey, head of Strategic Planning at the DIA, signed off on recruiting you. He oversees the Covert Operations Directorate. But you didn't hear that from me."

Teddy looked up. "Why you?"

"Because I speak five languages—German, Russian, Vietnamese, Spanish, and English," Stratton said. "And I've been behind the lines more than most of the CIA spooks they send out to pull triggers. And because when someone disappears in this country, I'm usually the one who knows why." He leaned forward. "You're not crazy, Colonel Roosevelt. You were burned—big time. I don't know why. I don't know who gave the original order. But I do know this—someone's trying to rewrite your history. And if you don't play this right and by the numbers, you're going to vanish one day, and no one's going to ask why. Your family will get a Western Union telegram delivered by a cab driver stating that you're missing in action."

Teddy scratched his chin. "That sounds like a threat."

"That sounds like Long Binh, one of the worst desk duty stations in this rotten ass country," Stratton replied. "Which is why we are here."

Teddy looked back down at the file. "When do I meet the rest of the team?"

"Soon," Stratton said. "But first, you and I need to spend some time rebuilding your cover. Shadow Lance doesn't exist yet. That means no one can screw it up—unless we do."

Teddy nodded. "Then let's get to work. Hooah!"

CHAPTER 8

0930 Hours
May 14, 1970
Provisional Staging Compound
5th Special Forces Detachment (ODA-332)
East of Biên Hòa
Republic of Vietnam

The morning haze hadn't yet burned off the treetops when the mud-splattered, olive-drab deuce-and-a-half truck rolled through the wooden gate wrapped in concertina wire. Dust trailed behind it like smoke from a battlefield, settling over the gravel motor pool and groups of green canvas general-purpose tents that formed the provisional compound. It wasn't marked as a firebase or a MACV post—just another unnamed Special Forces detachment camp hidden in the jungle east of Biên Hòa where records didn't matter and missions left no paperwork trail.

The heat arrived early, steaming off the jungle floor and turning the canvas tent flaps into damp curtains of sweat. From a shaded spot under the awning of the temporary command tent, Teddy sat with his injured leg elevated on an overturned ammo crate, a folded wool blanket cushioning the sharp edges beneath the new fiberglass cast—it was more water-resistant than plaster and wouldn't fall apart in the nearly drinkable humidity. The swelling in his ankle had decreased, the stitches had been removed, but the break was still fresh, and the pain manageable only when he stayed off it.

The dressings under his fatigues were clean, and the pain kept mostly at bay thanks to a cocktail of aspirin and grit. His crutches leaned against the wall beside him, but he didn't bother reaching for them now. Even short distances felt like punishment. His ribs ached with each breath, and the muscles in his left shoulder burned whenever he shifted his weight too far to one side. He'd rather nurse a mug of hot, thick instant black coffee—compliments of Jack and a package of *Coffee Instant Type II* from a box of C-rats.

Jack Stratton stood nearby, arms crossed over his chest, his eyes fixed on the cloud of dust rising from the road and the approaching deuce-and-a-half, engine downshifting with a screeching mechanical groan as it slowed near the motor pool.

"Is that him?" Teddy asked, squinting into the sun. "Is Sergeant Red Horse on that truck?"

"Yeah," Jack said. "Straight from the Iron Triangle. His team was ambushed outside Katum in the Central Highlands. He's one of three men who made it back. Officially, he's an engineer assigned to a transport unit, but his team needed to…ahh…remove a few obstacles."

Teddy chuckled. "You mean blow something up."

The tailgate dropped, clanging against the stops. A few battered men climbed out—lean, silent, and eyes hollow with exhaustion. Then came the last man, taller than the rest, his broad frame filling the space like a carved granite statue. He didn't rush, didn't limp—just moved with heavy purpose, his filthy rucksack and M16 slung over one shoulder, as if nothing on Earth could shake him.

He was tall—at least six four—weighing 250 pounds—with broad shoulders filling out sweat-darkened, dirty, blood-stained green ripstop jungle fatigues. His black hair was cut short in a military style, and his expression was unreadable. A long scar ran just below his left cheekbone, barely noticeable against the dark coppery tone of his skin.

"Eli Red Horse," Jack said. "Member of the Oglala Lakota Sioux tribe. Born on the Pine Ridge Reservation in South Dakota. Master Sergeant, specializing in demolitions, engineering, hand-to-hand combat, and heavy weapons. He even taught at the Special Warfare School for a while. They call him 'Stone.'"

"Why?" Teddy raised an eyebrow. "Because he doesn't talk?"

"No," Jack said. "Because when everything else falls apart, he doesn't. And he's impossible to move once he sets his feet. Think of an immovable object from physics."

Teddy studied the man as he paused to survey the compound's layout—not as a visitor but as someone analyzing cover positions, fields of fire, exits, and gun emplacements. The look of a consummate seasoned professional—a Special Forces soldier.

"He doesn't look like he missed a beat," Teddy said.

"He didn't," Jack replied. "Carried two wounded teammates a klick to the LZ while laying down suppressive fire with his M16. Then radioed their dust off and refused medical treatment until they were clear."

"Sounds like a brave man." Teddy reached for the crutches, dragging them to an upright position. He stood, relying on his right leg while his left one rested behind him, raised just enough to avoid putting pressure on the break.

"I'll stay here," Teddy said through clenched teeth. "Let's not put on a comedy show for everyone in the compound when I fall on my ass."

"That's for the best." Jack headed out to intercept the new arrival. "Master Sergeant Red Horse!"

The man paused and turned around, snapping to attention. "Sir."

Jack gave a quick nod. "I'm Captain Stratton. You're being reassigned."

"I wasn't told," Red Horse said.

"You weren't supposed to be. Classified. Come with me." Jack led him to the shaded awning where Teddy waited. Red Horse's eyes landed on the cast, the crutches, and the sweat beading on Teddy's forehead. He didn't ask any questions and stood with his hands behind his back at parade rest.

"I'm Colonel Theodore Roosevelt IV," Teddy said. "You've already met Captain Stratton."

Red Horse nodded. "Yes, sir. I've heard of you. They call you Bull Moose or Rough Rider. And Captain Stratton. They call him Ghost. You two are legends around here."

"I don't feel like a legend, more like a failure. My last team was killed in Cambodia two weeks ago."

"Mine was at Tay Ninh. Then you know the weight that I carry inside."

"I do." Teddy kept his eyes on them. "Are you ready to go off the books? Make a difference in this war?"

"Is that where we are now? Will they let us?"

Teddy smiled. Red Horse had good instincts. "Getting there. I'm forming a new team. Are you interested?"

"This will be covert ops. No written or recorded records. No chain of command or oversight. No guaranteed safe return for either us or our bodies," Jack said, drawing his thumb across his throat.

Red Horse looked between them. "What's the mission?"

"Classified. Not here. Too many unwanted ears. Our duties would include surveillance, interdiction, asset recovery, and intelligence gathering," Jack said. "You'll be fully briefed once we're in place, completely vetted, and in a secure location."

Silence settled between them.

Red Horse's eyes scanned the compound again before turning back to Teddy. "I'll need access to my demolition kit. And a forge."

Teddy raised an eyebrow. "Forge?"

"Yes. A portable field forge used by engineers that runs on propane or kerosene."

"Why?"

"To reshape charges. Humidity at this level and wild temperature fluctuations affect detonation patterns."

Jack looked at Teddy. "Told you. He's good."

Teddy extended his hand. "Welcome to Shadow Lance."

Red Horse grasped it without hesitation. His grip was calloused, firm, and bone-breaking.

"No turning back," Teddy added.

"I never turn back," Red Horse said. "I charge forward. Hooah!"

Teddy smiled. "Perfect. You'll fit right in." Just like him. One reason his superiors called him "Bull Moose" was because of how he fearlessly charged into battle—an homage to his great-uncle and his political party—President Theodore Roosevelt. The same goes for his call sign—Rough Rider—named after the 1st United States Volunteer Cavalry and their charge up San Juan Hill in 1898, led by his great-uncle, then Colonel Theodore Roosevelt.

CHAPTER 9

1510 Hours
May 15, 1970
MACV Staging Area/Officers' Quarters
East of Biên Hòa
Republic of Vietnam

The flimsy walls of the prefab building still smelled of plywood and insect repellent. Teddy shifted on the cot with a muffled grunt, placing his hands on the metal frame as he swung his casted leg over the edge. The makeshift quarters offered no ventilation except for the open louvered aluminum slats over the door as the jungle heat seeped in from all sides. Sweat clung to his green t-shirt like a second skin, the back soaked through to the dingy sheets hours earlier.

His ankle throbbed with a steady pulse—duller now, but still present. The wound in his left shoulder was healing more slowly, probably due to overuse. The doctor at the evac hospital did a good job, stitching the wound closed deep into the muscle wall. His only saving grace this far into the bush was that it stayed clean, thanks to diligent care from a local medic whose English didn't extend far beyond "Don't move."

He hadn't.

Much.

The crutches leaned against the wall within arm's reach but never close enough to feel like an invitation. He'd tried them yesterday. Once. It took every ounce of willpower to cross the narrow room without collapsing. He hadn't fallen. But it had been close.

He was out of the field hospital. But still healing. Still aching. Still not whole. That wouldn't happen for a while. A month, if he was lucky. Maybe two.

Outside, the compound barely stirred with signs of life—muffled voices, a radio broadcasting something half static from Armed Forces Radio Vietnam, and the distant clatter of a weapons check. No flags, marked uniforms, or signs were visible anywhere. This place didn't officially exist. Not in the Army or the CIA. But fully funded and stocked with weapons, food, and weekly supplies, it had to be in the records—somewhere.

A pitcher of tepid water sat on a wooden table next to an untouched box of C-rats labeled Beefsteak, Canned. While better than Ham and Motherfuckers, a disgusting mess even the VC wouldn't touch, he passed on the canned, flavorless fat glob and salty gravy. Instead, he reached for the canteen, lifting it to his lips with a slow, cautious breath for a drink of water. His ribs ached with the movement, but he ignored the pain.

Then he heard footsteps. Boots. Lighter in impact. More casual than regular soldiers.

Someone knocked once on the metal doorframe of his quarters.

Teddy lowered the canteen, wiping his lips dry with the back of his hand. "It's open."

The door eased inward.

Captain Jack Stratton was the first to enter—deeply tanned like a movie star, sharp-eyed and alert even while pretending to relax. He'd rolled the sleeves of his unmarked tiger-striped fatigues up to his elbows. His shirt hung open, revealing his muscular, sweaty, and somewhat hairy chest, and his jungle boots were covered with red dirt. "Afternoon, sir."

Behind him, Master Sergeant Eli Red Horse followed—bigger, quieter, with an unreadable expression behind dark eyes and a stillness that seemed carved from stone. He offered no greeting at all, just a respectful nod.

Teddy exhaled. "You're overdue and still alive. That's something. I was expecting bad news when you didn't check in on schedule."

Jack smirked. "Well, you gave us the boring part. Infiltrate the NVA supply depot, eyeball some troop movements, and report back. I thought we were here to make history."

"Maybe just history that doesn't involve body bags and family notification letters," Teddy said. He had too many recent deaths weighing on his conscience. "Sitrep."

Jack moved closer and placed a folder on the table. "Recon photos. Scribbled some notes. I can translate the field chatter, but most of it was routine—check-ins, patrol schedules, supply requests, and maintenance updates. No signs of any movement west of the ravine."

"And the NVA?"

"Mostly shuffling their assets further north. Moving artillery to the ridge. Pulling back their patrols but setting tripwires and booby traps as if expecting company. Nothing obvious. Pretty much standard stuff."

"The villagers are quiet. Too quiet. Something's wrong," Eli said, unslinging his M16 rifle.

Teddy absorbed the information, nodding. "Something always is."

A beat passed.

Jack pointed at the cast. "How's the leg?"

"Hurts, but it's still attached."

"That bad, huh?"

Teddy didn't answer right away. "It's coming along. I'll be on my feet again…soon." *Maybe in a month or two.*

Jack leaned against the table. "We're not going anywhere without you. You know that."

Eli, still standing just inside the door, nodded once. "Agreed."

Teddy looked into their eyes. "Thank you. You two were dragged into this mess, just like me."

"Maybe," Jack said. "But we chose to stay. That's the difference."

"You already knew about this kind of work, right?"

Jack gave a lopsided half smile. "Let's just say the CIA doesn't always knock when they want someone to disappear into Laos or some other country with a forged passport and a bad accent. I've been off the books longer than I've been on them."

"And you, Sergeant Red Horse?"

"I go where I'm needed," Eli said. "Always have. Always will."

Teddy picked up a pencil from the table to jot down a few notes for his weekly activity report. "Well. Looks like we're building something here whether we meant to or not."

Jack's smile grew wider. "Shadow Lance, huh? Sounds like the first edition of one of those dime-store war comics I loved as a kid."

"It wasn't my idea," Teddy said, stroking his chin. "But you're right, it does."

"It might not be your idea, sir, but it will be your legacy. That's the thing about shadows, Colonel Roosevelt. Sometimes they're all that's left when the light burns out."

Teddy leaned back on the cot's thin mattress, letting the words settle into the silence. For the first time since Operation Shatterhorn, the pain in his side, shoulder, and leg felt a little farther away.

He wasn't healed.

But he wasn't alone. Now he had two men he trusted standing beside him. Men he could call *friends.*

0740 Hours
May 18, 1970
MACV Staging Compound
East of Biên Hòa
Republic of Vietnam

The compound was quiet in the mornings just after mess call before the Hueys scattered red dust across the makeshift landing pad and the engineers started hammering down new pier sections on the east side of the canal.

Teddy sat in the shade of the communication tent's side awning with his crutches lying across a folding table next to a stack of field reports. His left ankle, still protected by a somewhat soft fiberglass cast, rested on an ammo crate labeled *FRAG*. The throbbing had decreased to a dull ache when he avoided putting weight on it. The ribs, however, healed much slower. He still took shallow, slow breaths, each exhale feeling like a struggle against the moisture-heavy air.

But he hated being grounded. Hated the inactivity. He would rather be out in the field with his new team, Captain Jack Stratton and Master Sergeant Eli Red Horse. He'd only known both of them for less than a week, but they had great chemistry together, much more than even his previous teams, including both SOG and the Special Forces. They gelled almost instantly, knowing each other's thoughts before they were spoken aloud.

From where he sat, he could see the perimeter trench line and the heat shimmer beginning to rise off the inch-thick steel plates shielding the west-facing watchtower.

Heavy footsteps approached him. He didn't look up—he knew the cadence.

Jack Stratton and Eli Red Horse entered the camp through the opening in the concertina wire—sweaty, exhausted, their faces and ripstop tiger-striped fatigues covered in dirt and grime. Both had efficiently slung their gear—clean weapons, mud-caked jungle boots, and, as experienced soldiers, pack straps adjusted mid-mission to evenly distribute the weight of their gear.

Jack removed his PRC-6 Radio Receiver Transmitter strap from his shoulder, the U.S. Army's version of a 5.5-pound "walkie talkie," and hung it on the rearview mirror of a nearby jeep then nodded at Teddy. "We were three klicks into Zone Echo-Five. No movement at the ridge line. But somebody's out there. One of the locals said his goats didn't come back this week. All of them went missing."

"That means they're being eaten by the local VC and NVA or being led away from the area to feed either an entire company or battalion of regulars," Eli added. "We found drag marks on the east trail. Too straight for tigers. They look man-made."

Teddy leaned forward, fighting through the sharp pain in his ribs. "Anyone on your six?"

"No," Jack said then grinned. "Not yet. But I think they want to say hello soon."

Eli pulled a green towel from around his neck and wiped his hands. "We left a few surprises on the trail for them."

"Non-lethal?" Teddy asked, knowing better. Eli was a demolitions expert who loved blowing things into tiny pieces. The surprises were probably a line of claymore mines linked in tandem, connected to a detonator and tripwire hidden on the trail.

"No promises," Eli said. "But I promise they'll slow down."

Jack slid a small pouch from inside his flak vest and placed it on the table next to Teddy's crutches. "These are my rough sketches of the terrain and villages, local intel on the Viet Cong, and a small hand-carved token— a good luck talisman, a gift to you from the local Montagnard chieftain, made from animal bone and strung on a leather cord. He hoped it would bring you protection in the days ahead."

"Good job. Let's hope it works. I could use some."

"I gave the crock of rượu cần to the medics to thank them for keeping you supplied with meds."

"Thanks, on both counts. I was so sick last time I'll never drink that nasty fermented rice and spit again. Anything else I should know?" Teddy asked as he slipped the leather cord around his neck next to his dog tags.

"Yes. The villagers said someone's been asking for 'the man with a cane,'" Jack said. "They think it's about you."

Teddy examined the pouch, checking the documents inside, then looked up at both men. "What in the hell did I do to get that kind of attention?"

"Bled in the wrong valley," Jack said, shrugging. "Who knows?"

Teddy smiled, then looked across the compound toward the portable command shack where the lead CIA agent had stepped out two days earlier. No uniform or insignia—just standard tropical khakis, available at any outdoor store, hiking boots, a clipboard, mirrored aviator sunglasses, and the confidence of someone who didn't need to explain anything.

Their conversation was brief. Teddy remembered every word.

"Who burned me during Operation Shatterhorn?"
"People who don't exist. But you already knew that."
"I'm not CIA. Neither were my men."
"You're not anything right now, just an invalid with a broken leg. That's the beauty of it. You want your war to mean something, Colonel Roosevelt? Just keep following orders."
"And if I say no?"
"Then they'll bury you under the wrong name in a file that never opens."

Teddy decided to end the conversation at that point. Why take the risk? Professional spooks weren't known for their humanitarianism or tolerance of unwanted questions. He might end up in a muddy hole with a bullet in the back of his head. That was enough of an answer.

Jack's voice snapped him back to the present. "We pulled a copy of the strike list from the CIA whiteboard at Tan Uyen. Someone marked off half the names in red grease pencil. Kohrs is the common link between them."

Teddy tightened his grip on the edge of the table. "Kohrs was last reported at Phnom Penh."

"Not anymore," Jack said. "They're moving him east to oversee operations in Vietnam. Probably to take care of anyone who steps out of line."

"And Dorsey?"

Jack shook his head. "Unknown. Still in the wind. But he's watching. You can feel it."

Eli dropped into a crouch near the table and began sharpening his combat knife on a whetstone. "This is going to go bad before it goes clean," he said without looking up, using long, straight strokes to produce a fine, razor-sharp edge.

"That's why we're here," Teddy murmured.

They sat in silence for a moment. No loud speeches, just an understanding that something greater than themselves was happening right now. Something they couldn't forget. But it would surely forget them if given the chance.

Teddy glanced down at his leg then up at the horizon. "I'll be cleared to move in ten days. Sooner if the med techs stop fussing about me staying off my feet."

"You'll be ready," Jack said. "One way or the other."

Eli sheathed his knife, stood, and slung his gear over one shoulder. "I'll prep the demolition satchels," he said. "Let me know if we need the shaped charges."

Jack looked at Teddy. "We will."

And with that, they walked off toward the armory together—two shadows cutting across the hot clay dust. Teddy sat alone for another minute, listening to the wind rustle through the canvas walls, thinking about how many things in this war came without a name.

CHAPTER 10

0830 Hours
May 21, 1970
Shadow Lance Compound/Operations Quarters
South of Biên Hòa
Republic of Vietnam

The map of Southeast Asia spread across the plywood table was streaked with pencil marks and faded grease pencil overlays—some from this week, some from last week, and some from long before Teddy arrived at the camp. Names and gridlines blurred together as the damp edges curled in the jungle humidity. No markings anywhere indicated this was a military command center. No PRC-25 radios tuned to monitor field units crackled in the background. No paperwork was needed to maintain a chain of custody. No written orders or official notices were posted on the corkboard.

The room had no official name.

Just like the team it housed.

Teddy leaned over the table, one forearm braced on the edge to support the strain, his casted leg stretched out to the side on a folded wool blanket. His crutches leaned against the doorframe within easy reach. He hated needing them. Hated the weakness in his ribs and shoulder more—the slow, deep ache that burned with every breath taken too sharply.

He squinted at the pinned sector map. Laos. Near Attopeu. Grid Nine-Zulu. The same quadrant that had swallowed a Special Forces observer team whole last month. Officially, they'd been reassigned to MACV. Unofficially, they'd disappeared into the shadows of forgotten paperwork and forged identities.

Outside, a jeep engine coughed once and died. Then the sound of two sets of feet hitting the ground. One heavy. One light.

He didn't look up when the door opened.

"Tell me it's done," Teddy said, glancing up to make sure they were unharmed.

Jack Stratton strode in first, his jungle boots covered in dried mud and his sleeves rolled up to his elbows. His fatigues were splattered with what could've been river mud or dried blood. Either way, his grin was too loose to be reassuring and came off as a bit creepy.

"Oh, it's done," Jack said. "The whole hut went up in a massive fireball like a bad joke. No more off-the-books black market ledgers. No more handoff points. One less shadow for someone to chase."

Behind him, Eli Red Horse ducked through the door. His sleeves were soaked up to the forearms in sweat from the jungle and God knows what else. He said nothing.

Teddy looked back and forth between them. "Casualties?"

"None of ours," Jack replied. "The target put up a fight. Tried to burn the ledger and hightailed it into the jungle. We beat him to it."

"You confirmed he was the contact?"

"Yes. He had the satchel and a pocketful of Thai baht. The wire connected to the roof antenna led to a clay stove concealing a Soviet-made transmitter and receiver. Whoever he was, he wasn't baking cakes."

Teddy pushed himself to his feet, leaning on the table to relieve the pressure on his leg. The pain shot up his shin then faded into the dull ache he was learning to ignore. "And the contractor?"

Jack's smile faded. "Dead. Took one in the neck when he lunged for a weapon. Eli dragged him outside before the det cord dropped the roof, destroying everything."

Teddy didn't say anything. He reached for the map, grabbed a grease pencil from the edge of the table, and marked an X through the grid sector. Just a mark. No initials, no date, no legend—nothing to identify him or his men to connect them to the mission. "He was ex-CIA, if that were even possible," he said after a pause. "Pulled from Laos last year. Wasn't supposed to be in country."

"Well, he was," Jack said. "And he knew our drop signal. That's not a coincidence."

Teddy set the pencil down and rubbed the tight line forming between his eyebrows. "So we're not just pulling assets anymore. We're burning them."

"No one ever said we were rescuing people," Jack muttered.

"That was the implication," Teddy said. "At least that was my impression."

"Then it was a lie. To all of us," Eli replied.

Silence settled over the room. They were being turned into murderers, not heroes saving the world.

Teddy eased back down onto the cot with a controlled breath. His ribs ached. His spine locked. Pain surged under the cast and spread from his ankle to his knee like a rising tide.

He reached for the logbook beside the cot. Not the one marked *Training*. The other one. The one with the hand-sewn leather cover and no identifying stamps. The one no one had authorized him to keep.

He wrote.

Grid 9-Zulu — Operation vector incomplete. Target terminated. Asset compromised. Orders given verbally. Chain of command unknown.

Then beneath it, in a smaller line.

Pattern repeats. Command divergence confirmed.

Jack looked down at the writing. "Do you really think someone's going to read that if we vanish?"

"No," Teddy said. "But if someone tries to erase us, I want the erasure to be incomplete. I want a record of the truth." He closed the book and set it beside him. "Get cleaned up then go check the radio logs from last week. If they're rerouting our communications through Luang Prabang again, we're being cut out of the loop. I want to know by whom and why."

Jack nodded. Eli stepped back through the door. Neither of them asked what would happen next.

Because they already knew.

This wasn't just about enemies in the jungle anymore.

It was about the hands pulling the puppet strings from behind the curtain.

2240 Hours
May 21, 1970
Shadow Lance Compound/Operations Quarters
South of Biên Hòa
Republic of Vietnam

The jungle at night always felt like it was breathing. Not in gasps or gulps, but in steady, quiet inhales—crickets whispering beneath the rustling tree canopy, frogs croaking far away in flooded ditches, wind sliding over canvas and wire like fingertips on stretched skin, creating an eerie off-key symphony. Even here, in a compound that didn't really exist, built on coordinates that changed every week, the darkness hummed with ancient life.

Teddy sat on the edge of his bunk, his casted leg stretched out straight and still on the chair in front of him. His crutches leaned against his issued footlocker. The dull but steady pain in his leg felt like a coil of heat wrapped around him, radiating up into his hip and ribs.

He held his leather-bound journal in his lap, closed. Nothing happened today to warrant an entry tonight.

Someone knocked once on the wooden-framed screen door—barely audible.

He didn't speak. Didn't move. Only waited to find out who decided to visit him at this late hour. It wasn't Jack or Eli. They had gone to bed early for a mission tomorrow.

The door eased opened.

The man who entered wasn't wearing a uniform or rank—only battered, worn-out tropical khakis, a tan field jacket, an unadorned black ball cap, and civilian hiking boots. He looked like a contractor, maybe a local fixer or courier—a nobody. The kind of ghost who passes unnoticed through checkpoints and kill zones alike.

But Teddy knew better. He checked to make sure his loaded M1911A1 was still on the table next to his cot within easy reach.

A real nobody wouldn't stumble onto this compound by accident or mistake—it wasn't marked on any map. Someone had to provide the coordinates and passcode for gate access.

"Are you Colonel Roosevelt?" his unknown visitor asked.

Teddy wrapped his fingers around the edge of the mattress. "I am."

The man stepped in, closed the door, and didn't salute—not that anyone did in Vietnam, considering it was a hazard to good health. He didn't sit either. Instead, he slowly reached under his jacket, as if gauging Teddy's reactions, pulled out a sealed envelope, and placed it on the wooden crate beside the cot. Plain. White. Unmarked. Thick and heavy with whatever was inside.

"You'll want to burn that after reading. The carbon paper inside logs the message in triplicate. Message destructs in thirty minutes."

Did he think Teddy was stupid? That only happened in spy movies and television shows. The technology didn't exist. He'd use the standard destruction method later—burning. "Who sent you?"

The courier gave him a dry half-smile. "Wrong question."

"What's the right one?"

"Who didn't?"

Teddy let his silence speak for him, continuing to watch his watcher. He could have kept the stare-down going all night, but he needed answers to his questions. "I'll ask again. Who sent you?"

The courier chuckled. "No one who'd sign their name."

"Great, another non-answer. You're not from MACV."

"Nope."

"CIA?"

"Not really. Close enough to smell their breath. Your team…is Shadow Lance, right?"

"That's not official."

The man nodded. "Exactly. Just be careful about who shakes your hand. Especially the ones who pretend they didn't ask for your file."

"You're talking about someone high up in the chain of command. Someone who shouldn't even know I or my team exists."

The man gave the faintest nod. "Bingo. Someone who knows how the game ends before it begins. Listen carefully. You don't know me, Colonel Roosevelt. You're not supposed to. I'm a grease point. A mail slot. Not even listed on the pay roster. But I've been running messages for a long time. Long enough to tell when one smells like bleach."

Teddy frowned. "Bleach?"

"Used to clean up blood and evidence." The courier tapped the envelope. "This one stinks."

Teddy didn't touch the envelope. "What am I looking at here?"

The courier looked at him with an intense, unblinking stare. "You didn't come back from Cambodia to rest, Colonel Roosevelt. You came back because someone wants you useful. Just not visible. And definitely not loud."

Teddy frowned. "Why me?"

"You're a legacy asset. Clean record. No scandals. Hell, you even look like your famous ancestor in a goddamn photo op and even share the same birthday—October 27th—except you're taller at six feet two and much more muscular. You're safe—on paper. That makes you dangerous to people." The courier leaned forward. Not threatening, just closer. "Ever hear the name 'Whiskey Actual'?"

Teddy narrowed his eyes.

It wasn't a name.

It was a callsign—high-level and not used by low-level grunts like him. One of the Pentagon's unofficial coordination terms for black-world directors, rarely spoken aloud and never inside a camp in Vietnam. Too many unwanted ears on both sides.

"I've heard of it," Teddy said.

"Good. Because that's who signed your unofficial reassignment—no written orders, just verbal ones through a backchannel courier three weeks ago."

The courier tapped the envelope again. "Your next mission's in there. But there's a postscript—hidden in the communication trail. An identifier. 'W.A.' and an authentication matrix used only by two people in the last year. One's dead. The other's on the Joint Special Plans Group. Ask yourself this—and don't quote me. Don't remember my face. Why would someone high up in black ops who's never set foot in this AO want a wounded colonel with a dead team reassigned without orders or paperwork?"

Teddy didn't have an answer. He picked up the envelope but didn't open it. "Name?"

"I didn't say a name."

"But you know it."

The courier met his gaze—something about him changed. Fear? Regret, maybe? "You didn't get it from me. But when you read it, and you find the name—don't say it out loud. Just think really hard about who gets to decide what a war is and who profits from it."

He moved to the door and paused, glancing over his shoulder. "You strike me as the kind of person who believes in right and wrong. The black-world doesn't. It believes in leverage. You're the real deal, Colonel Roosevelt—a true American hero. That's the problem. The black-world doesn't like patriots. It eats them."

He stepped outside and disappeared into the night.

Teddy sat still for several seconds. He placed the envelope next to his M1911. Did he want to find out? The courier said the mission was inside. Was he ready for this?

He opened the envelope.

Inside were two items.

1. A hand-drawn map overlay for an unnamed village near the Bolaven Plateau. No unit identifiers, just a handwritten note— *Confirm presence of PRC weapons.*
2. A single paperclipped line of communication chatter, buried in the margins.
   Asset reassignment confirmed by Whiskey Actual – MG Franklin A. Dorsey, DIA Strategic Planning.

Teddy set the map aside. His pulse started to tighten at the base of his throat. He had a name—the mysterious Major General Franklin A. Dorsey.

He reached for his journal, uncapped his pen, and wrote his nightly entry.

Courier arrived—no ID, unverified but cleared the perimeter with the correct passcode. Warning not about a threat but betrayal. Delivered mission data and a traced comm fragment identifying reassignment authority by 'Whiskey Actual'—Major General Franklin A. Dorsey. Name previously unknown except for brief mentions by Jack and in intel chatter. Connection suspected to unauthorized Cambodia asset withdrawal. No MACV paper trail.

He hesitated then added another line.

Start secondary logs. Record in parallel. Do not trust any external chain. Initiate the separation protocol. Trust nothing outside the team.

Outside, the jungle breathed again.
But this time, Teddy heard it differently.
Not like a breath.
Like whispers in the darkness and shadows, except these shadows had substance, a pulse, and death trailing behind them.

CHAPTER 11

```
0230 Hours
November 14, 1970
Operation Silent Arrow
Grid Sector Whiskey-Nine
Southern Laos
```

The jungle canopy overhead pressed down hard, its tangled branches dripping with dew, making the thick undergrowth slick and treacherous. Fog drifted through the trees in curling, smoky wisps, moving low and ghostly over mossy roots and half-hidden animal trails.

Even the moonlight struggled to penetrate the dense foliage, breaking into glowing shards scattered unevenly across wet leaves and tall elephant grass. Insects buzzed, frogs croaked, and the wind roared through the trees—too tall and too old to remember a time without war.

Teddy knelt beside the swollen banks of a nameless creek, shifting his weight onto his good leg. Six months after surgery, his ankle had healed, but a dull, steady ache remained, especially in cold weather or after long patrols like tonight's. He felt it now—a slow-burning pressure that reminded him of the cost of survival.

He scanned the distant riverbank, adjusting his grip on his CAR-15. The rifle's matte black finish was streaked with water, and the suppressor was wrapped in black cloth to reduce noise and thermal signature. He wore no insignia on his tiger-striped fatigues and had no dog tags around his neck. A camouflage, grease-painted shadow among shadows. His identity was left behind hanging on a hook above his cot.

To his left, Captain Jack Stratton emerged from the brush, crouching low and fluid like a jungle cat, holding his CAR-15 at the ready. "The camp's just past the next rise, about three hundred meters. Two roving patrols, two men each, rotating every half hour. Radios are Chinese-made—brand new. Someone's keeping them well supplied," he whispered just loud enough to be heard over the rushing water.

Teddy nodded. "Red Horse?"

"Covering the north slope on overwatch. He has already spotted one tripwire on the outer approach—probably more. He counted a total of twelve personnel—no civilians, no prisoners. Definitely not a village outpost."

Teddy adjusted his footing, careful not to put too much pressure on his barely healed leg. "Did you verify the supply crates?"

Jack nodded. "Yes. Stacked in the east quadrant. Marked in English. U.S. Army. Ammo crates from Da Nang, listed as missing on inventory reports. Someone's running weapons through U.S. black market channels—no question."

Teddy gazed into the night toward the hidden encampment. Operation Silent Arrow was supposed to be a simple infiltration mission—observe, confirm, and extract. A clean, non-contact reconnaissance operation. But nothing was ever that easy, not anymore. Six months in the black ops world had taught him that. He reached into his pocket, withdrew a small, waterproof notebook, and scribbled a few quick notes.

Silent Arrow – Grid sector Whiskey-Nine. Confirmed U.S.-marked crates in enemy possession. Chinese radio equipment verified. Source unknown.

He didn't bother recording anything else. Officially, they weren't even here.

Jack touched his shoulder. "Bull, are you all right?"

Teddy blinked and looked at him. "Just wondering whose poker hand we're really playing into tonight. Feels like we've been dealt a dead man's hand."

Jack's eyes narrowed. "Our orders were to confirm the presence of U.S. munitions. Nothing more. Then radio for extraction."

Teddy offered a faint, humorless smile. "Sure. Just like the last time. Verify and leave. Mindless robots in dirty uniforms."

Jack shifted his feet, uneasy about the implication as well. "Do you want to scrub the mission?"

"No. But we're not calling for extraction until I know exactly whose fingerprints are on those crates." Teddy paused. "If this goes deeper than local South Vietnamese corruption, I want proof. If someone's dirty, I want a name."

Jack nodded. "Understood. We go in quietly and handle our own intelligence gathering."

"Yes." Teddy braced himself against the muddy bank as the muscles in his leg twinged, sending a sharp pain up into his hip. He adjusted his grip on the rifle. "Get Red Horse on point. We move in ten. Tell him to watch for tripwires and boobytraps."

Jack slipped into the darkness.

Teddy paused a moment longer, inhaling the thick jungle air and tasting the sharp tang of decay and wet earth. Six months of covert operations had blurred the lines between friend and foe, patriotism and survival. He stopped believing in clean missions months ago. Team Shadow Lance wasn't a rescue mission anymore. They were janitors, cleaning up the messes others had created and left behind.

But tonight felt different. Tonight felt deliberate. Staged for someone's benefit. Theirs?

He took one last look at the notebook before securing it with a rubber band and slipping it into his pocket. Then he stood up and signaled Eli and Jack to move forward.

Time to find out who was really pulling the strings.

0425 Hours
November 14, 1970
Operation Silent Arrow
Grid Sector Whiskey-Nine
Southern Laos

They moved like smoke with the precision of a surgeon—Eli on point, Teddy and Jack fanning out to both sides, weaving through the jungle that separated them from the enemy camp. The outer tripwire was a simple setup—monofilament fishing line strung low between two branches, triggered to a signal flare. Eli cut it with his KA-BAR and tucked the cord beneath a root.

Next, they slipped past the two perimeter guards without alerting them. Eli took down one guard with a swift draw across the throat using his razor-sharp KA-BAR. The other guard was hit in the chest with a single shot from Jack's suppressed M1911A1.

Eli led the formation to within a hundred yards of the camp, sweeping the underbrush with preternatural focus, his M16 equipped with a Starlight scope and the safety off, ready to rock and roll on full automatic. Jack was close behind, guarding Eli's exposed backside. Teddy brought up the rear, his ankle supporting his weight for now, rifle steady, his breath controlled despite the sweltering hundred-plus degree heat rising off the wet forest floor.

At the outer perimeter, Eli spotted a single tripwire hanging low between two stumps. It was crudely set and connected to a stolen American Claymore mine, which was deadly if triggered—filled with explosives and stainless-steel ball bearings, its curved shape designed to focus the blast and shrapnel. He raised his fist, signaling everyone to stop, dropped to one knee, and carefully cut the wire before securing it to a nearby branch. A few more yards ahead, they reached the edge of the clearing.

The camp was arranged in a tight horseshoe shape. Two lean-tos built from corrugated tin and local wood, a radio shack with a tin roof, a mess area, canvas tents, and the crate stack—five wooden boxes, waist-high and stained with oil. Off-duty soldiers slept in outdoor hammocks with weapons within easy reach.

A kerosene lantern burned near the center of the camp illuminating two men hunched over a map spread out on a tree stump. As enemy camps go, this one was pretty amateurish—a five-year-old child with a crayon and some construction paper could have done a better job organizing it.

"Go!" Teddy waved them forward and gave a thumbs up.

Eli moved in first, taking out the lookout with his KA-BAR. A sharp, clipped, artificial bird call broke the silence. Two muffled thumps followed. No voices. No alarms.

Jack stealthily moved toward the radio shack and neutralized the radio operator before he could react. The two men by the lantern didn't even look up before Teddy closed in. He grabbed one from behind by the hair, yanked his head back, and sliced his neck clean through to his spine. The other man was taken down by a round fired from Jack's sidearm. The men sleeping in the hammocks didn't stand a chance as Eli silently eliminated them with his KA-BAR.

Teddy ran over to the crates, using the prybar hanging from his belt to pry open the lid of the top crate. It came off with a creak of damp wood and the squeal of rusty nails.

Inside were foam-packed, U.S. Army-issued M16 rifles, pristine, wrapped in wax paper and coated in cosmoline.

Teddy grabbed the packing slip.

Da Nang Ordnance Depot
Destination: Field Distribution—Special Logistics Route Bravo
Authorized Signature: MG F.A. Dorsey, DIA Strategic Planning

Teddy stared at the name as if a grenade had exploded in his hands, his mouth going dry. There was no mistaking it now. This wasn't just local corruption or black market dealings. It was official. Sanctioned. Dorsey's signature revealed everything.

Jack appeared beside him. "What is it?"

Teddy handed him the slip. "This isn't Army surplus. It's an underground weapons pipeline. Someone's diverting real-time supplies from our troops directly to these camps. We just found our proof. Dorsey's as corrupt as a politician on election day."

"Son of a bitch." Jack clenched his jaw. "So what now?"

Teddy looked up. "We log the coordinates, take the slip, and torch the crates. Then we disappear."

Eli joined them, already setting charges to destroy the camp. Small incendiaries designed to burn rather than explode. No bright flash, just flames, heat, and destruction. "Perimeter's clear. Clock's ticking, sir."

Teddy nodded. "We burn it all. Then we vanish. Fire and fade."

Jack pulled a small waterproof pouch from his vest and slid the manifest inside. "We get this stateside, we've got proof to nail Dorsey's hide to the legal wall."

"Assuming we live that long," Eli muttered. "Ten minutes, sir."

Teddy moved to the second crate, curious about its contents, and opened it—M7 bayonets. Another box contained medical supplies. A third was labeled with a black stencil—*5.56MM BALL M193 – LAKE CITY ARSENAL – LOT LC-71-D215-1*. Inside were rows of loaded magazines, still banded in green plastic. Beneath them were sealed paper-wrapped sleeves of boxed ammunition. Pristine. Ammunition intended for U.S. troops, not the NVA, Viet Cong, or black market buyers. The fourth box held more weapons—M79s and several boxes of M1911s. Everything was American made.

The last wooden crate left Teddy puzzled. It had no markings at all. He pried it open and froze. The only item inside was a three-ring, government-issue, waterproof binder—marked not in grease pencil or code, but with a typed manifest sheet attached to the cover with a duplicate one inside.

SUPPLY REQUISITION – ORD DEPOT: DA NANG (AO)
DESTINATION: PHANTOM SITE – BLACK LOTUS
SIGNED: MG F. A. DORSEY, DIA STRATEGIC PLANNING
HAND DELIVERY – DO NOT SHIP THROUGH REGULAR CHANNELS

"Black Lotus? I've never seen that on any chart or intel report," Jack said.

"You weren't supposed to." Teddy pulled the papers out of the binder, folding them to fit inside his shirt, and tossed the empty binder back into the crate. Loose paper was easy to hide. An entire plastic binder full of paper was not. "This wasn't a misdirect. It was a transfer. These weapons were never going to Saigon or Da Nang."

"Time to go, Colonel," Eli yelled from the gate. "Two minutes."

"Get going, Jack," Teddy ordered.

Jack nodded and took off.

Teddy took one last look at the site. It wasn't a camp. It was a node—part of a network someone like Dorsey controlled from behind a desk in a comfortable, secure office. Whatever was happening here wasn't about jungle tactics or lost supply crates. It was part of something bigger—something authorized, something that could be denied, and definitely arranged to avoid the Senate Armed Services Oversight Committee.

As they pulled back, the jungle around them remained eerily silent—no sign of activity from the enemy encampments farther east. Even the insects had gone quiet.

On the ridgeline, they turned to watch the fireball destroy the evidence.

The charges exploded in quick succession—precise and surgical. The fire soared upward in a powerful, choking wave of heat, sending smoke and ash swirling into the tree canopy.

"Dorsey's going to feel that," Jack said. "And his response won't be pretty."

"He already knows we're out here," Teddy replied. "Now he knows we're coming for him."

They didn't wait for the NVA to come looking for the source of the fire, heading south and vanishing into the jungle with stolen proof and a looming deadline.

The night swallowed their withdrawal, and the truth burned in their wake.

Smoke rolled into the jungle like a warning. Some fires weren't meant to stay hidden.

CHAPTER 12

0130 Hours
November 24, 1970
Operation Midnight Echo
Grid Reference Delta-Nine-Bravo
Laotian Border Sector

The jungle never slept. Instead, it waited—patient, dark, and heavy as wet canvas, every shadow in constant motion beneath a sky filled with low, oppressive slate-gray clouds. The monsoon season stretched into what would normally be the dry season due to a top-secret weather modification experiment called *Operation Popeye*, soaking the tall grass until water seeped through boots and fatigues. Everything here moved slower as if the darkness had taken on form and shape, creeping through the underbrush like a hungry tiger.

Teddy crouched low next to the massive trunk of a rain-slick banyan tree, every muscle tense and every nerve on high alert. The pain in his leg had eased to an occasional ache, a ghost of past injuries. He carried the lingering stiffness with every careful step. He'd never completely outrun it—but he could handle it and manage the pain. And tonight, he had to.

He moved forward along the animal trail, squinting through night-adapted eyes and holding a suppressed CAR-15 against his shoulder. The weapon's matte black finish reflected the moonlight. Twenty meters ahead, Jack Stratton blended almost seamlessly into the nightscape, moving in small increments and glancing back only to verify his position. Behind him, Eli was silent, carrying a bandolier filled with shaped charges and det cord wrapped securely in plastic sheeting to keep it dry in the wet conditions.

They'd done this so many times now, Teddy had lost count. Operations with no written orders, no oversight, and no after-action reports beyond the quiet scratch of a pen in his leather-bound journal hidden beneath his cot back at the compound.

But tonight's mission—*Operation Midnight Echo*—felt different.

The orders arrived by courier, the envelope delivered by a faceless local riding a stolen Honda motorcycle before disappearing into the night without even asking for confirmation. Teddy didn't know who had signed off on the mission this time—but he could guess—Dorsey. He'd long stopped asking aloud.

Their objective was straightforward enough—find a Viet Cong supply cache reported by local informants just across the border in Laos. No support. No extraction if things went sideways. Just three men, night vision, suppressed weapons, and enough explosives to destroy whatever they found. Standard procedure—except the map overlays had come in crystal clear, almost too precise. The intel felt wrong, cooked. But it wasn't their job to ask questions anymore. Questions were met with suspicion and silence.

They were armed ghosts, not strategists or intelligence analysts.

"Target hut. Twenty meters ahead. Three tangos visible, all armed with AK-47s. Two sentries, one inside," Jack said over the secure PRC-77 radio handset.

Teddy pressed the transmit button on his radio. "Any eyes on the weapons cache?"

"Negative. But the interior's set up like a staging point—supplies, ammo, and food."

"Does anything feel wrong?"

"Everything feels wrong about this mission, Bull," Jack whispered. "But we're already here."

Teddy let that hang. Six months of black-world ops had taught him one thing, especially after finding the evidence implicating Dorsey—hesitation meant someone else took the bullet. "Proceed," he whispered. "Set demolitions and withdraw. Engage only if spotted."

Eli moved forward, crouching low. Jack covered him, and Teddy remained on overwatch, scanning the perimeter with his binoculars for any movement. Raindrops rolled down his neck, under the collar of his unmarked tiger-striped fatigue shirt. He ignored it, keeping his eyes fixed on the hut.

Something moved near the back corner of the structure.

Teddy tensed, tracking the movement. A figure—slim, dressed in civilian clothes, baggy brown cotton pants, a shirt, and a floppy straw hat, possibly a local—emerged from the hut, carrying something small. He keyed the mic. "Hold—civilian spotted. Possible noncombatant."

"Demolition charges are already in place. Five-minute timer is set. Orders?" Eli asked.

Teddy hesitated, tightening his finger on the trigger. Should he fire? No. Not until he was sure. He adjusted his grip on the rifle and focused his binoculars on the figure. A boy. About fifteen, maybe younger. Not armed. Carrying a burlap-wrapped bundle of rice.

"Withdraw," Teddy ordered. "Abort! Civilian presence confirmed."

"Too late—the timer's live. Cannot disable without exposure," Jack said.

"Fuck!" Teddy slammed his fist into the mud, heart pounding in his chest. "Secure the kid. Now." This mission just spiraled out of control.

Jack moved, sliding out of the shadows. The boy jumped back, startled, eyes wide as saucers. Jack grabbed his shoulder and pulled him into the jungle, away from the hut.

"Clear," Jack said over the radio.

Then the night erupted into complete pandemonium.

The charges tore the hut apart—walls and roof exploding outward, fire surging upward in a blazing flash of heat and noise. The jungle erupted into chaos around them, insects screeching, birds scattering into the sky, small animals fleeing through the thick vegetation, away from the flames and the commotion.

Teddy sprang up from his crouch, rifle held ready in his hands. "Move—now! Back to the extraction point."

Jack grabbed the boy by the arm, pulling him away with fierce determination, eyes blazing in the firelight. Eli stayed close, weapon pointed behind them, watching their backtrail.

At the tree line, Teddy paused, glancing back over his shoulder at the hut. What remained of the building burned, orange flames reaching up like outstretched hands.

The boy stood trembling, eyes locked on Teddy's face, confusion and fear blending into a vivid expression of terror.

Teddy felt sick. The mission was over—but what had they destroyed tonight?

Jack touched his shoulder. "Colonel. We gotta move. Not even a blind man could miss that explosion."

"Go," Teddy said. "I'm right behind you." He followed a few seconds later, feeling every ache in his body and something deeper—something older. Something that hurt worse than broken bones.

This wasn't recon. This wasn't war.

This was something else entirely.

Back at their extraction point—an unmarked clearing north of the river—they waited in silence for the Huey from Biên Hòa, flying without running lights or radio contact with Shadow Lance. The only sounds were rotor blades slicing through the starless night. Teddy watched the boy, now seated, with his head bowed and shoulders trembling. Jack stayed close by, speaking softly in reassuring Vietnamese.

"Colonel," Eli whispered as he moved closer. "That hut wasn't VC. Not military. Too many personal effects. Civilians."

Teddy's chest tightened. "I know."

"Our orders were clear. But someone gave us a civilian target."

Teddy didn't respond. He knew exactly who had issued those orders—and what they had been used for.

And he knew, deep in his bones, there would be more nights like this one.

The black world didn't let go—not until it had taken everything.

In the distance, the faint chop of rotor blades grew louder, slicing through the jungle's heartbeat, coming to take them home.

But tonight, disgusted with himself, home was nowhere Teddy wanted to go.

CHAPTER 13

2040 Hours
June 16, 1971
Firebase Dragonfly
Undisclosed Location
Vietnam-Laos Border

Rain hammered the corrugated steel roof of the command bunker at Firebase Dragonfly, pounding out a steady heavy metal rock beat over the hushed whispers of radio static and muffled voices. The bunker was embedded halfway into a hillside, hidden beneath layers of mud-soaked sandbags and camouflage netting. A single bare bulb swayed from a wire overhead, casting shifting shadows across maps and red-marked photographs pinned to the rough wooden walls.

Teddy stood near the communications desk, watching the perimeter lights flicker through sheets of rain outside. His leg had healed enough for combat situations, but the dull ache around the titanium rod still crept back on damp, cold nights like this one—a silent reminder of Cambodia.

Behind him, Captain Jack Stratton and Master Sergeant Eli Red Horse waited, standing at ease near the back wall, their faces carefully neutral. They understood what tonight's visit signified. High-ranking officers didn't come this deep into the boonies without a good reason. And they definitely didn't show up for a casual chat.

The door swung open, allowing a gust of rain and cold, damp air to flow in. A young aide entered first, scanning the room. He moved aside, clearing the way for the man behind him.

Major General Franklin A. Dorsey entered the cramped bunker with the calm authority of someone accustomed to silence and obedience. He wore pressed and starched U.S. Army OD-green fatigues without any insignia, a simple web pistol belt with a black leather holster holding a standard-issue M1911A1 at his waist. He didn't remove his rain-soaked cap—just shook it once, causing droplets to scatter onto the wooden floor.

"At ease, gentlemen," Dorsey said, his voice deep and unhurried.

No one had moved into a position of attention anyway. Dorsey clearly wanted to assert his higher rank and authority. And no one cared.

"Colonel Roosevelt," he continued, eyes locking on Teddy. "Good to see you operational. I trust your team's been briefed on my arrival?"

"Yes, sir," Teddy replied. "Though the details were sparse." Almost non-existent.

Dorsey smiled, teeth bared, wolf-like. "In our line of work, sparse usually means important." He glanced at Jack and Eli, assessing them but said nothing. His gaze returned to Teddy. "Your team has an excellent track record over the past few months. Very quiet. Effective. Exactly what we need in this war."

"Thank you, sir," Teddy said, his voice steady and respectful. "But I doubt you came all this way just to compliment us."

Dorsey's eyes narrowed—appraising rather than annoyed. "You're right. I didn't." He moved forward, standing close to the table where maps and aerial reconnaissance photos lay scattered under waxy overlays.

"The war's changing," Dorsey said. "The American people are turning against us. Washington's tired of the controversy. Congress wants to wind down our involvement in Southeast Asia. Nixon wants results he can sell to the public and win reelection. But results, as you know, are not always about victories."

Teddy watched him closely. "Sir?" That callous remark wasn't part of any class he took at West Point. They were trained to win.

"Results," Dorsey continued, tapping his finger on a reconnaissance photo, "are sometimes about optics. Narratives. Justifications. The war behind the war. And when public support erodes, certain sacrifices become inevitable."

Jack and Eli exchanged a subtle glance at each other behind Dorsey's back.

"Sacrifices, sir?" Teddy repeated. He wasn't sure where Dorsey was going with this line of conversation.

"Nothing new," Dorsey said. "You've seen the memos— Vietnamization. Strategic withdrawal. Politically necessary actions. These are polite terms for ugly truths."

"Is this why you're here, sir?" Teddy asked. "To warn us we're on the wrong side of a drawdown?"

"On the contrary. I'm here to remind you exactly why teams like yours exist. Wars don't end quietly with a peace treaty, Colonel Roosevelt. They end loudly—or not at all. Sometimes loud enough to remind everyone why we were here in the first place. To fight communist aggression."

Teddy stared into Dorsey's pale blue, almost lifeless eyes, feeling a quiet chill settle between his shoulder blades. The man seemed a few donuts short of a dozen. Beaucoup dinky dau. "You're talking about engineered incidents. False flags."

Dorsey leaned back on his heels, hands clasped behind his back. "I'm talking about the world you signed up for the day you left Tay Ninh. A world where the truth serves no master. Where winning or losing doesn't matter as much as shaping what comes next."

"With all due respect, sir, that sounds more political than tactical," Jack said, weighing in on the conversation with his expert opinion.

Dorsey's gaze turned toward Jack. "Captain Stratton. You were an intelligence officer, known for slipping in and out of places like a shadow no one notices. You know better. All war is political. The tactical part is the easy part. It's what happens afterward that matters. How we shape the future."

Jack nodded, but Teddy could tell from his stern expression that he didn't believe a word coming from Dorsey's mouth.

Dorsey turned back to Teddy. "Shadow Lance is valuable because it does not exist. You are deniable. Invisible. Completely expendable if compromised. I trust you understand what I'm telling you, Colonel Roosevelt?"

"Yes, sir," Teddy said. "We've known that from the beginning."

"Good. Because soon, you'll have a mission—one that's crucial for all U.S. operations in the region. Something that will shape how the wind blows and how all U.S. foreign policy is conducted in the future. Consider this visit your official heads-up to start preparing for the mission."

Dorsey headed for the door, paused, then turned back to face Teddy. "Your men are exceptional, Colonel Roosevelt. But don't get attached to outcomes. That's how good officers get lost. You don't work for the Peace Corps."

Then he was gone—out the door and back into the jungle rain. The aide followed, closing the door behind them.

The room remained silent for a long minute.

"So that's General Franklin Dorsey. He reminds me of Fritz Haarmann, the 'Butcher of Hanover.' Looks like he'd slit your throat with a razor blade just to keep his boots dry," Jack said.

Teddy clenched his jaw. "He would. And call it necessary and vital to national security."

Eli moved closer, glancing at the closed door. "He didn't mention any specifics."

"No," Teddy said. "But whatever he's planning, it'll happen soon. And I guarantee it'll be bloody enough that he wants someone else's hands on the knife. Namely ours."

The bunker felt colder now, and darker somehow, despite the single overhead bulb still gently swaying above them.

Outside, the jungle continued whispering to itself, unbothered and indifferent to the men moving through its shadows.

CHAPTER 14

2303 Hours
November 19, 1971
Operation Wild Lantern
Ban Nasa
Laos

The clay sucked Teddy's jungle boots deeper into the ground with every step, irritating his left ankle as a constant reminder of Operation Shatterhorn and its aftermath. The rain had stopped hours earlier, but the ground still held onto the water like an unhealed wound. The heat hadn't broken, even this late into the evening, and the damp, heavy weight of monsoon season stuck to his skin like a second uniform.

Smoke hovered over the dense jungle canopy in a low-hanging haze, curling around the charred remains of the village. The huts, made of thatch and woven bamboo, stood gutted, walls scorched and sagging, the smell of burned wood—and worse—still hanging in the air. The entire area looked as if it had been shelled—yet no artillery rounds had fallen. The destruction was too precise. They had done this with small arms, grenades, and an M72 LAW—a portable, one-shot anti-tank rocket launcher.

Teddy moved like a man walking into the aftermath of his own betrayal. He held his CAR-15 against his shoulder, low but ready, sweeping through the remains of what was supposed to be a high-value target—a weapons cache linked to Chinese supply lines. That's what the classified briefing had claimed. The orders, issued by Lt. Commander Nathan Kaufman, Naval Intelligence, stamped under the black-world credentials of the Covert Operations Directorate—a group that didn't officially exist—were precise—neutralize the target, leave no survivors, destroy everything, and no retrieval if compromised.

They never learned the real name of the village. Only a grid square—Kilo Bravo Six-Two-Two—a tiny dot on the map, and a blurry satellite image. The operation was called *Wild Lantern*—just another meaningless code phrase hiding something much darker, much colder.

Somewhere behind him, Jack moved like a shadow through the broken palmettos and shattered thatch huts, sweeping his rifle back and forth, searching for movement.

But there were no enemy combatants, no weapons—only innocent civilians attacked in the dark of night without warning.

"Bull, we've got movement—north shack. It's just a woman. Not armed," Jack's voice crackled over the radio. "Looks about sixty or so."

Teddy keyed his throat mic. "Copy. Secure her. No sudden moves." He stepped over a collapsed basket of spilled rice mixed with still warm shell casings, careful not to look too long at the twisted, bloodied bodies that lay nearby—two men, both unarmed, one shot in the back of the head—execution-style. The other had taken multiple rounds in the spine while crawling, leaving drag marks in the clay at his feet. He clenched his jaw and swept the area again.

There had been no resistance. No return fire. No perimeter defense. Only screams, chaos, and now—total eerie silence. Not even insects, small animals, or birds remained in the area.

Teddy crouched beside the closest body and rolled it over. There were no tattoos or signs of military service—just a wooden Catholic rosary tucked into the man's waistband. He stood and continued his sweep of the area. The air reeked of wet wood and something sharper—something metallic—iron—blood and burned hair.

He found Eli crouched beside a hut in the center of the village, his hands covered with someone else's blood and face streaked with mud and ash. Eli had dragged a young boy into the open, maybe eight or nine, unconscious, his chest hastily wrapped in gauze pressure bandages.

"Nothing here but rice and corpses," Eli said, bitterness in his voice. "And they're all fucking civilians."

Teddy clenched his jaw at the inhumanity committed by their hands. "Weapons caches?"

Eli shook his head. "None. Checked every structure. Just food and rusted farming tools. No crates. No AKs. Nothing but what they used to survive. And even that wasn't much. Nothing here but death now."

Teddy felt it then—not just the weight of his wet gear or the dull ache in his left leg—but something deeper. A cold, hollow certainty twisted in his gut. They'd been given the wrong intel. Lied to. Used. Turned into murderers against their will. Except it wasn't bad intel—no one could ever mistake this simple village for an enemy stronghold. Intentional misinformation was the only explanation. A message to the other villages about what would happen if they sided with the VC.

Jack emerged from the swirling black smoke like a ghost, rifle down, face tight with anger. "You see the shack on the east end? It still had a lantern burning inside and a cooking pot still hot. Whoever was here didn't expect to be hit. This wasn't a militia camp, Bull. This was a village of innocent civilians."

Teddy didn't answer at first. He looked around again, taking in every detail. The bodies. The destroyed homes. The absence of anything even remotely threatening.

This wasn't collateral damage. This had been the target. Their target.

Teddy drew a slow breath, devastated by what they had done. "I know. We were set up."

"Agreed. Do you think it was Armstrong?" Jack asked.

"Not sure yet." Teddy looked back toward the jungle canopy, eyes narrowing as if trying to see through layers of smoke, lies, and politics. "But whoever gave us this target wanted us to pull the trigger. They just didn't want the world to know what was really here."

Eli straightened to his full height, the unconscious boy now bandaged and laid beside a fallen tree. "What now?"

"We get out of here. And we don't leave anything behind. Secure the area. I want us off this target zone in twenty minutes." Teddy turned, the heavy weight in his stomach growing with each step. The mission briefing had claimed this was a Vietnamese weapons depot, resupplied by Chinese traffickers moving through civilian networks.

They were instructed to go in hard, sweep and clear, and neutralize all occupants of the village with extreme prejudice. That last phrase had been underlined. No prisoners. Destroy the supply line. There were no weapons. No resistance. No return fire with AK-47s. Just old men, women, children, rice paddies. And now...corpses.

Teddy slung his rifle and adjusted the weight off his left ankle, pushing the pain down. "Jack, call for a chopper, ricky-tick. We're done here."

The helicopter extraction never arrived, forcing them to leave the boy at the nearest village instead of transporting him to a civilian hospital.

And two days later, as they humped through dense jungle and leech-filled rivers, Teddy kept those black-world orders close to his chest—knowing full well that what they'd done today wasn't a mistake.

It was part of the plan—whatever that was.

And what had happened to them? Those orders turned them into murderers. How could he live with himself? This wasn't part of the deal.

0057 Hours
November 22, 1971
Shadow Lance Compound
Quarters Bravo-2
Republic of Vietnam

The plywood walls of their quarters were thin—too thin to truly hide secrets—but tonight, they pretended they were alone. A kerosene lantern buzzed on a small table near the corner cot, giving off heat and the smell of burnt fuel. The metal fan overhead clicked with each rotation, its rusted blades barely stirring the thick, humid air. A wooden crate filled with unmarked ammunition served as their makeshift table, surrounded by three folding metal chairs. The heat hadn't eased even after sundown, and sweat still clung beneath the collars of their t-shirts.

Teddy sat on the edge of his bunk, one foot resting on the crate, elevating his wrapped left ankle to help reduce the swelling. His jungle boots lay unlaced beside him, covered in red mud and something darker— blood. He hadn't spoken since they returned to camp, didn't feel like it— just stared at the wall for the better part of an hour, letting the weight of what happened settle into his mind. His ankle still throbbed where the scar tissue had never quite smoothed out, serving as a subtle reminder of Cambodia. But that pain was nothing compared to the acid roiling in the pit of his stomach.

Jack leaned forward, elbows resting on his knees, holding a half-empty tin mug of black coffee in one hand with his sidearm still strapped to his thigh as if he didn't trust the quiet of the night. "That wasn't a mistake. Intel didn't screw this up. They *lied* to us."

"They wanted all the witnesses dead," Eli said. "Or simply didn't care who got caught in the crossfire. Fucking collateral damage."

"They used us to sanitize something," Teddy said. "Burn the evidence. Blame it on cross-border action with China or the VC."

"Except there were no VC," Jack said from the far bunk, sitting cross-legged in jungle trousers and a bare chest, his dog tags swinging around his neck. His CAR-15 was disassembled on his bunk, parts laid out on a clean cloth like a surgeon's tools. "We lit that place up for nothing. Intel said it was a logistics hub. I didn't see a single crate, not even a damn transistor radio. This whole thing is bullshit."

"They don't care. We were the match. They struck us and lit the flame. This wasn't just bad intelligence. This was a goddamn setup with us playing the executioner."

Except it keeps happening. We haven't had a single piece of actionable intel confirmed by a secondary source in over a month—just coordinates and corpses," Eli said in a steady, calm voice.

Their anger wasn't solely about Wild Lantern. There had been other missions with similar issues—minor inconsistencies in map coordinates, the number of combatants, missing intelligence, satellite photos of the wrong villages, and weapons caches that didn't match the briefings. Those missions felt more like executions. But this time, it was impossible to ignore. During the earlier missions, at least someone had been shooting at them, forcing them to defend themselves.

Jack shook his head. "I didn't sign up to slaughter innocent villagers."

"You didn't," Teddy said. "Neither did I."

Silence stretched long again, broken only by the faint hum of a fan somewhere down the hallway and the distant cough of a guard on duty outside.

Eli moved away from the window and sat on his bunk. "How far does this go, Bull? You've been running ops longer than we have. Do you think Dorsey's signing off on this shit alone?"

Teddy didn't answer because he didn't know.

"Is it the CIA?" Jack asked. "Is it Kohrs?"

"No one's admitted anything," Teddy said. "Everything we do gets burned upon arrival. No records. No logs. No accountability."

"Then we're mercs," Jack said, his voice laced with bitterness. "Paid killers, ready to disavow everything."

Another silence fell over the room, making it feel even colder.

"Do you ever think about walking away?" Jack asked, his voice softer than expected.

"Where would we go?" Eli asked. "We're in the middle of the damn fucking jungle with no passports and no papers. We wouldn't make it twenty klicks before someone put a bullet in our heads."

Teddy looked up. "I have, but not because I'm scared. Because I don't know who we're working for anymore. Not really. As for leaving, we'd never escape that easily. Hell, they probably already tagged us before this conversation even started."

"Do you think this Dorsey guy gives a tinkers' damn about what we think?" Jack asked.

"Nope. I do think he's playing a longer game than we realize, and that makes him even more dangerous."

Jack drained the last of his coffee and leaned back on his elbows, staring at the ceiling. "If we leave, we're dead. They'll hunt us down. Make us disappear."

"They wouldn't do it themselves," Teddy said. "They'd send someone else. A cleaner...a wet boy." He didn't say the name. None of them did.

But they knew who he was talking about—Kohrs.

CHAPTER 15

```
1945 Hours
November 24, 1971
Shadow Lance Compound
Quarters Bravo-2
Republic of Vietnam
```

The first thing Teddy noticed was how the compound fell silent. A sudden hush swept over the camp—a tense, uneasy quiet that spread faster than a wind-driven wildfire. Even the insects seemed to hold their breath, waiting for something unseen and hungry to pass by.

Teddy stood, setting aside the stripped M16 bolt he'd been cleaning, then moved to the doorway of his quarters. Next to him, Jack and Eli paused mid-motion, sensing the tension in the air. They'd spent too many years in jungles and war zones not to recognize the silence that signals a predator's arrival.

Outside, the gravel walkway crunched under steady footsteps. Purposeful. Unhurried. The sound of a man with nowhere urgent to go because no one dared to rush him.

The screen door swung open without any knock or warning.

Colonel Martin Kohrs filled the narrow doorway—average height, maybe five-ten, lean at around one-seventy, but built like a tempered steel sword beneath his simple, pressed green jungle fatigues and ballcap. He wore no rank insignia on his collar, no unit patch on his left shoulder, nothing that tied him to any recognizable military service branch—except he wore the air of authority like a crown. His boots were spit-polished to a deep, shiny black, free of mud or jungle rot. His sleeves were rolled exactly two folds above the elbow, revealing sinewy forearms crisscrossed with faint old scars—thin, pale reminders of violence that no records existed for, and if they did, they had been destroyed for convenience.

His face was narrow, almost hawkish, with sharply angular cheekbones framing eyes so pale they blended into the faint yellow glow of the single light bulb hanging from a wire overhead. His eyes moved across the room, noticing every detail without missing anything. His dark hair was cut short in a military-style crew cut, but it seemed colder—and more clinical, like everything else about him.

Kohrs closed the screen door behind him, soft enough that the latch bolt barely clicked. "Gentlemen," he said. His voice was smooth and unremarkable—no accent, no emphasis on any particular letter—yet it carried an underlying physical threat. "We need to talk."

Teddy didn't move from his spot, didn't salute, didn't greet the man. They were the same rank. He stood very still, studying the man who was rumored never to leave a trace—the U.S. Army's top-secret version of a CIA "wet boy."

Kohrs stepped forward, hands clasped behind his back, his posture rigid and precise, like a ramrod nailed to his back. He moved smoothly like someone trained to kill in the shadows, each step placed exactly where he intended, each movement controlled and subtle.

"Colonel Roosevelt," Kohrs said, meeting Teddy's eyes with unsettling directness. "You've had a difficult few days."

"You might say that," Teddy replied.

Kohrs turned, giving Jack and Eli an appraising glance, evaluating rather than acknowledging. "I understand that Operation Wild Lantern presented some…irregularities."

Jack shifted his feet, tension tightening along his shoulders. Eli stood motionless, his massive frame poised, eyes locked on Kohrs with a cautious sharpness—ready to jump into action to protect his teammates if necessary.

Teddy met Kohrs' unblinking stare with one of his own. "Irregularities is a polite way of saying massacre."

Kohrs blinked once, deliberately. "I don't deal in politeness. I deal in containment."

"Meaning?" Teddy asked.

Kohrs' eyes narrowed. "Meaning, when a team starts to have second thoughts, it becomes a concern for everyone in the chain of command. Especially one responsible for operations sensitive enough to alter geopolitical realities."

"We're soldiers, Colonel," Teddy said. "We do our jobs, nothing more. Politics is General Dorsey's responsibility."

"Yes," Kohrs said. "But your job isn't to question your orders. Your job is to follow through with them smoothly, quietly, and without hesitation or doubt. Especially without leaving behind whispers of uncertainty." He stepped closer to Teddy, just within reach, as if daring him to move.

Teddy remained perfectly still. This lunatic might stab him in the gut out of spite.

"You're very good, Colonel Roosevelt," Kohrs continued. "All three of you. Exceptional soldiers. But even exceptional men become expendable if they stop being useful. If they talk too much."

Jack's jaw tightened, but he said nothing. Eli didn't move, yet his eyes burned with an intense fire behind them.

Teddy leaned against the center support pole with his arms crossed. "We know our role."

"Do you?" Kohrs tilted his head. "Because recent...private conversations suggest otherwise."

The words hung in the humid air. Were their quarters bugged?

"We do what's in the orders," Teddy said.

Kohrs shook his head, as if correcting a child. "That's not enough, Colonel Roosevelt. Not anymore. You're not MACV. You're not CIA. You're not even soldiers now. You're shadows in the dark. Shadows don't ask questions. They don't wonder about morality. Shadows only move—cleanly, quietly—and then disappear. Anything more is dangerous...to everyone's safety."

He stepped back, pacing across the narrow room with deliberate grace, fingers brushing the lockers as he passed, as if inspecting them for future reference.

"Understand this," Kohrs said, turning back to face them again. "This isn't a reprimand. It's not even a warning. It's clarification. We placed you here because you're exactly the kind of men who believe in service. In patriotism. In duty. Those beliefs are useful, but they're also your greatest vulnerability."

He paused intentionally, allowing his words and the implied threat to linger in the air.

"Because patriotism becomes complicated when orders get ugly," Kohrs continued. "Duty turns painful when those giving the orders wear your own uniform. But remember—your official uniforms were removed when you entered this world. Your orders don't come from national flags. They come from whispers in the dark."

Another carefully measured silence made the tent feel colder, like a deep freeze in the jungle.

Kohrs' gaze hardened. "Whispers that I control. Whispers that Major General Dorsey controls. You know these names. You understand their reach. What you may not fully appreciate is how effectively we clean up our own messes."

His eyes slowly, purposefully shifted to look at Jack and Eli.

"The next time you consider walking away," Kohrs said, his voice growing even softer, "think carefully about whether you'd prefer bullets or sharp blades—because one of those is how this always ends. Every time."

He allowed the threat to hang in the air, then gradually turned toward the door and opened it. Cool night air rushed inside. "Goodnight, gentlemen. Sleep lightly." Kohrs stepped outside, closing the door behind him, leaving only silence and the lingering heaviness of his warning.

Outside, the insects resumed their quiet chirping as though nothing had happened.

But Teddy knew something had changed forever. The black world had just become even darker.

CHAPTER 16

2235 Hours
December 1, 1971
Shadow Lance Compound
Quarters Bravo-2
Republic of Vietnam

The room was filled with thick, oppressive shadows, the flickering glow of a kerosene lamp casting pools of amber light across intelligence reports scattered across his desk. Teddy sat hunched over, one hand lazily tracing the edges of a mission map, the other holding a half-empty glass of cheap bourbon. His left leg throbbed, a bitter reminder of recent betrayals, both mental and physical. The quiet hum of insects outside was interrupted by a soft creak as the screen door eased open—barely audible, but loud enough to cause an adrenaline dump.

Teddy's heart rate sped up as his instincts, sharpened by weeks of threats and lurking dangers, kicked into overdrive. In one smooth, practiced motion, he stood, grabbed his loaded Colt M1911 from the desk, thumbed back the hammer, and aimed at the shadow slipping through his doorway.

"Take one step closer, and I'll put two dead center in your chest," Teddy warned, his voice low, steady, and dangerous.

The intruder stopped, slowly raising his hands, palms facing forward as a cautious gesture of surrender. "Easy, Colonel Roosevelt. It's me— Lieutenant Colonel Harry Desmond. We met at Long Binh."

Recognition dawned gradually. Teddy squinted, maintaining his firing stance, finger tight on the trigger, breathing controlled. "Step forward, slowly. Keep your hands where I can see them."

Lieutenant Colonel Harry Desmond moved cautiously into the dim glow of lamplight, revealing tired eyes and graying hair beneath a battered OD-green field cap. His plain clothes—a tan shirt and wrinkled tan pants—suggested a desire for anonymity, his posture relaxed despite the tension thick in the air between them. "It's been a while, Colonel Roosevelt."

"Forgive me for being cautious, Colonel Desmond," Teddy said, lowering and decocking the hammer—but not holstering—his pistol. "But after the recent visits from Dorsey and Kohrs, I'm not exactly welcoming to unexpected guests."

Desmond nodded. "Understood completely. Which is precisely why I'm here."

Teddy studied him, placing the pistol on the desktop but leaving it within easy reach. "Then talk."

Desmond approached the desk, pulling a plain white envelope marked *Eyes Only* from his shirt pocket. He placed it in front of Teddy. "This is your emergency ripcord. Directive Seven-Two and the legacy protocol are your only lifelines left. If they're circling you now, you need this."

Teddy opened the envelope, handling the papers with cautious suspicion. He skimmed the typed pages, the details sharp and unsettling.

TOP SECRET // EYES ONLY
SPECIAL ACCESS REQUIRED
DIRECTIVE SEVEN-TWO
OPERATION SUBNET ECHO PROTOCOL

CLASSIFICATION: TOP SECRET
SPECIAL ACCESS PROGRAM (SAP)
COMPARTMENTALIZED / NOFORN

AUTHORIZED PERSONNEL ONLY:
By direct order of the Joint Chiefs of Staff (JCS) and under the explicit authority of the National Command Authority (NCA) and the U.S. Army Office of Covert Operations (OCO), this document and the information contained herein are strictly forbidden from unauthorized distribution. Violators are subject to prosecution under applicable laws, including the Espionage Act, 18 U.S.C. §§ 793-798.

PURPOSE OF DIRECTIVE:
Directive Seven-Two is a classified fail-safe protocol operated by Operation Subnet Echo. It is only activated when a buried or presumed-dead asset is reactivated in hostile threat zones. When triggered, Directive Seven-Two permits the automatic exposure and dismantling of compromised internal command structures through targeted intelligence leaks, controlled asset exposure, and strategic disruption of financial and operational systems.

Directive Seven-Two is not an extraction or rescue protocol. Its purpose is the targeted and controlled exposure of compromised command-level assets and networks that pose existential threats to national security interests and personnel safety.

ACTIVATION PROCEDURE (LEGACY PROTOCOL):
Code Phrase: DELTA-ONE-NINER-BLACK
Activation Method:
The asset must establish direct contact through a secure, pre-approved legacy telephone number on a secure, pre-approved network.

LEGACY CONTACT NUMBER:
(212) 555-7483 (rotating secure trunk line monitored 24/7 by Operation Subnet Echo)

Once a secure line connection is established, the asset will wait five seconds as a failsafe in case the number is called intentionally or by mistake, then verbally state their full legal name, call sign, and the authentication phrase DELTA-ONE-NINER-BLACK. Condition—compromised. Confirm legacy protocol. No additional authentication is required. The agent receiving the call may respond with additional questions.

EXPECTED EFFECTS OF DIRECTIVE ACTIVATION:
Upon valid protocol activation, Directive Seven-Two will immediately:
1. Trigger pre-positioned intelligence leaks via trusted media and allied covert channels, outlining targeted corruption, compromised operations, and rogue command elements.
2. Deploy immediate asset-protection countermeasures designed to disrupt adversarial surveillance, monitoring systems, and command & control infrastructure within a 24–48-hour window.
3. Enable direct intervention by allied, vetted internal counterintelligence personnel committed to the asset's survival and operational security.
4. Implement minimal, covert operational disruption sufficient to allow the asset time for relocation or additional defensive measures.

Warning:

Once initiated, Directive Seven-Two actions are irreversible and will result in immediate, widespread internal and external consequences. Collateral damage within the affected structures is unavoidable and deemed acceptable under the directive's guidelines.

HISTORICAL CONTEXT (REFERENCE – MONGOOSE LIST):
Established in 1961 under joint CIA-DIA-MACV operations, the "Mongoose List" was initially created to track and disrupt financial and operational networks supporting communist insurgencies and hostile state actors across Southeast Asia. It was officially terminated after the Bay of Pigs and publicly disavowed by the Kennedy administration in 1962.

Unofficially, the Mongoose operational framework remained active, evolving into covert assassination and targeted intimidation operations throughout Vietnam, Cambodia, and Laos—later integrated into the Phoenix Program. In recent years, the framework has been taken over by unauthorized command-level personnel (notably Major General Franklin A. Dorsey, DIA Strategic Planning) for blackmail, political coercion, elimination of inconvenient personnel, and illegal manipulation of national security policy within his own private agency—Covert Operations Directorate.

Unauthorized use of Mongoose methodologies continues to pose a direct and ongoing threat to operational security and institutional integrity.

DIRECT THREAT ASSESSMENT (FRANKLIN A. DORSEY):
1. Confirmed unauthorized appropriation and misuse of intelligence infrastructure.
2. Verified use of blackmail and direct threats against U.S. Senators, Congressmen, senior Pentagon personnel, and foreign diplomats.
3. Direct involvement in orchestrating clandestine operations resulting in the extrajudicial elimination of allied assets, informants, and political opponents.
4. Responsible for organizing coordinated disinformation campaigns aimed at influencing national security policies for personal and ideological reasons.

5. Currently, the listed threat cannot be neutralized due to external factors beyond the control of the JSC, NCA, and the OCO.

ADVISORY AND RECOMMENDATIONS:
Directive Seven-Two is authorized as a final protective measure. The use of the legacy activation phrase DELTA-ONE-NINER-BLACK should only occur upon confirmation of an imminent threat or compromise by hostile internal actors. Asset discretion is advised. All consequences are solely determined by the asset's judgment.

DISTRIBUTION:

Original copy – Recipient asset only
Secondary copies – None authorized
Destroy immediately after activation or upon compromise.
End of Directive Seven-Two // Operation Subnet Echo

Harry Desmond

Lieutenant Colonel Harry Desmond
Authorized Liaison Officer
Operation Subnet Echo
MACV-SOG / Special Intelligence Division

"Directive Seven-two is a fail-safe, last-resort firewall. It's designed to dismantle any internal command structures compromised by black-world infiltration. When activated, it triggers controlled intelligence leaks, exposes financial ties, destroys corrupted assets, and disrupts operations," Desmond said.

Teddy rubbed his stubbled chin. "And this legacy protocol? What exactly is it?"

"A hidden line beyond anyone's ability to trace. One phone call, one phrase—Delta-One-Niner-Black—and you set the network ablaze. It alerts every sleeper agent still active, every covert asset loyal to us. It disrupts surveillance, scrambles orders, and creates brief windows of opportunity—short moments you'll desperately need if Dorsey sends Kohrs back here with kill orders."

"Dorsey's made it clear exactly where we stand," Teddy replied, bitterness coloring his words. "But why are you here risking your neck?"

Desmond sighed. "Because Dorsey's organization isn't just rogue—it's institutional. He uses threats, blackmail, and even outright coercion against senators, congressmen, and senior military officers to get what he wants. His influence runs deep, and his methods are ruthless. Have you ever heard of the Mongoose List?"

Teddy narrowed his eyes, wary of the implications of that list. "Officially, that was the CIA's failed covert operation against Castro in Cuba. Shut down by Kennedy after the Bay of Pigs. I saw that listed in the paperwork. Is there anything else I should know?"

"Officially, yes, the list was disbanded," Desmond agreed, leaning closer and lowering his voice. "But unofficially, the Mongoose framework never disappeared. Instead, after Kennedy dissolved the original operation, the CIA, working with elements of the DIA and MACV, quietly repurposed it in Vietnam for their own use. They transformed it into a secret elimination list—a precursor to what we now know as the Phoenix Program. Originally, it targeted enemy financiers and informants. But Dorsey and his people hijacked the structure and expanded its purpose far beyond that. By 1970, the Mongoose List had become something darker— a targeted assassination and coercion network. Informants, journalists, diplomats, even our own senior military officers and politicians—anyone who threatened to expose or obstruct their covert activities—ended up on that ledger."

Teddy absorbed this information in silence, tension coursing through his body. He knew how far Dorsey's influence extended—he'd experienced it firsthand—but hearing the historical facts laid out clearly gave him a new, chilling perspective on how deeply he had been pulled into Dorsey's dark world.

Desmond stood straighter, locking his gaze onto Teddy's. "Dorsey didn't just inherit the Mongoose List. He weaponized it. Senators who oppose his plans are suddenly faced with scandals or career-ending threats. High-ranking generals found themselves abruptly retiring, being reassigned, or under JAG investigation on charges fabricated by Dorsey's internal network of loyal officers. Anyone who opposes him finds themselves sidelined—or worse, under a kill order with Kohrs doing the dirty work. That's why the black world wants you gone. You've seen the ledger. You know too much."

Teddy examined the documents in his hands, now understanding the full weight of the papers before him.

"You've always played by the rules, Colonel Roosevelt, a patriot and loyal Army officer, adhering to the regulations, but this is no longer a game of rules. Activate Directive Seven-Two, use the legacy protocol—but know this—once it's started, there's no going back," Desmond said in an urgent but calm voice.

"Where do you stand in all this, Harry?" Teddy asked.

Desmond offered a faint, weary smile. "Same place I've always stood—with good soldiers like you caught in the crossfire of a dark shadow government. Keep those papers hidden. Memorize that number, and never hesitate to use it. The next time Dorsey sends Kohrs, you might not get another chance."

Without another word, Desmond turned toward the door, his footsteps silent on the weathered wooden planks. He paused in the doorway, glancing back over his shoulder. "Good luck, Colonel Roosevelt. You'll need every bit you can muster. I hope you have a leprechaun on your shoulder and a four-leaf clover in your pocket."

Then he was gone, leaving Teddy alone again with secrets heavy enough to change history—or to bury him beneath it.

CHAPTER 17

1630 Hours
May 29, 1972
Shadow Lance Compound
Firebase Apache
Republic of Vietnam

The secure briefing hut at Firebase Apache was barely more than a wooden bunker with a corrugated sheet-metal roof, buried halfway into the slope of a muddy hillside. Layers of sandbags reinforced the sides, and camouflage netting draped over the roof, blending it into the jungle terrain to prevent artillery strikes. Inside, the air was thick with cigarette smoke, diesel and exhaust fumes from the generator, and the acrid tang of insect repellent.

A battered aluminum table sat in the middle of the room, covered with laminated grid maps, grainy black-and-white aerial photographs, and intelligence folders marked with cryptic identifier codes. An overhead lamp cast sharp, focused circles of light, the glare spilling over the faces gathered for the briefing.

Teddy leaned over the table, forearms resting on the edge, his eyes narrowed as Lt. Commander Nathan Kaufman—Naval Intelligence—systematically laid out the briefing materials.

Kaufman moved with precise control, every gesture deliberate, as if choreographed in an over-rehearsed play. He wore green jungle fatigues stripped of insignia, sleeves cuffed at the wrists, and a stainless steel Rolex Submariner on his left wrist—practical and exact, like everything about him. Also, it cost about a third of what a U.S. Navy Lieutenant Commander earned each month.

"We've been monitoring increased Chinese logistical activity in southern Laos," Kaufman said, his voice cool and professional. He glanced up at Teddy, making direct eye contact before turning back to the photographs. "Satellite passes confirm significant movement along these coordinates—Grid Sector Lima-Seven. Approximately twenty kilometers northeast of Paksé."

He tapped the aerial photograph with his index finger, a thin, pale line of light reflecting off the crystal of his Rolex watch. "These roads didn't exist four months ago. Heavy machinery and freshly cut jungle trails have appeared. More notably, aerial infrared photography shows fuel drums and suspected ammunition caches buried near these structures."

Jack leaned in, examining the photo. "That's a hell of a lot of activity for an area supposedly empty with no strategic value."

"Precisely," Kaufman said. "Intercepted radio chatter—encrypted Chinese frequencies—suggests an inbound shipment within seventy-two hours. Possibly weapons, possibly something bigger. Whatever it is, they've committed significant assets to safeguarding it."

"What about the locals?" Teddy asked. "Are there any villages in close proximity to the target location?"

Kaufman looked at a black-and-white, grainy secondary photo showing the outlines of thatched huts barely visible through the jungle foliage. "Two minor villages within five klicks. Nothing suggests direct involvement, but it's unclear how much they know."

"Do you suspect a trap?" Eli asked from the corner.

"I always suspect a trap, Sergeant Red Horse," Kaufman replied, meeting Eli's suspicious gaze. "But we can't ignore what we're seeing here. This level of enemy activity demands an appropriate response."

Jack shot a quick glance at Teddy, both men sharing the same unspoken suspicion.

Kaufman must have sensed their hesitation, drawing his shoulders back. "I've triple-checked these intercepts myself. This isn't questionable village intel or hearsay from defectors. It's verified satellite reconnaissance passes and communications intercepts." He leaned over the table, locking eyes with Teddy. "Colonel Roosevelt, your team is being tasked to verify and neutralize this shipment. Your authorization comes from General Dorsey himself, directly from DIA Strategic Planning."

Teddy clenched his jaw at the mention of Dorsey's name. He didn't reply right away, letting the silence drag on a few moments too long before responding. "You verified these orders personally?"

"Yes," Kaufman replied without hesitation. "They're officially verbal with no written paper trail beyond my own secure channels. Plausible deniability remains intact. I'm here only to provide the intelligence packet. Execution of the order remains entirely at your team's discretion."

Jack shook his head. "We've heard that one before."

Kaufman's expression remained neutral, but Teddy noticed something in his eyes—maybe concern, maybe understanding. With eyes that cold, it was hard to tell.

Kaufman paused, choosing his words carefully. "Off the record, Colonel Roosevelt, this mission feels crucial to our continued support in this region. Possibly decisive. If these supply caches contain what we suspect, it could alter the political and military landscape in Southeast Asia overnight. And we both know what happens to teams who carry out decisive operations."

The implication hung in the air. Kaufman didn't need to elaborate.

Eli shifted his weight, breaking the tense silence. "What about our extraction? The chopper failed to show during Operation Wild Lantern. Flight operations would never tell us why."

Kaufman turned to the logistics folder. "Standard LZ, roughly one klick southeast of the target area. You'll have priority evac once you signal the forward air controller mission complete."

Teddy nodded, studying the aerial photos spread out under Kaufman's hands. His stomach tightened. Kaufman's intel was professional, precise, and thoroughly vetted—exactly what the black ops world demanded. Still, something felt off, incomplete, maybe even fabricated. Familiar warning bells, quiet but persistent, rang in the back of his mind. Now he faced a choice—believe Kaufman or trust his gut. He met Kaufman's gaze evenly. "Anything else we should know?"

Kaufman hesitated for just a split second. It was barely noticeable, just a flicker of something deeper behind his carefully rehearsed composure. "Just remember…operations like this leave very little room for error. Trust your instincts. Officially, nothing about tonight exists." He stepped away from the table, signaling the end of the briefing.

Teddy glanced at Jack and Eli, both watching him, their faces serious but alert, minds already preparing for what would come next.

As Kaufman reached the door, he paused and looked back over his shoulder. "Good luck, Colonel Roosevelt. For what it's worth." Then he exited the bunker, closing the door behind him.

In the silence that followed, Teddy examined the photographs again, studying the faint trails and hidden caches, the unclear shapes of huts and abandoned roads. Kaufman had given them everything—and yet, somehow, nothing at all.

Teddy picked up the map. Whatever awaited them at Grid Sector Lima-Seven was already planned, already decided.

And once again, Shadow Lance would walk in blind.

CHAPTER 18

2215 Hours
May 30, 1972
Shadow Lance Compound
Firebase Apache
Republic of Vietnam

Under the harsh yellow glow of portable floodlights, the staging area in the middle of the compound was organized chaos. Heavy canvas tarps, marked ammunition crates, neatly arranged weapons, and tactical gear sat in precise rows, each item inventoried and ready for final inspection.

Teddy walked through the setup, examining each piece of equipment. He still wore jungle fatigues with his sleeves rolled up to his elbows, jungle boots, and his M1911 pistol strapped to his hip. The familiar ache in his ankle whispered with every other step, a quiet reminder of past missions. He brushed it aside and continued his inspection.

"Explosives?" he asked, glancing at Eli.

Eli knelt beside his demolition equipment, which included ten one-pound blocks of C-4, wiring harnesses, and radio detonators—enough to demolish a two-story building. He looked up, meeting Teddy's eyes. "Charges shaped and sealed. Det cord checked and bagged separately. All detonators accounted for. Ready to rock and roll."

Teddy nodded. "We're going in heavy enough to take out any buried cache we encounter."

Eli nodded. "Understood. I'm ready for anything."

Teddy moved further along, stopping beside Jack, who was inspecting their suppressed CAR-15 rifles, each disassembled and laid out on a clean oilcloth, parts arranged like surgical instruments. Jack's face stayed calm and focused, his eyes sharp as he oiled a bolt carrier.

"Weapons?" Teddy asked.

Jack looked up before returning to his task. "Cleaned, checked, and sighted in. Zeroed at fifty meters. Suppressors tested and sound tight. Ammo loads are marked and counted. All mags fresh from the box to prevent jams."

Teddy visually inspected the weapons without touching them. He had complete confidence in Jack's precision. The man handled rifles and optics as if they were an extension of himself, a perfectionist in all things lethal.

"Sidearms?" Teddy asked.

Jack tilted his head toward a nearby, smaller tarp-covered table where three suppressed M1911s lay disassembled, parts gleaming under the lights. "Same. Function checks completed and test-fired."

Teddy nodded again, pleased that the equipment was ready. "Good job."

Eli joined them. "Comm gear?"

Teddy turned toward the compact prototype radio sets arranged on another table with the labeled frequency cards tucked beside each handset. "Checked by Kaufman himself. Sat-burst capability through DSCS confirmed. Backup frequencies are in place. All encryption and codes were validated through approved channels."

Jack set down the rifle bolt and looked at Teddy. "Then we're as ready as we'll ever be."

Teddy nodded, turning his gaze to the floodlit perimeter fence. His gut tightened at the thought of what lay ahead—Kaufman's intelligence, Kohrs' warning, and Dorsey's orders all tangled in his mind like booby-trap tripwires hidden beneath the mud.

"We'll know soon enough," Teddy said. "Wrap it up, gentlemen, pack everything, then get some rest. We move out for the border tomorrow night for our final briefing."

2335 Hours
May 30, 1972
Shadow Lance Compound
Operations Tent
Firebase Apache
Republic of Vietnam

The single kerosene lamp on Teddy's desk cast a faint, uneven circle of light, leaving the edges of the small room in shadows. Outside, the jungle had fallen silent—its usual nighttime chorus of insects muted by the heavy tension hanging over the compound.

Teddy sat alone, staring at the sealed white envelope on the battered table in front of him. The paper had no official seal or signatures—just a small notation scribbled in one corner—*Eyes Only – Colonel Roosevelt. Destroy after reading.*

He picked up the envelope and slit it open with his pocket knife, removing a single folded sheet of paper. It was plain, typed on a manual typewriter—clear, precise lettering. His pulse quickened as he unfolded it and began to read.

Operational Directive – FIRELIGHT
Classified: Eyes Only
Covert Operations Directorate
Authorization: MG Franklin A. Dorsey, DIA Strategic Planning
Date: 30 May 1972

Colonel Roosevelt,

You and your team are tasked with neutralizing suspected high-level Chinese military caches located at Grid Sector Lima-Seven (see coordinates provided by Lt. Commander Kaufman). Target location confirmed through satellite photographs and SIGINT intercepts. The mission is urgent and politically sensitive. Absolute discretion is required.

Mission Parameters:
1. Confirm the presence of advanced Chinese weaponry.
2. Destroy caches using explosives.
3. Ensure no traceable evidence remains at the target location post-operation.
4. Engage any hostile forces as necessary to uphold operational security.

Extraction and Contingencies:
1. Evacuation point secured in the southeast (LZ coordinates attached).
2. Emergency extraction only if the mission is compromised.

Note: Mission success is critical. The operation must conclude with zero identifiable U.S. presence. You and your men will maintain absolute silence regarding mission details at all times, before, during, and after execution. Dismiss all previous operational doubts. You are officially unacknowledged until further notice.

The significance of the final sentence weighed heavily on Teddy's mind. He stared at the words, jaw clenched, pulse steady and pounding against his temples. *Officially unacknowledged* was a code he understood well—no rescue, no backup, and no accountability. If they died, no one would recover their bodies—food for worms and scavengers. Just like his team in Cambodia.

He set the paper down slowly, exhaling through clenched teeth, eyes fixed on the words—*Absolute silence.*

The room around him felt colder and heavier, as if the shadows themselves had pressed in closer. Dorsey's words—cryptic but clear—left no doubt. The implications were obvious—if anything went wrong, Shadow Lance had already ceased to exist. They'd become disposable. Expendable.

A memory of Kohrs' pale, watchful eyes surfaced in his mind, the ghost of a warning clear in every carefully chosen word the man had spoken. Teddy realized then—Firelight was not just an ordinary operation. It was the culmination—the mission for which Shadow Lance had always been intended, knowingly or not.

Teddy glanced again at the envelope's quiet directive—*Destroy after reading.*

He folded the paper and placed it into the small metal trash can next to his desk. Reaching for a pack of matches, he struck one on the edge of the desk, the small flame flickering as it cast shadows across the surface while he lit the directive.

The paper blackened and curled, the edges glowing red before turning to ash. Teddy watched until the last ember died out, leaving only dust and smoke behind.

He leaned back in his chair, his eyes drifting toward the dark window as he listened to the oppressive silence of the jungle outside.

Whatever awaited them in Lima-Seven, there was no turning back now.

CHAPTER 19

0930 Hours
June 1, 1972
Undisclosed Forward Operations Center
Grid Sector Kilo Bravo Six-Zero
Cambodia-Laos Border

The room had no windows, only plain concrete walls. A long metal table sat in the center with a single yellowed light bulb hanging from a wire overhead. A portable air conditioner hummed in the corner window like an afterthought. Everything about it screamed temporary but not improvised. It was the kind of room where decisions were made without oversight—and then erased.

Teddy sat at the far end of the table, his arms crossed over his chest. Next to him were Captain Jack Stratton and Master Sergeant Eli Red Horse—both silent and alert. Jack's eyes scanned the few visible details in the room—the sealed door behind them, the metal ceiling fan overhead spinning just enough to remind them it was working. Eli didn't fidget. He never did. One of the reasons they called him "Stone."

The door opened.

The man who entered looked as if he had been plucked straight from a Washington D.C. cocktail party and dropped into a war zone without advanced warning. Slate gray slacks, a khaki shirt under a lightweight tan jacket, and black patent leather dress shoes. He moved purposefully but lacked military discipline. Too smooth. Too clean. And so perfect, even the ever-present dust wouldn't stick to him.

"Colonel Roosevelt," the man said as he took a seat across from them without offering a hand in greeting. "Captain Stratton. Sergeant Red Horse. I'm Christopher Armstrong, your CIA liaison officer for this phase of the operation."

Teddy didn't reply. Neither did Jack or Eli.

Armstrong smiled as though he expected their reaction. He pulled a battered manila folder from his briefcase and placed it in front of him.

"Operation Firelight," he said, voice low but highly rehearsed, ready for an audition to star in the latest blockbuster movie. "This mission is not listed on the MACV-SOG mission board. You are not under Group command for the next seventy-two hours. Operational authority has been verbally reassigned to the Special Projects office." He tapped the folder once. "That's the extent of your official paperwork."

Jack's eyebrows twitched. Eli stared straight ahead. Teddy clenched his jaw, fighting the urge to make a sarcastic comment about the situation or the man in front of him who acted like an arrogant royal class jerk.

"You're being tasked with a high-value reconnaissance run," Armstrong continued. "Insertion into a village near Grid Sector Lima-Seven. You'll confirm the presence of Chinese-manufactured weapons— Type 56 rifles, 82mm mortars, and crates marked with PLAAF stamps. We have reason to believe they're being diverted to Khmer Rouge assets operating along the Ho Chi Minh Trail."

"Who confirmed that?" Teddy asked.

Armstrong smiled, thinner this time. "Multiple intercepts from military officials in Phnom Penh and Vientiane. Secondary verification from our own assets on the ground operating under commercial cover identities in Phnom Penh."

"Names?" Jack asked.

"Not relevant to your mission."

Teddy leaned forward, placing both hands on the table. "I don't move my team solely based on intelligence coming from the CIA, Mr. Armstrong. Most of the time, it's absolute garbage that even a blind man can see through the lies. I want the names of your sources."

"You don't need them." Armstrong's tone never changed. "Your job is to confirm the material presence, document it with photographic proof, and transmit the coordinates to a forward strike team operating under separate authorization. You're not responsible for the follow-up. Just focus on painting the target for us."

"And if there's nothing there?" Eli asked.

"There will be," Armstrong said. "Our reports are solid. The intel is beyond reproach, no matter what you think of us, Colonel Roosevelt."

Jack shifted in his seat. "And if they're not?"

Armstrong didn't blink. "Then you get back on the chopper and head back to the base. Simple, even for grunts."

Teddy remained silent for a long moment, biding his time, aware that Armstrong had just called them stupid. He tapped his fingers twice on the table—once out of habit, and once to get Armstrong's attention. "We'll need independent satellite imagery and overflight access. I want to interpret the information myself."

"You won't get it."

"Then you're asking us to go into Laos blind."

"I'm asking you to do what you've always done," Armstrong replied. "Get the job done without asking for more than what's already on the table."

"This operation...is part of a broader push, isn't it?" Teddy asked. "Something to justify re-escalation across the border into both Laos and Cambodia. A narrative to fit the current political landscape, using defeating communism as the rally cry to invade a country that doesn't want or need us."

Armstrong smiled and closed the folder with one finger. "Sometimes the truth is defined by whoever prints the report first. You're soldiers, Colonel Roosevelt. Not investigative journalists. Let's keep it that way."

Teddy kept watching Armstrong. Cold. Assessing. Already calculating the weight of what wasn't being said.

Armstrong stood and walked away without shaking anyone's hand, as if simple human contact and acknowledgment were beyond his reach or understanding. "Wheels up at 0100 hours on the fourth. The insertion point's already been confirmed. The village's name is Chum Nhi." He paused at the door. "And before you look, you won't find it on any map."

He exited the room, the door closing behind him.

The silence in the room grew thicker.

Jack looked at Teddy. "Does that smell like truth to you?"

"No," Teddy said. "It smells like current political policy wrapped in a multitude of official lies."

Eli rose from his seat, every movement quiet and deliberate. "Do you believe him?"

"I believe he knows exactly what he's not saying."

"Me too." Jack glanced at the door. "Do you think we just got handed a fuse?"

Teddy sighed. "I think we were just handed a box of matches. Whether we light that fuse or not is up to us."

CHAPTER 20

0115 Hours
June 4, 1972
Operation Firelight
Insertion Point Grid Sector Lima-Seven
Laos

The dense jungle canopy beneath them was an endless sea of blackness, gently rippling under the steady, rhythmic pulse of rotor wash. The moonlight cast a ghostly shadow skimming the treetops. Teddy sat quietly on the open side door of the UH-1 Huey, one leg hanging into the dark emptiness below the skids, his gloved hand gripping the web strap above him tightly. The wind tugged at his unmarked tiger-striped fatigues as the helicopter skimmed treetop level, swaying softly beneath a moonless sky.

To his left, Jack shifted his weight quietly on the canvas bench, his blue eyes calm and steady beneath streaks of green, black, and brown camouflage grease paint. Eli sat across from him, his massive frame unmoving, carved from granite, face impassive under the same camouflage grease paint as he checked the equipment lashed to his combat web gear. Demolition charges. Extra mags. Field medical supplies.

"Thirty seconds out," the pilot's voice crackled over the internal speakers, barely audible through the rotor noise.

Teddy raised his fist with a thumbs up, signaling readiness. Jack and Eli responded with firm nods, their fingers checking weapon safeties and flipping them to the off position.

The helicopter slowed to a hover, engines roaring against the dark night. Teddy leaned forward, eyes struggling to pierce the thick jungle canopy below, searching for the faint glow of chemlights marking their landing zone. A single small green flicker appeared, then more in a circle, exactly on schedule.

"Go!" Teddy ordered.

He dropped first, the world vanishing beneath his feet in a rush of cold night air and branches slapping hard against his body. The rope hissed under his gloves, burning through the leather as gravity pulled him down into the jungle's oppressive embrace, using his foot looped around the rope to slow his descent. He landed on the ground, rolled sideways, absorbing the impact with bent knees. Sharp pain shot through his left ankle—brief and familiar—but he ignored it, raising his suppressed CAR-15 to his shoulder in one smooth motion.

Jack arrived a few seconds later, crouching with his rifle raised and scanning the perimeter. Eli followed, heavier and more solid, hitting the ground with a muted grunt as he released the rope and rolled clear.

The helicopter disappeared into the darkness, low and fast, engines fading into the distant silence. The jungle muffled the sound of the rotor wash. They were alone, far behind enemy lines, with no extraction scheduled until the mission was complete.

Teddy keyed his throat mic. "Shadow Actual. On the ground. Moving to the target. Radio silent."

Two quick mic clicks in response. Message received.

Teddy adjusted his pack straps, redistributing the weight on his shoulders, and took one last look around the LZ before signaling the team to move out. The air was thick with humidity, carrying the scent of mud, moss, and distant wood smoke rising from the valley below.

The jungle closed in around them, thick and humid, alive with distant animal calls and rustling leaves. They moved in a tight formation along the trail, guided by a compass and the stars, making almost no sound— shadows within shadows. Jack took point with Teddy in the middle and Eli watching their backs. The ground beneath them was soft, yielding, and covered with wet leaves and tangled roots.

Ten minutes in, Jack paused and raised a closed fist at head level. The team froze, crouching low with their weapons sweeping outward—three points of a compass instead of four. Teddy moved forward, eyes fixed on where Jack pointed—a thin strand of wire, nearly invisible, stretched taut at ankle height between two slender trees.

"Tripwire," Jack whispered.

"Claymore," Eli confirmed, pointing at the faint outline of a rectangular explosive half-buried in the foliage.

Teddy nodded once, signaling them to proceed. On a tight schedule, there wasn't time to disarm it.

They skirted the booby trap, their senses sharpened by adrenaline and the heavy silence around them. According to the briefing, Grid Sector Lima-Seven overlooked a suspected Chinese arms transfer site, a relay village used by the Pathet Lao to move crates along the Ho Chi Minh Trail. Their mission was to confirm the weapons cache, plant a signal beacon, and get out. No engagement unless fired upon. No deviation. No questions.

Twenty meters further ahead, the trees thinned out. Jack dropped down, signaling the team to move forward. Teddy took a position beside him, peering through a gap in the dense vegetation.

Ahead, the jungle opened into a clearing. Two low huts made from bamboo and thatch stood silent and dark, surrounded by shallow defensive trenches dug into the earth. Faint lantern light spilled from half-open doors, casting uneven shadows. Stacked wooden crates sat beneath a camouflage netting, their outlines dark and bulky against the night.

"Looks like Kaufman was right," Jack whispered. "For once."

"Move in slow," Teddy ordered. "Confirm the weapons, rig the beacons, and move out."

The team split up—Jack went left, Eli turned right, and Teddy headed straight for the stacked crates.

Teddy hugged the treeline, scanning for sentries. None were visible. It felt wrong. The village was unnaturally quiet. Not just "enemy evacuated" quiet—but staged for their benefit. Campfires burned in perfect circles. Cooking pots remained warm. Deliberately placed footprints in the mud led nowhere.

He crouched beside the nearest wooden crate, slipping his combat knife under the nailed edge and prying it open. Inside, gleaming in the faint glow of a chem-light attached to his web gear, Chinese characters were etched onto black metal ammunition tins. Dozens of them were stacked on top of each other. The next crate revealed rocket-propelled grenade launchers, oily and new.

"Jack," Teddy whispered. "We've got Chinese ordnance here...I think." Something about it felt...off. This was way too easy.

Jack appeared beside him, inspecting the cache. "This is fucking surplus Soviet shit, Bull. Look at the stenciling on the crates. It's spray-painted in Mandarin to look like Chinese issue."

Teddy pried off the lid of another crate—inside were AK-47s, spare parts—everything he'd expect in a Chinese-run operation—except it wasn't. He reached in and pulled out a grease-covered bolt carrier, then froze. He turned it over in his hand.

The serial number was in Cyrillic lettering—Russian. More Soviet surplus.

Jack pulled out an AK-47. "This isn't Chinese or Russian. That's Vietnamese script and a poor copy at that. They didn't even weather the damn paint properly. This crap was made in Vietnam, probably in Hanoi or Haiphong."

"These weapons aren't cached. They were planted. Here for show." Teddy moved crate to crate, discovering more inconsistencies. A Chinese crate filled with Soviet parts. Sandbags filled with the wrong grit—brown and coarse, not the red clay native to this region. And a burned-out Jeep frame with deflated tires still bearing U.S. tread patterns and a partial serial number dating back to the Korean War.

"Someone staged this," Teddy muttered to himself.

Jack entered one of the huts and returned with a bundle of documents. "Orders in Chinese…except the font's wrong. It's not even the paper stock they use. This is U.S. Signal Corps stationery with hand-inked Chinese Hanzi logographs."

Teddy's breath cooled inside his chest as he turned and looked out over the dark ridge. Everything became clear—the briefings that didn't add up, the refusal to allow his team to conduct pre-insertion reconnaissance, the fact that Kaufman hadn't shown up in person, and that Armstrong passed orders through cutouts.

The mission wasn't about gathering intelligence. It was stagecraft, and poorly executed at that—a hastily planned operation.

And they were the final piece of the puzzle.

"Shit!" Teddy exclaimed. "This whole site is fake."

Jack blinked. "You're saying it's not a Chinese arms route or command center? That our orders are total garbage."

"Yes," Teddy said, his voice low. "It's not even Pathet Lao. Look around—no defensive perimeter, no guards, no civilians—nothing. Just abandoned props and empty huts. We were sent to verify enemy aggression…so they could use it as a pretext in Congress to justify escalating U.S. military action in the region." He looked back toward the jungle. "This is a false flag operation. They want us to call in confirmation so the press has proof splashed all over the newspapers by nightfall. We're the evidence chain and now a bunch of damn fools caught in the middle of a lie."

Eli's hand hovered near his weapon. "So what now?"

"We don't plant the beacon." Teddy stood and scanned the ridgeline one last time. "We vanish. Backtrack west toward the rendezvous point. We're not playing into their hands."

Jack glanced over. "You sure?"

"Yeah," Teddy said. "Too sure." Because deep down, he'd seen this before. In Cambodia. In the quiet fallout of Shatterhorn. But this time, they weren't just being used.

They were being set up to take the fall.

And now he knew.

They were alone—deep in Laos, compromised and abandoned.

Teddy's blood ran cold. They'd walked into a trap—a trap set from the inside. And now they had to fight their way out of it.

1750 Hours
June 4, 1972
Operation Firelight
Rendezvous Site Grid Sector Delta-Six
Laos

The jungle clearing was eerily silent. No birds, no bugs, not even a breeze to dry the sweat on Teddy's forehead. Only the distant echo of artillery in the hills and the smell of smoke—coming from the wrong direction, the wrong village. Teddy could feel it in his chest. This wasn't a cleanup job. This was a burn—and unknown who was going to take the heat—the enemy or Shadow Lance.

He stepped into the clearing with Jack and Eli flanking him. The oppressive humidity clung to them like wet gauze, shirts soaked with sweat, mud caked on every inch of their fatigues. They were scraped raw from humping through dense jungle to reach the rendezvous point—mud-covered boots, torn sleeves sliced from sharp elephant grass, and the stench of blood from all their scratches and cuts. Teddy's ankle ached, but it was nothing he couldn't handle with a couple of aspirin from the small bottle in his pack.

None of them had spoken much since Lima-Seven. Not after what they'd seen—or rather, what they hadn't.

The village was deserted. Nothing remained in any of the huts—abandoned too neatly, as if someone had staged the mess and taken the elaborate play elsewhere.

And now their handler, CIA agent Christopher Armstrong, stood in the middle of the clearing beside a still-idling U.S. Army green UH-1, its blades still turning in the rising heat. He wore spotless, pressed khakis and mirrored Ray-Ban aviator sunglasses, as calm and composed as ever. Clearly, he was not worried about attracting the attention of enemy patrols. His two escorts, dressed in green jungle fatigues and armed with M16s and sidearms—quiet and impassive—stood alert just behind him.

"Colonel Roosevelt, you made it," Armstrong said with a hint of amusement in his voice. "Glad to see you're on time. Although I expected you to follow the plan, plant the beacons, transmit the information, and pull out through the northern ridge."

Teddy didn't smile. He stood, rifle still in hand, the muzzle pointed downward as he fought the urge to point it at Armstrong. "The operation is scrubbed on my authority."

Jack and Eli flanked him without a word.

Armstrong raised an eyebrow. "Oh? You found something at Lima-Seven—Chum Nhi?"

"We found nothing," Jack said, anger filling his voice. "That's the problem."

"Not a single Chinese crate. No shell casings. No intel. Not even a whisper of enemy presence. It was all a load of fucking bullshit," Eli added.

"Then I assume your after-action reports will reflect the ambiguity of the site minus the profanity," Armstrong said.

"There were no Chinese weapons," Jack said. "Not real ones. I spent six months learning the production marks of every Soviet bloc weapon. I know what a Type 56 looks like. The crates were stamped in the wrong language and lacked the proper manufacturing symbols. And the mortars—Soviet tubes with stripped serial numbers, not PLA stock."

Armstrong shrugged. "You confirmed the presence of weapons. That's what matters."

"That's all you have to say," Teddy said, flipping the safety on and off on his CAR-15 with his thumb while fingering the trigger.

"Colonel Roosevelt, I think your team's been in country too long. You've lost perspective."

"No!" Teddy stepped forward. "I finally got it back. The intel you gave us—garbage. That village was empty of anything of strategic value. You sent us to stage something. We didn't. And we won't in the future."

Armstrong let that hang for a moment then tilted his head. "No, Colonel Roosevelt. You didn't. But that part didn't require your team."

Jack stiffened. "What does that mean?"

"It means we already handled it," Armstrong said. "Downriver from your sector. A different village. One with...let's say...more useful optics and strategic value. You'll be credited with the forward recon. Langley will file it accordingly in your service records. Congratulations on the victory."

"You murdered civilians?" Teddy asked, his voice deadly calm.

"We conducted a field operation…with extreme prejudice," Armstrong replied. "Same as you've done for the last nine months. The difference is that this one mattered. It will shape future U.S. foreign policy."

Teddy stepped forward, closing the gap. "The crates we found were Soviet surplus with Chinese spray paint. The weapons were stamped incorrectly. The maps were faked. You didn't want us to verify Chinese arms smuggling. You wanted to create it. This was a false flag operation. Firelight was never about weapons tracing or Chinese intervention. It was about creating a justification for U.S. intervention in Laos and, by extension, Cambodia, to avenge Nixon's failed invasion and political gain. You needed a spark."

Armstrong smiled. "And I found one. You. Perception shapes policy, Colonel Roosevelt. Always has. Always will."

"We're done," Teddy said. "Firelight is over."

"No," Armstrong said. "It's complete. Mission accomplished. And so are you."

The tension between them snapped tight like a sunbaked cowhide drum head.

Teddy reached into his shirt and pulled out his extra set of folded mission orders—damp, torn, and stained with his own blood. He tossed them at Armstrong's feet. "You used my team to frame an atrocity. You burned a village we never saw or knew about. Then tied it to our operation so the record would show we were boots on the ground when it happened. Not a mistake. A plan."

"The plan was for you not to make it to this meeting," Armstrong said, his voice cold enough to flash freeze on contact.

Jack tightened his grip on his rifle sling.

Eli moved nearer to Armstrong, hand on the handle of his KA-BAR.

"You were supposed to go quietly," Armstrong continued. "A lost team. Shot down, overrun, missing in action—something clean. Something final. Not three exhausted men limping out of the jungle asking the wrong questions."

"Well," Teddy said, "here we are."

"Not for long," Armstrong said. "The fallback LZ has been scrubbed. No extraction. No air cover. Your CO thinks you're in Saigon for reassignment. The Army has no record of your presence in Laos. Your radios were spiked minutes after your insertion, before you reached Lima-Seven. You're ghosts now. Disavowed, unclaimed, off the books, never to be heard from again."

Jack stepped forward, unslinging his rifle, anger blazing in his eyes. "Then we'll do what ghosts do best. Disappear."

Armstrong took a deep breath and backed up toward the Huey. "One more thing, Colonel Roosevelt."

Teddy stared him down. "What!"

"When you're found—if you're ever found—there will be photos of you participating in the raid on the village. Witnesses. Reports. All pointing to your team's involvement in what happened today. You can run. You can hide. But when the curtain rises, you'll be holding the torch, and you will get burned by it."

"You fucking son of a bitch. You used us to light the fuse. You wanted the press to find those bodies—blame the Pathet Lao, tie it to the Chinese, and drag the U.S. back into this war. A war the American public doesn't support."

"That was the mission," Armstrong said. "You don't get to rewrite U.S. foreign policy because you had a moral epiphany."

Teddy raised his rifle—not aimed, but with the safety off, ready and waiting in his hands. "As I said, we're done. We quit."

"You don't get to walk away," Armstrong said. "You know that."

Eli adjusted his stance, digging his boot into the wet ground. "Then try to stop us."

"I don't have to. The jungle will do it for me." Armstrong climbed into the Huey and signaled the pilot.

The rotors picked up speed.

Teddy didn't move.

Neither did Jack or Eli.

They stood in the rising dust cloud, watching the chopper lift off and disappear into the sky—leaving only silence behind.

Teddy turned to the others. "We head east. Cambodia's two to three days on foot."

Jack nodded. "And Firebase Buttons four days after that."

Eli adjusted his pack. "Let's move."

There was nothing else to say.

They started walking—three men with no country, no command, and a convenient truth too dangerous to die for.

CHAPTER 21

0420 Hours
June 6, 1972
Bolaven Plateau
Southern Laos

They had been walking for almost two days, their jungle boots heavy with mud and skin rubbed raw underneath their soaked fatigues. Each step was slower and more deliberate due to exhaustion, not caution.

Any conversation had ceased hours ago, replaced by the sound of labored breathing and their boots crushing damp jungle undergrowth.

Teddy led the way, on point, every inch of him covered in layers of sweat and grime. He kept his eyes locked forward, never looking back. Every step sent sharp bolts of pain through his left ankle, threatening to buckle under the strain of climbing slick, root-covered, muddy slopes and sliding feet first down the other side. He ignored it, having run out of his limited supply of aspirin yesterday.

Behind him, Jack moved silently, scanning the jungle's green walls. Eli trailed last on rear guard, stoic, silent, steady. The three men carried their weapons close, barrels down, safeties off. They were beyond cautious—instincts sharpened to a deadly edge, survival honed to something primal.

Hours earlier, Teddy had given up calling for air support. At first he thought it was terrain interference—deep gullies and thick jungle canopy—but over time, the truth sank deeper into his chest. They had been radio-silent for too long, and even after Armstrong's warning, the promised extraction was now hours overdue. It wasn't coming.

They were alone. Ghosts walking toward either safety or destruction.

Teddy hadn't told Jack or Eli yet. But he could tell from their silence—they already knew.

Just before dawn, Teddy paused at the top of a ridge. He raised his hand to halt their advance and lowered himself to the ground, his knee aching from fatigue and his ankle swollen beneath his torn pant leg. Jack knelt beside him, looking westward. Eli kept a silent vigil behind them, watching their six and scanning their exposed backtrail for any movement.

"What do you think, Colonel?" Jack asked. "How long until we reach Paksé?"

"Another day, maybe," Teddy replied, voice hoarse. "If we can avoid the patrols."

Jack stared into the valley below, wiping sweat from his forehead. "Extraction's not coming, is it?"

Teddy shook his head. "No. Armstrong sold us out."

Jack clenched his jaw but didn't respond, watching the horizon through narrowed eyes. Eli said nothing, but Teddy felt the heavy weight of his silent realization.

"The fallback safehouse is our only option now," Teddy said. "We hit it, resupply, then cross into Cambodia."

Jack exhaled sharply in a rare moment of frustration. "Do you trust Armstrong's safehouse?"

Teddy's hesitation to answer spoke louder than his words. "No. But we're running out of options. We can't go much longer without food, water, and a safe place to rest without constantly looking over our shoulders."

Jack nodded once. Eli adjusted his pack, his face blank, as he prepared for whatever was coming next.

They kept walking, quieter now, nerves stretched tight, every jungle sound amplified, danger lurking all around them. Teddy's mind raced through the briefings, Armstrong's words, the staged crates and fake documents back in Grid Sector Lima-Seven, the village of Chum Nhi. The same dark thought kept circling—how far was Armstrong willing to go to silence the truth?

CHAPTER 22

They reached the outskirts of Paksé with the last of their strength scraped raw. Every step pushed their endurance to the limits, every breath filled with dirt and rot from two days of crossing jungle terrain without support, rest, or backup. Mud covered their boots. Blood—their own—dried in black rivulets along torn sleeves and sweat-soaked shirts. The jungle had stripped them bare, but they were still alive. That had to count for something.

The small cabin appeared through a gap in the trees—a squat, weathered structure pressed low to the ground, hidden by thick underbrush and camouflage netting, barely visible in the fading twilight. It should have been a secure fallback.

Teddy slowed down, raising a hand to stop the others. He surveyed the perimeter—no footprints, tire tracks, visible sentries, or movement in the windows.

He moved forward anyway, leading with the muzzle of his rifle, safety off, finger resting beside the trigger guard, every instinct burning sharp and cold. They had been walking toward this safehouse for two days—a place that was supposed to have water, rations, maps, dry uniforms, and an encrypted communications unit—hell, even a damn PRC-77 radio pack would have been useful. He could call for a chopper extraction at the Vietnamese border.

Once he reached the door, Teddy pushed it open, letting it swing inward. The hinges squeaked—a loud, dry rasp that seemed out of place in a building meant to be silent and prepared. He stepped inside, systematically clearing the narrow front room, then the back. Nothing. No signs of a recent occupant. No gear. No crates. No codes scribbled on laminated cards.

Just a room with drag marks on the wooden floor where the equipment was hastily removed.

Dust covered the single table in the center. The floor was swept clean—too clean—sending a subtle chill down Teddy's spine. This place had been stripped bare, not abandoned. The kind of emptiness that echoes when help never arrives.

On the far side of the room, tucked under a loose corner of the wall paneling, Teddy spotted the envelope. It was wedged there like an afterthought, resembling a scrap someone had left behind either by accident or on purpose.

He peeled it loose and opened it. A matchbook dropped into his hand—labeled *The Half Moon Club*. Inside was a handwritten message—a burn notice—*Roosevelt. Silence Order. Watch your six.*

Jack stared at it, breath catching in his throat.

Eli clenched his fists at his sides, knuckles turning white, as his expression darkened with silent rage.

Teddy's shoulders sagged, weariness sinking deeper into his bones than any exhaustion ever could. He remembered *The Half Moon Club*, having a drink there with his friend Vince Cross. He read in *Stars and Stripes* that it had burned down four months ago under suspicious circumstances. Rumors in the MACV grapevine suggested Dorsey had it torched to tighten his grip on the intelligence network he'd built—the classified Covert Operations Directorate—a NGO with no Congressional oversight.

No signature, no ciphers, no classification markings—just a final confirmation on a plain paper matchbook.

Teddy stared at the message for a long moment before slipping it into his breast pocket. "We've been abandoned. The matchbook is our burn notice. No one's coming."

Jack slammed his fist on the table. The truth they already knew was now unavoidable. "So, we are ghosts?"

"No," Teddy said. "We're targets."

Eli leaned against the doorframe. "So that's it. They've cut us loose."

"They never planned to get us out," Teddy said, his voice low and gravelly, not from fatigue or rage, but heavy with understanding. "The extraction plan was never real. Just an effective placeholder to keep us heading toward the burn point."

Jack looked around the empty space, putting the pieces together on his own. "They wanted us to die out there."

"They still do," Teddy said.

Eli tightened the sling on his rifle, jaw clenched. "Orders?"

Teddy turned toward the open door, determined to prove Dorsey wrong…again. "Same plan. We move northeast. Firebase Buttons. We have to cross Cambodia on foot."

Jack shook his head. "That's enemy territory. The Khmer Rouge has patrols everywhere. If they catch us…"

Teddy locked his eyes on them, unblinking. "I know. We're dead, but we're ghosts now. And we finish this on our terms."

No one spoke after that.

They moved again, shadows within shadows, headed west, deeper into hostile territory—three men betrayed, hunted, and officially erased, moving toward whatever small hope still existed beyond this jungle hell.

They didn't know what awaited them at Firebase Buttons.

But at least they now knew exactly what was behind them.

CHAPTER 23

June 8–11, 1972
Crossing toward Firebase Buttons
Unknown Map Grid Location
Eastern Cambodia Jungle

The jungle was a realm of damp silence and constant danger. Every leaf shimmered under the weight of heavy monsoon rains. Fog hung low to the ground, curling around roots and ferns like smoke. The dense, vine-covered canopy above blocked out any moonlight, leaving the forest floor cloaked in endless shadow. The only light came from the occasional glint of a mosquito's wing or the dull shine of sweat and misery on skin.

They moved mostly in silence. When they spoke, it was either to warn the others of movement, change the watch rotation, or pull each other out of mudholes that sucked their boots down like quicksand. The jungle canopy above offered little relief from the heat—only deeper shade—and the constant drip of moisture from leaves that never dried. Somewhere ahead was Firebase Buttons—if the map still mattered, if the map provided by Armstrong wasn't just another lie.

Jack led the way, his sharp machete carving a silent path through the underbrush, while Eli followed him, his eyes watchful for movement—VC patrols, trackers, predators, and snakes. The worst were the spiders—large, silent, hanging in the trees and crawling across their boots in the dark.

Teddy limped behind the others, bringing up the rear, gritting his teeth and pushing forward, favoring his swollen left ankle. The bruising had turned purple-black, and the pain gnawed into every step like a dull, grinding handsaw. He kept his rifle shouldered, but each mile made the sling feel like a blade across his back. His fatigue wasn't just his—Jack and Eli bore their own scars of attrition. Not one of them was unscathed. They'd been soaked to the skin since the first hour out of Laos, and they hadn't been dry since.

Their jungle boots were soaking wet, water dripping from the drain holes—leather blistered with the finish peeling off. Socks had long since stopped providing comfort—now they were barely more than friction rags, rubbing the skin raw. The sharp sting of jungle rot had begun to creep into the gaps between their toes, and the constant wetness caused small weeping ulcers to form unchecked on the soles of their feet. Teddy recognized the signs. So did Jack and Eli. But they had no choice but to keep moving—walking toward what they hoped was safety, salvation, a hot meal, a hot shower, and, more importantly, dry clothes.

Each day merged seamlessly into the next. The jungle was relentless and unforgiving. The rain came and went in heavy, thunderous bursts, muffling the sounds of patrols but never the smell—smoke, sweat, rotting vegetation, and the faint chemical scent of diesel that revealed the location of passing NVA trucks somewhere deeper among the trees.

At night, they huddled under their rain ponchos stretched low between the trees, draining the pooled water into their canteens and purifying it with a bitter-tasting iodine tablet. None of them had eaten in two days. Their rations were intended for a three-day reconnaissance mission, not a week-long trek through hostile territory. The jungle offered little—what fruit they found was bitter and questionable. Roaches hid in the underbrush from the constant rain. Catching small ground vermin to eat raw required setting traps, and that took time they didn't have.

No fires. No light or warmth. No sound louder than a whisper. Nothing to alert the patrols to their presence. Just the soft clicks of insects, the occasional hiss of a snake sliding through leaf litter, and the biting whine of mosquitoes feasting their fill of blood on any exposed skin they could find.

They rotated watches. No one slept longer than ninety minutes. There was no safety here—only constant motion and survival. And always, the knowledge that one mistake would end them. There was no backup—just a narrow trail heading east and the hope that Firebase Buttons would still be standing when they arrived.

On the fourth night, they found a small incline beside a dry gully and settled there for the night. Jack was on watch duty when Teddy stirred from a shallow sleep, leaning against the gnarled trunk of a rubber tree, trying not to shiver, cold sweat sticking to his chest. The pain in his leg had grown sharper, throbbing up into his hip. Mosquitoes swarmed relentlessly, biting through his soaked uniform, his face, and the raw skin on his neck. His feet were numb, the skin blistered and wrinkled white from days of soaking in wet socks. He could no longer feel his toes.

"You awake, Bull?" Jack asked.

"Barely," Teddy muttered. "My ankle feels like it's on fire."

Jack knelt beside him, handing over a damp canteen. "You should've let us splint it."

"With what? We don't have a splint. Just jungle, rain, and a lot of bad luck."

"Fair point," Jack said, chewing on a leaf for moisture. He sat back on his haunches, scanning the tree line. "Used to think this kind of thing only happened in spy novels. Jungle insertions, hiking out of enemy territory. Now it's just the same old Tuesday. Do you ever think about why the hell you joined up in the first place?" he murmured. "Some nights, I can't remember."

"To get off the reservation. Wasn't much else in Pine Ridge. Just dust and waiting for something better. Thought the Army might be it." He shifted in the mud, adjusting the sling on his rifle. "My granddad was in Korea. Came back with nothing but shrapnel in his hip and stories no one wanted to hear. But he stood tall when the American flag went up the pole in front of government offices every morning," Eli said from the shadows.

"I know the feeling." Teddy gave a quiet grunt. "Jack, you never told me how you ended up in Intelligence. Most guys with your background would have drifted toward training the incoming volunteers at Special Forces selection…been part of the cadre."

Jack leaned his head against a tree. "Yeah…well, things didn't work out that way. Bounced through foster homes in Southern California for most of my life and endured one nasty winter in Connecticut that I'd rather forget. Moved around a lot—never stayed in one place long enough to matter. Got good at listening and picking up languages. By the time I hit eighteen, I could speak five languages fluently. Figured if I had to keep moving, might as well wear a uniform. The Army saw potential. And the intelligence unit scooped me up fast. Intel was supposed to be safer—desk jobs and paperwork. But I kept volunteering for field rotations. You don't learn shit about people from behind a desk."

"Is that why you don't sleep much?" Teddy asked.

Jack's eyes narrowed, not unkindly, more as a way of acknowledging Teddy's question. "That, and too many nights waiting for someone to kick in a door and put a bullet in my head."

"We didn't have doors on the reservation," Eli said. "Just canvas flaps on the old Army surplus tents. At Pine Ridge, winter makes you tough, but it doesn't teach you much about trust."

Teddy could barely make out Eli's shape in the darkness. The Lakota sergeant hadn't complained once since they crossed the river, but his face showed signs of exhaustion.

"Tell me something good," Teddy said, knowing he had to keep things upbeat. A trick he learned commanding troops in the field, not in any classroom.

"My grandfather taught me how to hunt when I was five. Taught me patience. I think he'd like you, Colonel. You're a pain in the ass, but you don't quit—just like him."

Teddy managed a dry chuckle. "Coming from you, I'll take that as a compliment."

"You should," Eli replied. "Now it's your turn. Start talking."

"About what?"

"Come on, you know."

Teddy let the silence stretch before speaking. His voice was rough, worn down by exhaustion and pain. "My first year at West Point, I was assigned to a Firstie named Charles McCray. Son of a senator on the Armed Forces Service Committee. He hated my guts from day one as part of a legacy family, someone who didn't earn their appointment but had it handed to them. I sure as hell earned mine, but try telling that to a self-important asshole who's already made up his mind."

He took a deep breath, fighting the urge to fall asleep. "McCray called me everything from dumb squat, smackhead, beanhead, ghost, even a tool, which I sure wasn't back then. He quilled me every chance he got. I had ten demerits before the end of the first week of Beast Barracks, walking the area for hours. I was sure to be a century man before the end of the first term. Made me clean his gear with a toothbrush, run his boots across the quad like they were parade banners. Yelling at me to brace or grab some wrinkles. I hated punitive neck retraction. One day, he graded me naked in the shower like a side of grade A prime beef. It was humiliating."

Eli let out a low, guttural, amused laugh. "Really. How did you rate…in his opinion?"

Teddy grinned. "Above average. However, that didn't help me. Every mistake I made, I had to memorize the Corps of Cadets roster backward, recite every bit of Plebe knowledge from Bugle Notes, perform Swim to Newburgh on the alcove rail, and drink a White Tornado." He made a yuck face, remembering the horrible taste of every condiment on the table in Washington Hall, including an entire bottle of Tabasco sauce, mixed together in a milk slurry. "One night, I was ready to quit and go home. Had my duffel bag packed and everything. Then this old, crusty Master Sergeant stopped me at the Thayer Gate before I could leave the post. Didn't say a word. Just handed me a cup of coffee and told me to wait in the guard shack for the morning bell. 'Quitting's easier in the dark,' he said. 'But the new day will find you eventually.'"

He fell silent again, as the memory of that first semester cut through the damp air like fire.

Eli looked at him. "Did it help?"

Teddy nodded. "Yes. I unpacked the duffel bag, sucked it up, and here I am, trussed up like a turkey ready for Thanksgiving dinner."

Eli laughed. "Sometimes I can imagine you behind a desk teaching history to a bunch of high school students."

Teddy shook his head. Eli unintentionally brought up his family history. "A high school teacher, huh? Never in a million years. My full name's Theodore Roosevelt the Fourth."

Eli raised his eyebrows, surprise on his face. "As in *that Roosevelt*? The one on Mount Rushmore?"

Teddy grunted, almost like a laugh. "Yeah. Distantly. Great-nephew of the old Rough Rider himself. My family tree gets murky after the second generation, but the name stuck. My father insisted on it—said it was about legacy."

"Damn, no family pressure there," Jack said, his voice laced with sarcasm.

Teddy nodded. "Tell me about it. My great-grandfather fought in the Spanish-American War, my grandfather in World War I. My old man served in Europe during World War II, earning his reputation at the Battle of the Bulge. Now me. Fourth generation in uniform, three tours in this hellhole. I was supposed to be a legacy, not a weapon." He paused for a second as pain shot up his leg. The swelling had spread up his calf now, hot to the touch and pulsing in time with his heartbeat. He took a breath and pressed on. "West Point was a foregone conclusion since my father and grandfather graduated from there. I didn't even apply anywhere else. Went in at seventeen, plebe year in '51—smack dab in the middle of the Korean War. Beast Barracks was a fucking wake-up call. I learned real fast how much they didn't give a damn who my ancestors were or their proud history in the U.S. Army. You earn your name at the Academy—every single damn day."

Eli nodded in approval. "Sounds about right."

Jack glanced sideways. "So how'd the Rough Rider legacy lead you here? Shadow games and ghost orders?"

Teddy didn't answer right away. The jungle around them shifted—dark, wet, and endless. "Because when someone told me the mission mattered more than the medals, I believed them," he said. "That's what makes a

Roosevelt, isn't it? Charging up the hill, whether it's San Juan or a lie wrapped in a flag."

"Speaking of that," Jack said. "How in the world did you make full Colonel by thirty-five with only fifteen years in the Army? That takes about twenty years or more to accomplish. Does it have anything to do with your name and a certain relative?"

Teddy rolled his eyes. Jack wasn't the first person to ask that question. "Yes and no. Some of it probably was my famous last name, family legacy in the Army and at West Point, but that's not listed in any official promotion criteria." He held up one finger. "There were other factors involved."

"Like what?"

"West Point graduates, as a rule, get promoted faster than those going through ROTC and OCS if they demonstrate exceptional leadership and perform well in challenging environments. What they call 'Below the zone' or 'accelerated' promotions that shave years off the typical time in rank norms. Wars also often require quicker promotions due to higher personnel needs and increased operational tempo."

"True. I get that. I've seen guys get battlefield commissions," Jack said. "It still doesn't explain how you were a major before you turned thirty."

Teddy chuckled. "Yeah, I got some flak about that. I was called baby face, toddler, and a few other, let's say…less-than-respectable…things by more than a few combat-hardened, grizzled sergeant majors in front of my battalion. But to answer your question, mine were based on entering the Special Forces and volunteering for a few successful black ops assignments, so I fit the criteria of exceptional performance during high-stakes missions. I was promoted right before Operation Shatterhorn. It was my first operational command as a full colonel, and it all went to shit. I'm sure there were a few generals who sat on my promotion board wishing they'd never recommended me for accelerated promotion."

The silence returned—a deeper one. Not hostile—just worn down. Woven with the kind of exhaustion that ran bone-deep.

Teddy could feel the fever building behind his eyes. He pushed it down. They were close now. Firebase Buttons was ten, maybe fifteen klicks away. They would reach it sometime tomorrow. He just had to keep moving. Keep breathing. One step at a time.

CHAPTER 24

1215 Hours
June 12, 1972
Firebase Buttons
Song Be Province
Republic of Vietnam

They staggered out of the jungle like ghosts—three men covered in mud, their uniforms soaked, torn to shreds, and their boots falling apart with every step. Their weapons were carried low and slack, muzzles wrapped in cloth to keep out the mud, but no one had the strength to lift them now.

Teddy could barely walk. His left leg was swollen from the knee down to the ankle, the boot bulging grotesquely where jungle rot and infection had taken hold. He leaned on Eli with every third step, grinding his teeth to keep from crying out.

The distant outline of the firebase looked like heaven on Earth—low concrete bunkers, sandbagged machine gun nests, and antenna towers reaching upward like skeletal fingers. The American flag hung limply on the flagpole in the center of the main compound.

The sun was just rising over Firebase Buttons, casting long streaks of orange and crimson through the lowland haze. The sharp crack of distant gunfire echoed from the northeast, but the base itself remained quiet—smoke curling from burn barrels and cook fires, diesel fumes hanging heavy in the air.

They didn't speak, just trudged forward, one step at a time. They were alive, but every inch of them had been paid for in absolute misery.

Acrid smoke drifted from a burn pit near the perimeter, the tang of diesel, cooked human waste, and charred trash mixing with the iron taste of dried blood in Teddy's mouth.

He struggled through the last few yards of tangled brush, his right leg nearly giving out on the downhill slope. The swelling around his left ankle had grown, hot and angry. His boot, waterlogged and caked with heavy jungle mud, felt like a vice tightening around the wound.

They hadn't seen another soul since crossing the Cambodian border—seven days of wet socks, hunger, infected cuts, and whispers in the dark. Teddy hadn't slept more than two hours at a stretch, and his leg throbbed with every step. He carried the original mission orders tucked under his shirt, sealed in a bloodstained waterproof pouch.

Jack raised his hand toward the nearest guard post, waving to get someone's attention. "Shadow Lance…approaching from the east…don't shoot," he yelled.

There was movement behind the sandbags—rifles snapping into ready position, helmets lifting as soldiers manning the mortar and machine gun emplacements looked at them. The sentry on top of the watch tower raised his binoculars, then reached for the field phone.

Two M60s tracked them from behind a sandbagged gun emplacement.

"Hold your position!" a male voice shouted. "Hands where I can see 'em!"

The three men obeyed, moving together as one. Teddy's legs buckled as he tried to straighten up, and he dropped to one knee with a ragged grunt. Eli didn't flinch—he stepped forward, lowering his rifle to the dirt.

"Special Forces. Shadow Lance. Bolaven escape route," Eli yelled loud enough for the sentry to hear. "Roosevelt, Stratton, Red Horse. We're coming in."

There was a long pause. Then the concertina wire-wrapped outer gate creaked open, and two MPs moved shoulder to shoulder with their M16s raised but not aimed at them. A third man—older, rail-thin, with captain's bars and red-rimmed eyes—strode out behind them. He wore the faded green jungle fatigues of a field officer and moved as though he hadn't slept in three days. "Jesus Christ," he muttered. "Get them inside."

The MPs slung their rifles and hoisted Teddy upright, throwing his arms around their shoulders. He sagged between them, unable to hide the pain any longer. Jack looked worse than he did—cheeks hollow, bloodshot eyes, lips split down the middle. Eli was still standing, but his knuckles were blackened with dried blood, and his face was streaked with semi-healed, yellowish bruises and mud.

The captain ran toward them, shouting over his shoulder, "Get the aid station prepped! We've got wounded! I want a medic and a goddamn stretcher yesterday!"

"Who in the hell are you?" one of the MPs asked, eyeing Teddy with suspicion.

Jack spoke on Teddy's behalf. "Colonel Theodore Roosevelt IV. Special Forces. Clearance Whiskey Echo Seven. Get your CO."

The MP's eyes widened. "Roosevelt…like in *President Roosevelt*?"

Teddy tried to smirk but couldn't. "Not the one you're thinking of. I bleed easier."

The men around them moved faster after that.

They were taken past the motor pool and the ammo dump, down muddy lanes between sandbagged hooches. Firebase Buttons looked like every firebase Teddy remembered—temporary, brutal conditions, and bustling with activity. Radio towers loomed overhead, surrounded by barbed wire and gun emplacements. Helicopters sat on the landing pad, tied down with the rotors swaying in the breeze. Half the base was asleep, the other half pretending it wasn't, and all of them looked as if they'd been on the edge of something bad for weeks.

The field medic's tent smelled of iodine, sweat, and damp canvas warmed by the sun, blending with the copper tang of old blood and the wet rot of worn uniforms. Inside, flickering lanterns cast uneven light across the cots.

Eli sat on the edge of a nearby cot, stripped to the waist, his copper-colored skin marred by scrapes and deep insect bites that hadn't healed. Jack leaned against a support pole, arms crossed, his fatigue shirt hanging open. They all looked like hell—exhausted, starved, and limping.

The medic didn't ask questions. He took their vital signs, recorded temperatures, and handed out canteens of clean water like holy grails. "You all need a malaria workup," he muttered. "Hell, I'm surprised you aren't already positive and showing symptoms."

The medic with Teddy began removing his clothing and boots even before laying him down. He didn't complain as the sharp knife blade sliced through leather and into the swollen, discolored skin of his ankle. The gangrenous, rotting smell caused one of the medics to gag, and he turned to vomit into a nearby trash can.

"Infection's set in," the medic muttered. "This leg's bad. We need IVs, broad-spectrum antibiotics, and transport to Tay Ninh ASAP. Someone get me a damn helo manifest!"

"Name?" another medic asked, clipboard in his hand, pen poised over the blank form.

"Colonel Theodore Roosevelt...the...fourth," he managed to say, sinking into the gurney as the edges of the world started to blur together. "Serial number...oh hell, ask me again in a few minutes. My brain's a bit fuzzy."

"How far did you boys walk?" a medic asked, glancing between them.

Jack didn't answer. Neither did Eli.

"Far enough," Teddy said. "We came in from the southwest, across the border."

The medic paused for a moment at that. He didn't ask for any more information.

Jack stood next to Teddy, hand on his shoulder. "Don't you die on us now, sir."

Teddy smiled. "Too stubborn. Besides…I have paperwork to file."

The tent's hanging canvas door fluttered as an officer entered, flanked by two armed MPs. He looked young—a butterbar second lieutenant wearing a neatly pressed uniform and holding a clipboard like a shield. Probably fresh from OCS or ROTC. He didn't carry himself like a West Point ring knocker.

The MPs didn't draw their sidearms, but their presence was enough to mark this as an official visit.

"Are you Colonel Roosevelt?" the lieutenant asked, tapping his foot.

Teddy didn't have the strength to look up. "Colonel Theodore Roosevelt IV. Serial number O—"

"That won't be necessary," the lieutenant interrupted him. "Colonel Roosevelt, you and your men are hereby placed under military arrest pending an investigation and an Article 32 hearing into conduct unbecoming, dereliction of duty, insubordination, and suspected war crimes. The orders are signed."

The medic didn't even look up from Teddy's leg, busy applying ice packs and setting up the IV. "Yeah? Well, he's not going anywhere."

The lieutenant blinked. "Excuse me, sergeant? Is this a joke?"

"You're excused," the medic muttered without looking up. "This leg's borderline septic. I've got lymphangitic streaking, a fever climbing above 102, and he's dehydrated. If he doesn't get broad-spectrum antibiotics soon and an immediate evac to Tay Ninh or Cu Chi, all you'll be transporting is a corpse."

"They're to be taken into custody immediately. I have written orders, Sergeant—"

"And I've got medical authority," the medic snapped while threading an IV catheter into Teddy's forearm. "You want to override that? I'll need it in writing, preferably signed by a general and notarized in blood. You move him without medical clearance, he could go into systemic shock. Do you want to be the reason a colonel in the United States Army dies in your custody because you overrode medical protocol? Be my guest. I'll make sure the JAG boys have this on record."

The MPs shifted their weight from one foot to the other, uneasy with the ultimatum. Even Jack tensed at the clear threat—one the medic could back up in the regulations.

The lieutenant appeared conflicted—caught between his orders and the harsh reality in front of him.

Jack sat up on the next cot, face bruised but alert. "What he's trying to say, Lieutenant, is that arresting someone mid-infection isn't exactly protocol. You let him crash en route, and it's your gold butter bars on the line, not whoever issued those orders in a safe office in Saigon. Not a good look for a brand new shavetail louie."

"Let them treat us, Lieutenant. You'll still have your prisoners in the morning. Or do you want the paperwork to say I died under your command?" Teddy asked, dry and raspy.

The medic snorted. "Try explaining that to CID."

The lieutenant hesitated, then—reluctantly—he nodded. "Fine. You have forty-eight hours. They're not to leave this facility."

"They won't," the medic muttered. "Not under their own power. I guarantee that."

The MPs stepped aside but remained close to the door. A silent reminder that freedom has an expiration date.

The medic peeled back the edge of Teddy's makeshift dressing, squinting at the clean, puckered scar running along the inside of his ankle. "You've had surgery on this leg before."

Teddy didn't answer right away. His breath caught as the medic lifted his leg again to check the range of motion—there wasn't much left due to the excessive swelling.

"Tay Ninh," he whispered. "Two years ago. Broken ankle. Compound fracture. Tib-fib. They put in a nail."

The medic grunted, already probing the swollen tissue around the old incision line. "Looks like you've pissed it off again. Infection's spreading from the lateral side—could be around the implant. I can't believe you humped out of Laos on this leg and were still on your feet at the main gate."

Jack looked over from his cot. "We didn't have a choice. The radio went dark. Air cover and our extraction helo never showed up. It's been swelling for days. He didn't say a word."

"Didn't need to," Teddy ground out.

The medic looked up, his expression a mix of professional detachment and quiet concern. "You're lucky it hasn't gone septic yet. That leg's angry, sir. We'll give you cefazolin and gentamicin now to get the process started, but you'll need surgical debridement if the infection doesn't respond to treatment. You might have an abscess around the implant. We've got a surgeon here, but he's overloaded with wounded, and your leg's not something I want half-done in a tent." He glanced at the other medics. "Get this man ready for evac, priority one for Tay Ninh tonight. Let Battalion argue about his status after he's treated and still breathing."

Outside the tent, Huey rotors kicked up dust and loose paper, but nothing landed. Just another fly-by. Maybe someone was leaving the base before the weather turned for the worse.

One of the MPs came forward, clearing his throat. "We need to speak with the patients. Orders from command—"

"No, you don't," the medic snapped. "Not until they're stable. Do you see a JAG directive stapled to any of these beds? No? Then step your ass back and wait. These men are casualties of war, just like everyone else here. If you want to arrest them, you wait until they're out of triage and stable."

The MP tensed up, appeared ready to argue, then noticed the withering look from the other medic and stepped back. "Fine. We'll keep the external guard in place until orders arrive."

"You do that," the medic said. "And stay out of my way." He turned back to Teddy and lowered his voice. "Sir…you've got about six hours before that infection forces my hand and the surgeon has to amputate. We'll do our best to stabilize you until the helo's ready."

Teddy nodded. "Understood."

Then, with the medic gone for a moment and the tent a little quieter, Jack moved over to his cot and pulled a stool next to it. "You know they're not here just for us," he said, voice low enough for only Teddy to hear him.

"No," Teddy said. "They're here to make sure we disappear before anyone upstairs has to explain what the hell Operation Firelight actually was."

Eli chuckled on his cot. "Let 'em try. We're still breathing."

"For now," Jack said, glancing toward the flap. "But we both know what happens when command wants you gone."

"You disappear into paperwork and burn notices. Or a shallow grave just south of Paksé," Teddy said, sounding flat and bitter.

The senior MP paced outside the triage tent flap, his PRC-6 radio pressed against his ear. "Yes, sir. All three accounted for. Receiving medical treatment now. No, they're not ambulatory. One's likely surgical. Yes, sir. We'll hold position."

Inside, another MP hovered near the edge of the room, one hand resting on the grip of his M16 but not making any move to intervene.

"Orders, sir?" Jack whispered, nodding toward the guard.

Teddy shook his head. "None...for now. It's no longer their decision. Ours is already written. They're just here to make sure we don't vanish before someone rubber-stamps it."

Across the room, Eli shifted uncomfortably under his blanket. "Let them watch. Ain't the first time."

The medic applied a cooling pack around Teddy's leg. "As long as they don't get in my way, they can play sentry all night for all I care."

The three of them sat in silence for a moment, the weight of what they'd just endured pressing heavier than their wounds. Outside, lightning streaked across the jungle canopy, thunder rolling in the distance like incoming artillery.

They had made it back. But the war—*their* war—was just beginning.

CHAPTER 25

0500 Hours
June 13, 1972
Firebase Buttons
Medevac Flight to Tay Ninh Army Hospital
Republic of Vietnam

The relentless monsoon rain stopped as the first light of dawn began to seep through the gray canopy overhead, casting the jungle in shades of wet stone and faded orange, leaving a layer of mist clinging to the treetops like a funeral shroud. It carried the scent of rust, aviation fuel, and blood.

The UH-1 Huey sat idling on the landing pad outside Firebase Buttons, its rotors chopping the air like dull razor blades, and the tail rotor stirring the haze into low whorls of grit and exhaust. Lit only by the perimeter lights and the pad's rusted floodlamp, the chopper looked more like a silhouette carved from steel and noise than a dust off chopper, its nose and doors painted with a red cross on a white square.

Teddy lay strapped to the middle stretcher, barely conscious, clenching his jaw against the pain radiating from his left leg. His new ripstop jungle trousers had been sliced open to expose the angry, blistered mess of his lower left leg for treatment. The entire limb had swollen overnight, the skin stretched tight and inflamed from the ankle to mid-thigh. Red streaks now traced faint lines toward his groin—early signs of lymphangitis or cellulitis, the medic had warned. Everyone in country knew what it was— a tropical curse that festered in boots worn too long through swamps and streams, untreated under stress, and covered in germ-filled dirt.

He'd walked out of Laos on that leg, enduring seven brutal days through leech-infested lowlands, across thorn-choked trails and rice paddies contaminated with human waste the locals used as fertilizer and chemical runoff from air-sprayed defoliant. His feet had never dried. Now, his left leg was trying to rot itself from the inside out.

The antibiotics administered at Firebase Buttons had slowed the infection, but it was still not under control. Every jolt of the stretcher sent agony piercing through the bone.

Jack climbed in beside him, still bruised but able to move. "That leg looks like it's about to come off."

"It won't," the medic said. "But we're racing against the clock. We need to get to Tay Ninh fast, or he's going septic."

"Antibiotics?" Jack asked.

"Wide-spectrum ones started in the triage area, cefazolin and gentamicin. Not much more I can do up here unless he codes."

Teddy raised his head, dropping it back to the tiny pillow. "Not...dead yet."

Across from them, Eli sat with his back against the cabin wall, quiet and alert. His face was hidden in the shadow of his boonie hat, but his eyes tracked every movement like a hawk hunting for the next ambush. His ribs were taped under his fatigues, a result of a fall during their final scramble out of Laos. He hadn't said a word about it, not even when they half-carried Teddy out of the jungle.

The crew chief gave a thumbs up to the pilot and yanked the side door shut.

"Dust Off Bravo-Two-Zero, wheels up, cleared hot to Tay Ninh. Weather's holding, turbulence light. ETA two-three minutes," the pilot's voice crackled through the internal speakers.

The chopper lifted off the pad with a jarring lurch, rattling every panel as the engines fought against gravity. The vibration shot straight into Teddy's bones. He clenched his teeth, trying to stay conscious, every nerve in his left leg burning as if soaked in hydrofluoric acid. Sweat poured off him despite the artificial wind blowing through the gaps in the fuselage, saturating the canvas pad beneath him.

Jack steadied the IV bag overhead as it swung sideways. He leaned in closer. "Stay with me, Colonel. You didn't come this far to rot away from a goddamn fungus."

Teddy managed a weak grunt. "Hell of a war."

"You don't know the half of it," Jack muttered.

The medic adjusted the IV drip to wide open and pulled Teddy's blanket higher on his chest. "We'll push fluids until we reach the hospital. He's stable—for now." He placed two fingers on the carotid artery in Teddy's neck. "Still thready. Nothing more to do until they get you on the operating table."

"Bone's probably fractured again," Jack said. "Took everything we had left to him out."

"You could've told me that before I loaded him," the medic muttered, half-joking. "Let's just hope gangrene doesn't set in before the orthopedic surgeon cuts him open."

Teddy managed to lift his head. "Appreciate the optimism."

"Sir, I've seen worse," the medic said, rolling his eyes. "But not by much."

The Huey banked left to avoid something—a bird, maybe—rattling every panel and sending a surge of white-hot pain behind Teddy's eyes. He clamped down hard on an involuntary scream, grinding his teeth as he fought to stay conscious. Sweat poured down his temples, soaking the canvas pad beneath his skull.

Eli leaned forward to look Teddy in the eyes. "Hang in there, Colonel."

Teddy didn't answer. He was too focused on breathing and trying to hold back the nausea as the vibrating deck twisted his insides into tight knots and made his leg feel as if it was packed full of broken glass.

The medic pulled a morphine vial from his pocket. "This is almost empty. Gave him the last field dose right before we left the firebase. You'll get more at Tay Ninh. Hang on, sir."

Teddy gripped the stretcher rail, his knuckles turning white. "Yeah. I understand." He really didn't, but he didn't want to upset the medic. Morphine was never denied to a soldier in pain without a reason. Someone probably ordered him to withhold the medication. And Teddy had a pretty good idea who—Dorsey or Kohrs. Him dying en route to the hospital would solve a problem.

The sky outside began to brighten with the first light of dawn as the Huey banked eastward toward Tay Ninh. Below, the jungle stretched on endlessly—green, tangled, and mysterious.

Teddy closed his eyes. The pain in his leg throbbed in sync with the beat of the rotor blades, but deeper than that, something colder had taken hold—a feeling that whatever lay ahead, it would be worse than jungle rot. Worse than infection. Something had burned deeper than skin, and it hadn't started in the jungle. Firelight had reduced everything they knew to ash.

Now they were flying toward the only place remaining that might still hold answers—or justice. But on which side of those legal scales would they land?

CHAPTER 26

```
0530 Hours
June 13, 1972
Emergency Intake and OR Prep
45th Surgical Hospital
Tay Ninh
Republic of Vietnam
```

The Huey flared on the pad outside the field hospital, its skids slamming into the ground with a crunch of gravel and torn grass. A team of medics rushed forward as soon as the crew chief yanked open the side door, their faded jungle fatigues soaked with sweat and stained with who knows what. A battered gurney clattered alongside Dust Off Bravo-Two-Zero as the medics pulled Teddy's litter out, their boots pounding on the hard-packed clay.

"He's febrile—104-degree temperature and rising. Two saline IVs are running wide open. It's jungle rot, but there's a complication," the medic shouted over the idling rotors. "Previous injury. Internal fixation device— probably an intramedullary nail—feels like it's failed. The tibia's unstable. Infection's flaring along the old surgical path."

The triage officer's face drained of color. The nauseating stench was a dead giveaway. "Jesus, this one's already septic?"

"On the edge. Push him straight through—let the surgeons sort it out."

Teddy didn't speak as they rolled him inside. He couldn't, fighting back nausea that threatened to overwhelm him. His uniform shirt had been peeled down to his waist, revealing tanned skin shining with feverish sweat and muscles trembling from exhaustion. His lower left leg told a different story—red, hot, misshapen, and angry. Just below the knee, the swelling had distorted the normal shape of the tibia. Beneath it, buried deep in the muscle, the titanium rod inserted two years ago had probably shifted.

A young nurse ran alongside the gurney, checking the IV drip. "We need full cultures—blood and wound. Start vanco and gentamicin pending ID confirmation of a possible Staph infection. Get the ortho in here now."

They wheeled Teddy into a surgical prep bay, one of six converted tents separated by canvas and thick plastic sheets. A combat field surgeon— rank of major—rushed in, pulling on surgical gloves. He squatted beside the gurney and palpated the leg with clinical precision. "He's guarding hard—percussion tenderness. This isn't just cellulitis. I want X-ray confirmation, but if that rod has shifted, we've got to go in."

Jack Stratton stood nearby, his sweat-soaked fatigues drying under the hot lamps, his eyes locked on the gurney. "Will he lose the leg?"

The surgeon didn't look up. "If the infection's into the marrow and the implant's compromised, maybe. If the bone's already necrotic, it's a yes. But we're not there yet. We'll go in, debride, stabilize, irrigate the hell out of it, and pray we're not chasing sepsis up his spine."

Eli, as quiet as ever, posted himself near the door like a sentinel.

The nurse placed her hand on Teddy's chest. "Sir? You'll feel some pressure. We're giving you something now to help with the pain."

Teddy nodded, the tremor in his jaw noticeable to more than himself. "Don't let them cut it off. I walked out of Laos on that leg."

The surgeon met his eyes. "We found your case from two years ago in our records. We'll do everything we can to save it, Colonel Roosevelt. You've got my word."

Then the curtain closed.

0615 Hours
June 13, 1972
Operating Room
45th Surgical Hospital
Tay Ninh
Republic of Vietnam

The lead surgeon—Major Halverson—lowered his magnifying glasses and adjusted the sterile drape. "Let's make it quick, everyone. The clock's ticking on this one."

The overhead surgical light buzzed as it warmed up, casting a stark white glare over Colonel Roosevelt's leg. The prep nurse had finished the final Betadine scrub, the angry red stain extending from mid-thigh to ankle. His boots were long gone. The field dressing around his lower leg had already been removed, revealing clear signs of jungle rot—mottled skin, patches of necrosis, and pustular breakdown around the old surgical scar, along with a raw, pus-filled drainage tracking along the tibial shaft.

"Vital signs are holding steady," the anesthetist confirmed from the head of the stainless steel operating table, a steady hand on the Ambu bag, breathing for him in rhythm with the rise and fall of Colonel Roosevelt's chest.

"Scalpel," Dr. Halverson's assistant called, slapping it into his palm.

With a steady hand, Halverson cut along the medial border of the tibia, reopening the previous scar with precise skill. Yellowish purulent drainage surfaced, confirming his suspicion. The tissue beneath was inflamed, swollen with edema, and hotter than the air inside the stifling operating room.

"Suction."

The surgical tech inserted the Yankauer and suctioned away thick greenish-white fluid as Halverson peeled back fascia and dissected deeper. The steel glint of the intramedullary rod appeared beneath infected muscle tissue.

"There it is," Halverson muttered. "The nail is loose. The bone around it looks osteomyelitic. We'll debride the hell out of it."

Halverson switched tools, grabbing a curette to scrape away tissue slough and necrotic bone. The sound it made—a faint, sickening grind—was met with quiet professionalism. There was no time to hesitate. He irrigated the cavity with liters of warm saline mixed with an antibiotic solution, the spray catching the light like a smoky mist under the surgical lamp.

"We'll leave the rod in place for now—removing it in a field hospital could destabilize the entire shaft. External stabilization once he's stable, if needed, then send him to the 95th Evac for a full ortho workup."

"Cultures were sent to the lab," the nurse confirmed. "Temp was 104.4 before induction."

Halverson nodded. "He bought himself this infection walking out of Laos, a country off limits to U.S. troops. Hell of a thing."

When he was satisfied that the dead tissue had been removed and the infection flushed out, they packed the surgical cavity with antibiotic-soaked gauze and closed what they could using wide interrupted sutures—minimal tension, just enough to protect the wound bed.

"Done for now. He lives. Whether the leg does is up to God and the antibiotics."

They removed their gloves, gowns, and masks as the orderlies prepared to wheel Colonel Roosevelt to the recovery ward.

0930 Hours
June 13, 1972
Recovery Ward
45th Surgical Hospital
Tay Ninh
Republic of Vietnam

The first thing Teddy noticed was the weight. Not pain, not light, not the usual drift that comes after anesthesia—but the crushing, immovable weight of exhaustion. His body felt as if it had been buried under heavy, wet concrete with every muscle refusing to obey. He couldn't move. He couldn't speak. But he was aware of his surroundings.

A dull ache pulsed through his left leg—deeper than bone, hot and throbbing. It spread upward into his hip and downward into his toes, but it wasn't sharp. Not yet. Not while the morphine still worked its way through his bloodstream. He could feel the IV catheter taped to the back of his hand pulling the hairs, and the steady pressure of the IV lines snaking into his arm. A nasal cannula was looped beneath his nose, supplying oxygen—not much—just enough to ease the grogginess from anesthesia in the heat and humidity inside the tent. And he had a damn Foley catheter shoved up his penis. He hated that uncomfortable thing, except it served a purpose. He couldn't get up to pee. Not that he needed to…yet.

The canvas walls fluttered in the breeze outside. Somewhere, a generator coughed and whined. He could smell alcohol, iodine, old blood, and the constant mildewy scent of the tropics. The field hospital was crowded—cots lined shoulder to shoulder under mosquito netting, IV poles hanging from the frame of the GP medium tent. Muffled groans sounded nearby, low and rhythmic, occasionally broken up by a barked order from a nurse or medic moving between beds.

"Colonel Roosevelt?" The voice was close, calm, and female.

Teddy blinked. As he turned his head, everything came into focus. A young Vietnamese-American nurse stood next to him, clipboard tucked under one arm, her expression both professional and kind.

"You're at Tay Ninh. You had surgery a few hours ago. The infection in your leg was serious—osteomyelitis. They performed a debridement and stabilized it as best they could," the nurse said.

He nodded—barely—and swallowed, trying to moisten his dry throat.

She held a cup with a bent straw to his lips. "Easy. Small sips. We don't need you vomiting after surgery and ripping out your sutures."

133

The water hit like cold fire—cooling his throat and awakening his senses. As he drank through the straw, he noticed more—his chest was bare except for EKG pads stuck to it. A heart monitor chirped beside his cot. His leg was elevated and splinted with a thick cotton and gauze dressing damp from saline.

He tried to speak, swallowing to soothe his sore throat. "Rod…still in?"

"Yes, sir," she said. "Too risky to remove it here. If needed, you'll be transferred to the 95th Evac once you're stable enough. For now, they're treating the infection with everything they've got—gentamicin, clindamycin, cephalothin. Triple-line coverage."

"Fever?"

She nodded. "Still high, but falling. You've had two bags of chilled fluids and antipyretics. Temp's down to 102.6, and you tested negative for malaria."

He closed his eyes. That explained the chills and the pounding migraine headache. Every part of his body ached, worn out after days on foot with no food and no sleep—just the jungle, fear, and the weight of betrayal.

"Your team's here. Sergeant Red Horse and Captain Stratton. They're stable. Some dehydration, foot damage—minor jungle rot, and mild respiratory distress, but nothing surgical. We are currently treating them with IV fluids and antibiotics."

That brought him a great deal of relief. His men were safe. He didn't try to speak again. Not yet.

She adjusted the morphine drip, checked the Foley catheter, and pressed her palm to his forehead. "Get some rest, Colonel Roosevelt. The MPs are outside, but no one's coming in here right now. Your one and only job is to heal."

She turned and disappeared down the aisle, her footsteps lost in the multitude of patients in the recovery ward.

Teddy stared at the khaki-colored ceiling. The fan above him didn't spin fast enough to lower the temperature. The heat suffocated him like a living thing.

He lay there in silence, the steady beat of his heart on the monitor beside him, the infection still smoldering beneath the surface. Whatever came next, he'd need his strength to fight. And time was quickly running out.

CHAPTER 27

1110 Hours
June 13, 1972
Recovery Ward
45th Surgical Hospital
Tay Ninh
Republic of Vietnam

The humidity had crept in early like a phantom skimming across a graveyard, sticking to every surface in the recovery tent like an unwelcome second skin. Teddy lay still, propped up on several pillows, his leg elevated and heavily bandaged, supported by a mobile metal traction frame. The pain was constant now—a deep, throbbing ache that even morphine couldn't drown out. Beads of sweat formed on his chest despite the oscillating fan next to his cot, more for show than effectiveness.

He heard them before he saw them.

Boots—worn, slow-moving, dragging a bit. Familiar rhythms. One lighter, the other heavier, both limping. Two silhouettes appeared in the aisle between the cots, framed by the hazy sunlight filtering through the canvas.

Jack Stratton and Eli Red Horse.

They moved like men who had seen too much and slept too little— bandaged, bruised, and still wearing borrowed jungle fatigues faded several shades off from regulation. Eli's arm was wrapped in gauze from elbow to wrist. Jack had a deep abrasion on his temple, butterfly-bandaged together. But they were standing. Alive.

"Permission to come aboard, sir?" Jack asked with a tired grin as he reached the foot of the cot.

"Not exactly a ship, Jack. But I'll allow it, permission granted," Teddy rasped, his mouth and throat dry and cracked from fever and days of dehydration.

Eli didn't smile, but his eyes softened. "Heard you finally stopped moving long enough to let someone fix that leg."

"Didn't have much of a choice," Teddy said, chuckling. "They knocked me out and cut me open before I could argue."

Jack moved to the side of the cot and pulled a metal stool closer. "Debridement?"

"Yeah. Twice. Bone's still infected. The rod might fail."

Eli glanced at the frame around the leg and let out a small grunt. "That thing held you through a week of mountain crossings. It's earned an early retirement."

Teddy exhaled, the sound halfway to a chuckle. "What about you two? You look like hell."

"We smell worse, or did before a long, hot shower," Jack said, leaning forward with his elbows on his knees. "But we're still standing. Jungle rot on both feet, dehydration, and enough mosquito bites to draw a map of Cambodia on our legs. We tested negative for malaria. I'm so glad I don't have to take chloroquine and spend time in the nasty latrine with the runs. That field medic at Firebase Buttons wasn't gentle, but he knew what he was doing."

"Yeah, he did. I still have my leg thanks to him and the doc." Teddy leaned back into the pillows, clenching his teeth as pain shot through his hip. "You've got to tell me we made it in time. That the orders are still intact."

Jack's grin faded. "They're safe. I never took them out of the bag. Still sealed in my ruck. Makes for one hell of a souvenir and some pretty damning evidence against Dorsey."

Eli sat in the metal folding chair at the head of the cot. "They'll try to make that disappear if anyone finds out we have them. Those papers aren't supposed to exist."

"That's why we'll need more than just paper," Teddy said. "We're not just witnesses anymore. We're evidence."

A pause hung in the air—thick and heavy.

"Any word on how long we've got before the hammer falls?" Jack asked.

Teddy glanced toward the flap at the far end of the tent where two MPs had been posted just out of sight. "They're giving us time to stabilize. That's all. After that? Who knows? Transport, charges, and silence. Whatever Dorsey and Kohrs have lined up for us."

"Then we don't waste any time. If they want to burn this, we need to dig in and make sure what's left survives the fire," Eli said.

Teddy nodded. "Agreed. But right now, we heal. Then we plan."

The three men sat in silence for a while—one on a cot, two on steel chairs—listening to the low hum of machines and the quiet groans of wounded soldiers. It wasn't a strategy session, not yet. But the bonds formed in blood and betrayal didn't need instructions to grow stronger. They already understood what had to be done.

They had survived Operation Firelight.
Now came the fight to expose it to the world.

2300 Hours
June 13, 1972
Interior Supply Closet
45th Surgical Hospital
Tay Ninh
Republic of Vietnam

Jack stopped in front of a door in the hospital hallway, one hand inside the front pocket of his faded ripstop fatigue pants, fingers gripping the waterproof envelope. Inside was everything—a copy of Armstrong's original mission briefing, the hand-drawn map of the fallback locations, and even a fragment of coded frequency assignments that had changed halfway through the mission without warning. Things no one would believe unless they saw them with their own eyes.

He looked both ways, opened the door, and went inside. The air in the supply closet was heavy with the scent of alcohol wipes, surgical gloves, sterile gauze, and iodine. Outside, the distant whop-whop-whop of helicopter blades faded into the darkness of the jungle, swallowed by the night.

The fluorescent lights buzzed overhead, casting a dull yellow glow over stacks of gauze, morphine vials, and unopened mailbags waiting to be flown out with the next batch of field reports. No one had noticed Jack slip away from his bed in the VIP quarters, guarded by two MPs. No one ever did when he didn't want to be seen. He'd been trained by the best. Any MPs in the Vietnam theater were mere amateurs.

Jack pulled open a canvas pouch labeled—*NON-MILITARY MAIL POUCH – INCOMING/OUTGOING*. The stenciled black label was faded, but the rules hadn't changed. If it was sealed tight and marked for civilian postage, no one opened it unless ordered to do so. Especially during late-night shifts, when the admin clerks were more concerned with heat rash and powdered eggs than with regulations regarding mail sent stateside to the U.S. Post Office.

He had addressed it earlier—handwritten in block letters, careful and deliberate, to a false name he kept using out of habit—*Mr. Carter E. Stroud, P.O. Box 452, Alexandria, Virginia*. He had used that box once during an infiltration operation in Laos before he met Teddy—untraceable unless someone knew what to look for.

Jack slid the sealed bundle deep into the bottom of the outgoing canvas mail sack, beneath routine correspondence going stateside and private letters written by U.S. Army soldiers, then zipped it shut.

He glanced over his shoulder. Nothing but shadows, the faint click of someone typing in the next room, a nurse moving boxes, and footsteps that didn't get any closer.

Teddy wouldn't have approved—he would've said it was reckless to hide evidence instead of passing it up the chain of command. But then again, after the betrayal, after Operation Firelight, maybe he wouldn't now, convinced the system was the problem.

Through countless covert missions in Vietnam and the Soviet Bloc, Jack had witnessed firsthand how the chain of command truly functioned. It looped back on itself, coiling like a snake eating its own tail. The truth wouldn't survive the journey—unless someone kept it alive.

He stepped back into the corridor, looked left then right, holding a cigarette he didn't bother lighting. Somewhere down the hallway, an MP shifted his feet near Teddy's cot. Eli sat in a folding chair nearby, arms crossed and still. Jack gave him a faint nod as he passed. Eli didn't respond, but his eyes followed Jack all the way back.

Tomorrow, everything would be different.

But for tonight, Jack had just given them a fighting chance.

0935 Hours
June 14, 1972
Recovery Ward
45th Surgical Hospital
Tay Ninh
Republic of Vietnam

The hum of a nearby generator droned through the canvas walls, steady and dull, blending in with the usual camp sounds—the clanging of the mess hall bell, soldiers passing by on their way to somewhere, and the constant wop-wop-wop of incoming and outgoing dust offs.

Fluorescent light bars buzzed overhead, their yellowish, off-white glow casting a washed-out hue across the triage ward. Teddy sat upright on a cot, what passed for a hospital bed in a field hospital, propped up on a couple of pillows and a folded wool Army blanket. His leg was splinted, wrapped in fresh bandages, and elevated on two more pillows to reduce the swelling. An IV hung on the steel stand beside him, the slow drip of broad-spectrum antibiotics and morphine flowing into his arm.

Jack sat near the cot on a folding metal chair, arms crossed. Eli, silent and stoic, leaned against the tent's support pole, a fresh dressing taped over his ribs. Their gear was gone—confiscated during triage. Teddy's boots had been cut off at the seams to expose the swollen, red flesh around his lower leg. The previous surgical scar—still prominent—was now bordered by inflamed, angry skin mottled with early signs of necrosis. They caught it in time. Barely.

The curtain surrounding his bed rustled, a poor attempt to create an illusion of privacy for a wounded soldier. The orthopedic surgeon entered wearing green scrubs still stained with blood—Major Halverson, a broad-shouldered Army doctor with the lined face of a man who'd seen too much battlefield triage in Vietnam in too few years.

Most Army doctors—draftees—spent a year in country before being rotated back to the States—DEROS—and usually celebrated with a party, complete with alcohol and living party favors. Halverson felt more like a seasoned, career Army doctor, ready to make a positive impact on the world.

"Good morning, Colonel Roosevelt. How are you feeling?" Halverson asked.

Teddy shrugged. "I'm still here. That's about it."

"I've stabilized your leg the best I can," he said, glancing at the notes on his clipboard.

"And I thank you for that, Doc. So, how did I rank in your experience saving men from a slow, lingering death from an infection?"

"I've seen worse," Haverson said, nodding at the IV bag. "But not by much. You're lucky to have arrived when you did. If you'd spent another day in the mud outside the wire, Colonel Roosevelt, you'd be in a meat wagon headed for amputation...or, as you aptly put it, lingering death, headed for Graves Registration."

Teddy nodded. "I know."

"You're not out of the woods yet," Halverson continued. "The intramedullary nail held, but the tibia hasn't healed. You're still non-weight-bearing on your left leg. You'll need a proper orthopedic follow-up, possibly a medevac to Japan if the infection flares up again. But we've stabilized your leg for now."

Jack pointed at himself, Eli, and Teddy. "What's next for us?"

Halverson sighed. "The good news ends there. This morning sealed orders arrived from MACV. You're all to be taken into custody for immediate transfer to a secure holding facility in Saigon pending special transport back to the States."

Eli looked up.

Teddy said nothing, but the tension in his shoulders tightened like a drawn, tempered steel sword.

"What are the charges?" Jack asked

"They didn't say," Halverson replied. "Just that they came in a sealed packet from MACV headquarters with instructions to process you as detainees. Effective immediately."

"Is that why the MPs haven't left since we got here?" Teddy asked. What happened at Firebase Buttons was a bit unclear. He wasn't sure if he was remembering everything correctly.

Halverson nodded. "Yes. They were told not to interfere with your medical care but to be present at all times. The rest is above my pay grade and security clearance, Colonel Roosevelt."

Two military policemen entered, both dressed in standard tropical fatigues and web gear. One carried several sets of handcuffs tucked over his web belt. The other held a clipboard with paperwork—a manila envelope stamped *TRANSFER ORDERS—SEALED.*

The lead MP cleared his throat. "Colonel Theodore Roosevelt IV, Captain Jack Stratton, Master Sergeant Eli Red Horse—under the authority of the Uniform Code of Military Justice and according to orders from MACV-Saigon, you are hereby placed under arrest pending a full investigation into events in Laos and court-martial proceedings under Article 118 of the UCMJ. You will be detained and transported to a secure holding facility pending transport back to the United States."

Teddy gave a slow nod, looking down at his bandaged leg. "I'll need assistance moving. And I'm sure not ambulatory unless you're planning to drag a stretcher into a cell?"

"You'll be stretchered to the helipad," the MP replied. "Per protocol, sir, you'll be cuffed during transport regardless of your medical condition. You'll remain under armed escort until cleared otherwise. The orders say you remain under full medical care, but you're officially in custody."

Halverson raised an eyebrow but remained silent. He knew better than to argue.

Jack looked at Teddy but didn't say anything. His silence spoke volumes.

Eli pushed off the tent pole, calm as always, holding his hand out in front of him.

"You don't have to cuff us," Teddy said, his voice low, using his best command tone. "We're not going to run or cause any problems."

"No exceptions, sir," the MP replied.

"Then make it quick," Teddy muttered, shaking his head. What did they think he was going to do, crawl away on the ground like a baby?

The second MP grabbed Teddy's right wrist and secured it with a metal cuff. The chain was threaded under the IV line and attached to his left wrist across his chest. A third MP entered and adjusted the stretcher straps. For now, Teddy lay shackled, eyes straight ahead, wondering how his career had been turned upside down.

Jack and Eli were next—wrists cuffed behind their backs. Neither resisted or spoke.

Outside, a medevac Huey was already spooling up, its rotor blades churning the morning haze into loose, swirling sand. Inside the canvas tent, the air carried the sterile weight of iodine and resignation.

As Teddy was carried outside the tent, one of the MPs walked beside the stretcher, rifle slung. Another kept his hand on Jack's elbow while a third MP escorted Eli.

They weren't soldiers anymore.

They were prisoners.

And the long war was only just beginning—orders, politics, and betrayal—closing in once again.

CHAPTER 28

1700 Hours
June 24, 1972
3rd Field Hospital
Saigon
Republic of Vietnam

The fever had broken hours earlier, but Teddy still felt a deep ache as if the jungle itself had climbed inside his skin and found a permanent home. He lay flat on a canvas hospital cot in the recovery ward of the 3rd Field Hospital in Saigon, eyes half-lidded, the aftertaste of salt and penicillin drying his mouth.

He couldn't move much, not yet. His muscles protested every time he shifted his weight on the cot. His leg was elevated on two pillows, wrapped in layers of gauze and cotton. The skin underneath was raw, red, and hot to the touch.

A new antibiotic dripped into his right arm from the IV bag hanging beside the bed. Now, between the ache in his bones and the warming sting of whatever was in the IV, sleep came in brief, haunted moments. The MPs stationed outside his curtain offered no comfort and weren't subtle. One stood at the head of his bed—rifle slung barrel-down, hand resting on the stock. Not a threat, not explicitly. But not optional, either. Neither was the message—he was a prisoner.

The sound of boots on the concrete floor signaled the opening of the curtain flap. He didn't bother lifting his head, recognizing the gait before the face.

General Dorsey.

The man didn't offer a greeting. He pulled a metal folding chair closer to the cot, sat, and crossed one leg over the other. His tan class B uniform, devoid of any rank, ribbons, or accomplishments, was immaculate, with highly polished black shoes and the creases in his slacks as sharp as a scalpel. He looked at Teddy with the same polite, unreadable expression he always wore—like a man reading a eulogy written in advance.

"Colonel Roosevelt, I thought I'd stop by to see how you're holding up. I must say, you look better than I expected," Dorsey said. "You've always been too damn stubborn to die clean."

Teddy ignored the barb. The IV line continued to drip into his arm. He allowed the silence to remain.

Dorsey leaned forward. "Let's not pretend. You and I both know how Firelight was supposed to end."

"With a report and extraction," Teddy said, his voice rough from the ongoing dehydration and painkillers.

"No." Dorsey smiled. "With confirmation of Chinese weapons, a body count, and no survivors. You made a mess by walking out alive, Colonel Roosevelt."

Teddy clenched his jaw but didn't take the bait. Not yet.

"I've read the reports," Dorsey continued. "What's left of them, anyway. Armstrong's in the wind. Kohrs is cleaning house for me. And you're here, sitting up in a hospital bed, leaking intel with every breath."

"You mean breathing," Teddy said, his voice low and sharp, "which wasn't in your plan. And I haven't told anyone a God damn thing about the mission, only that we humped out of Laos. Since having U.S. soldiers over the border isn't exactly a secret anymore, I read about it in the *Washington Post*. What's your point?"

"That's exactly the problem." Dorsey stood, walking to the foot of the bed and tapping the steel frame. "You've been too loud for too long, Teddy. The kind of loud that echoes." Dorsey paused and turned. "But there's still a way through this. Quietly. You've got a name the Army still respects. Make this easy. Testify to nothing. Contest nothing. Let the courts do their job. Take your lumps, keep your men in line, and this will go away— eventually."

"And if I don't?"

Dorsey's smile grew wider. "Then you don't go back to Bragg. Not intact."

Teddy paused for a moment then smoothed out the wrinkles from his blanket. "That line always comes before a knife or a gunshot to the head under suspicious circumstances. Are you going to frag me in public inside a U.S. Army hospital with all these witnesses?"

"What do you think, Colonel Roosevelt? You were never meant to be part of this world. With your family legacy, you were made for medals and ceremonies, not shadows. But once you stepped through that door, you stopped owning your famous name. That's the thing about ghosts. They don't get marble headstones at Arlington."

"This isn't about me being related to President Roosevelt or my family's legacy in the U.S. Army. Stop trying to manipulate my emotions. It won't work."

"Ah," Dorsey said, gesturing at the IV bag. "You're recovering. Don't get overly dramatic on me, Colonel Roosevelt. The Army appreciates what you've done. And the CIA—well, they appreciate results. Sometimes operations don't go as smoothly as we'd like. You know how it is."

"I'm figuring that out."

"You and your men will be heading back stateside soon." Dorsey adjusted his tie with practiced indifference. "Medical evac flight, priority handling. There'll be hearings, of course—Article 32, formalities. However, you should know…the official narrative is already under construction. Best not to add anything that could complicate it."

Teddy locked his eyes on him. "You burned a village and murdered innocent civilians?"

Dorsey didn't flinch. "Some regrettable actions took place in your area of operations. That's not the question. The question is—did your team act outside its official parameters?"

"You tell me," Teddy said, keeping his tone level. "We followed your orders."

"Precisely." Dorsey leaned forward. "And those orders, as filed, will support that. If you keep things tidy and clean."

Teddy said nothing.

Dorsey's smile never reached his eyes. "I like you, Colonel Roosevelt. Your record is spotless. West Point, top ten percent of your class, and First Regimental Commander. Three combat tours in Vietnam. More awards for bravery than entire platoons—Two DSCs, Silver Star, Legion of Merit, Soldier's Medal, four Bronze Stars with Valor device, four Purple Hearts, an Air Medal, and numerous Army Commendations. Frankly, we expected a little more…alignment from someone with your background."

"I didn't realize that patriotism involved killing innocent civilians."

Dorsey let out a soft, disappointed sigh. "Patriotism means following the chain of command without question. And understanding when silence does more for the country than noise." He stood, brushing invisible lint off his pant leg. "Get some rest. You'll need to be on your feet soon. For your sake, I hope you're ready to play the part they expect."

And then he was gone, the curtain swaying in his conceded wake.

Outside, the MPs moved closer to the door, rifles held with safeties on but ready.

Teddy closed his eyes, but sleep eluded him once more. Too much noise in his mind. Too many promises made in the dark.

This time, he'd keep them to strengthen his resolve.

CHAPTER 29

0310 Hours
June 26, 1972
Recovery Ward
3rd Field Hospital
Saigon
Republic of Vietnam

The hallway outside Teddy's room had fallen silent. It wasn't shift change for the medical staff—no squeaking carts on the tile, not even the whispers of nurses behind the curtain. Teddy's senses, dulled by medication but still alert, picked up on it first—not a sound but the absence of one. Silence carried weight—a kind of pressure in the air. That's when he knew.

The man who entered didn't speak, announce himself, or glance at the MPs who decided to take their break ten minutes early without anyone assigned as relief to replace them. He wasn't openly armed, but Teddy knew instinctively he was more dangerous than anyone with a weapon.

Kohrs.

Medium height, built like a long-range shooter with too much restraint to waste on unnecessary movement. Civilian suit—gray and crisp—creased in the right places but not tailored. Off-the-rack. Forgettable. Intentional. His walk was smooth and silent, like a man accustomed to working in carpeted embassy halls and concrete safehouses where footsteps meant death.

He pulled up a chair but didn't sit. Instead, he placed a manila folder on the steel bedside table and tapped it once with two fingers.

"Your name's not in this one," he said, holding up one finger. "Yet."

Teddy met his gaze without flinching. "And?"

Kohrs glanced down at Teddy's leg under the blanket. "We gave you a way out. Dorsey explained the boundaries."

"You mean the fucking lie!"

Kohrs ignored his outburst. He opened the folder, flipped a page, then closed it again. He didn't need to read it. That wasn't the point.

"You're thinking about what comes next. I'll save you the trouble. There is no next. There's only how clean we make this." Kohrs moved closer, close enough for Teddy to see the old scar on his neck beneath the collar—thin, pale, and surgical—like everything else about him. "People like me don't issue threats, Colonel Roosevelt. We carry out policies. I don't argue ethics. I don't debate morality. I erase problems. It's that simple."

Teddy remained still, watching Kohrs' body language for any attempt to reach inside his coat. Men like him never went anywhere unarmed.

Kohrs sat in the chair, but it felt more like a countdown than a conversation. "You're a fourth-generation soldier. I get that. It makes you feel like you still have some control. But this world doesn't run on honor or duty. It runs on containment. Operation Firelight was never about intelligence. It was about outcome. You weren't sent to gather facts—you were sent to make a certain precisely chosen conclusion unavoidable."

"And when I didn't play along?" Teddy asked, his voice dry and low to avoid collateral damage if someone on the hospital staff overheard their conversation. The chances were extremely high that person would become the target of an unfortunate accident.

Kohrs smiled. "That's why I'm here." He leaned in, his presence suddenly more imposing. "We don't burn men like you unless we have to. But the second you stop being useful to us, you become expensive. And you're racking up debt exponentially, Colonel Roosevelt."

Teddy clenched his jaw but kept his composure. "Is that what this is? A bill? And you're here to collect?"

Kohrs stood again, picking up the folder. "No. This is the receipt." He turned to leave, pausing just long enough at the curtain to glance over his shoulder. "Your five-minute window will come," he said. "Use it. Or next time, I won't be knocking."

Then he vanished into the hallway. No footsteps. Only silence.

Teddy leaned into his pillows, staring at the ceiling. Everything was in motion now. The wheels kept turning. And every one of them had blood on the spokes.

June 28, 1972
1022 Hours
3rd Field Hospital
Saigon
Republic of Vietnam

It took him five minutes to walk the short distance from the recovery ward to the debriefing room—ten steps with a cane, his left leg still burning with each one of them. The MPs didn't assist him, but they watched him closely. He was no longer just a patient. He was something between an officer and a detainee. Neither free nor quite yet imprisoned—living in the limbo of innocence and guilt.

He sank into the chair, one arm resting on the edge of the table, jaw clenched from the pain. The room was sparse except for the ticking wall clock, a single pitcher of water, and two empty glasses.

When the door opened, Dorsey was the first to enter.

His class B tan uniform was spotless, exemplifying regulation perfection, right down to the polished black Corfam shoes and a faint scent of tobacco clinging to him. He carried nothing but a smile. Behind him, Kohrs appeared—silent as always, one step to the rear and ten degrees colder.

"Colonel Roosevelt," Dorsey said, pulling out the chair across from him. "Good to see you vertical."

Teddy didn't answer. He didn't need to, since something he shouldn't say in front of women or generals might slip out. But he could definitely think it. What a fucking arrogant son of a bitch.

Dorsey sat with calm authority, arms relaxed, fingertips steepled in front of him. "Your vitals are holding steady. The infection is responding well to the antibiotics. You'll be cleared for transport stateside within forty-eight hours. We've already arranged for a priority medevac out of Tan Son Nhut—nonstop to Fort Bragg." He waited as if expecting a thank you.

Teddy didn't oblige him. No one thanked their jailer.

"You'll be held temporarily at the Fort Bragg stockade while the Article 32 hearing date is scheduled and placed on the docket," Dorsey continued, his tone unusually pleasant. "Just routine, you understand. You'll have your hearing. An assigned JAG lawyer. All the proper channels will be followed. And in the end, the truth will come out."

The word *truth* hung in the air like something spoiled, stinking up the place like rotten cabbage.

"You already know how it ends," Teddy said without emotion.

Dorsey didn't blink. "That depends on your cooperation."

Behind him, Kohrs remained still—hands at his sides, posture stiff, and expression unreadable. He hadn't spoken a word, but his presence was louder than a gunshot as a threat of what could happen.

Dorsey leaned in close enough for Teddy to smell the garlic on his breath. "You're going to play the role we write for you, Colonel Roosevelt, and act it out to perfection. Disavowed hero. Unwitting scapegoat. A few years in confinement, then quietly reassigned to another duty post.

Something offshore. Guam, maybe. Somewhere warm and comfortable. A discreet and controlled paradise to live out your remaining years."

Teddy looked at him through narrowed eyes. "And if I don't play along?"

Dorsey smiled again, this time colder than Siberia. "Then the file grows longer. Witnesses vanish. And the men you lead begin to question if your silence is worth their lives."

The room remained quiet.

Dorsey stood and straightened his shirt cuffs with meticulous care like a man finishing a job that hadn't quite required him to break into a sweat. "Let's not make this messy," he said, and turned toward the door.

Kohrs stayed behind.

For three seconds, neither man moved. Then Kohrs took a few steps closer—not much, just a fraction inside Teddy's personal space.

"You continue to breathe because we allow it. You're no longer assigned to the recovery ward. Enjoy the private room and more privacy, compliments of the general," Kohrs said, then he turned and walked out after Dorsey, his steps perfectly spaced, perfectly silent.

The door clicked shut behind them.

Teddy let out the breath he hadn't realized he was holding, his grip still tight around the handle of the cane. Outside, the corridor resumed its usual activity.

But the chill in the room still hadn't gone away.

They had finished warning him. Now they watched, wondering what he would do next. The next move was his. The problem—he had no idea what he was going to do now.

CHAPTER 30

0620 Hours
June 29, 1972
Private Room
3rd Field Hospital
Saigon
Republic of Vietnam

Teddy woke up to the gentle rustle of sheets, a soft, comfortable mattress, and the quiet hum of a ceiling fan barely stirring the thick, humidity-laden air. The antibiotics had lowered his fever but didn't help him fall asleep. Nightmares hovered at the edge of consciousness—images of Laos, Cambodia, Firelight, and the sounds of villagers screaming under a burning sky.

He shifted in the bed, grimacing as the pain from his leg throbbed under the bandages. The IV remained in place, as did the armed MP standing outside the room. But this morning felt different.

A gentle knock sounded on the door. Someone eased it open, then a familiar blond-haired head peeked around the doorframe.

"Sir? Are you busy?" Jack asked. "The head nurse said I had five minutes."

"Busy? No." Teddy waved him into the room. "I'm just lying here like a damn vegetable, waiting for a roasting pan."

Jack closed the door. He stood between the bed and the window. "You need to know—somebody's already rewriting our footprints or, at least, trying to."

Teddy sat up, his abdominal muscles tightening from the effort. "What do you mean?"

"I stopped by the communication room yesterday while walking down the corridor for my daily exercise with my watcher in tow. I told him I was checking on any communications received about our charges and used my rank as an added advantage. The private decided to follow my order after I threatened to write him up. Your name's been removed from the medevac manifest—twice. Someone corrected it back by hand both times, but that doesn't happen by accident."

Teddy absorbed that information. Was it Dorsey? Kohrs? Or was there another player involved in this macabre, almost Shakespearean play?

Jack pulled a folded scrap of paper, no larger than a dog tag, from the front pocket of his jungle fatigues. "I mailed your copy of the orders. The originals. Everything you tucked into your shirt before we went dark. Everything was sent to my PO box stateside under the old code name. It's off-the-grid. Safer than keeping it on base."

Teddy took the slip of paper with the name and address of the P.O. Box—*Mr. Carter E. Stroud, P.O. Box 452, Alexandria, Virginia.*

"Also…one of the nurses mentioned something strange. She said a CID officer asked about your condition. Not your injuries. He wanted to see your chart—what was recorded in your medical file—and who had access to it, but he didn't leave a name."

Teddy raised an eyebrow. "Kohrs?"

Jack shook his head. "She said it wasn't him. An older guy around your age. Tall, about six feet, short-cropped brown hair, wearing a gray suit, and flashed an Army ID card, but no unit was listed. Polite, well-mannered, and confident, but he seemed...off. She thought he might be someone from the Inspector General's office until she saw him walking with someone from Langley later."

Teddy didn't say anything. He didn't have to. They were already rewriting history and erasing the damage. The verdict wasn't being decided in a courtroom—it was being built in silence, file by file, erasure by erasure. Then a thought struck him, slowed by the medication in his system. Jack had just described Lieutenant Colonel Vincent "Iron Vince" Cross. Was Vince searching for him? Was he still a friend, or had he become an enemy? That was something he needed to find out if he ever got the chance.

Jack straightened. "You've got maybe one day left before they move us. After that, we'll be separated. Different cells, maybe different locations, and definitely different backstories."

Teddy gripped the paper tighter. "Then make sure ours stays true."

Jack nodded once. He was already halfway to the door when he stopped. "I'll see you at Bragg, Colonel."

Teddy watched the door close behind him then folded the paper and tucked it under the gauze bandage beneath his hospital gown.

The war wasn't over yet. It had just gone underground.

0445 Hours
June 30, 1972
Medical Transfer Bay
3rd Field Hospital
Saigon
Republic of Vietnam

It was still dark, pre-dawn, when the transport detail arrived before reveille. Prisoner transfers never involved any ceremony—only handcuffs and a wheelchair. A pair of MPs stood outside Teddy's room—the same ones from yesterday. Both of them looked at him with an indifference that bordered on hatred.

"Colonel Roosevelt," the staff sergeant said, clipboard in hand. "Orders are in. The transport window opens in twenty minutes. You're being moved under Article 32 into pretrial confinement. Destination—Fort Bragg."

Teddy sat on the edge of the bed, his wooden cane leaning against the wall. His leg still ached, but he could stand and take a few steps, aided by the cane. Jack had left him a set of unmarked OD-green fatigues and a pair of jungle boots.

He dressed, fingers moving slowly over each button. Eli and Jack would already be in the holding area. He'd see them again soon, but not as soldiers. Not as free men.

The medic arrived a moment later with his final clearance. "Vital signs are holding steady. Fever's broken, and your temperature has returned to normal. IV's out. You're stable enough for transport. Pain management's your call, Colonel Roosevelt. Do you want ten morphine tablets you can take orally when needed to get you through the next twenty-four to forty-eight hours?"

"I'll manage without it," Teddy said, grabbing his cane. He didn't want to be doped up when he landed, so he could remember everything that happened on that transport plane.

Eli and Jack waited for him in the hall, both wearing plain jungle fatigues.

"Look who finally decided to join the party," Jack said, smiling like a Cheshire cat. The MP beside him silenced him with a hand on his shoulder.

"Keep it quiet," the sergeant warned. "No talking unless addressed by one of us."

As they made their way down the hall, hospital staff averted their eyes. The same nurses who had treated his wounds, made small talk, and

151

checked his vital signs, now concentrated on patient charts. No goodbyes or heartfelt farewells—just silence and paperwork.

Two more MPs flanked them as they moved through the ward and outside into the suffocating, almost drinkable humidity. A waiting ambulance idled at the concrete curb, its rear doors open. Not for show. Standard procedure.

"The medical directive signed by your doctor says you shouldn't put too much weight on a compromised limb while cuffed," one MP said.

Jack climbed inside first, then Eli. Both men sat on the bench. Now it was Teddy's turn. He placed his right foot on the bumper and held out his hand to Eli, who pulled him up and into the ambulance. The effort left him winded, but he was inside, sitting next to Eli.

The handcuffs went on next. First Eli, then Jack, their wrists cuffed in front of them. Teddy received the same treatment. Leg irons weren't used on him because of his medical exemption—but the message was clear. He wasn't boarding the ambulance as a patient. He was cargo—a prisoner.

As the doors slammed shut, Teddy leaned back against the wall, looking up at the ceiling. Next to him, a clipboard hung from the ceiling bulkhead. He read the names on the transport manifest.

Colonel Roosevelt IV, T. – Article 134, UCMJ, Unauthorized Detention, Pending Review

Captain Stratton, J – Article 134, UCMJ, Unauthorized Detention, Pending Review

Master Sergeant Red Horse, E – Article 134, UCMJ, Unauthorized Detention, Pending Review

Status: Red-Level Custody
Visibility: Classified (Eyes Only)

He closed his eyes. *Red-Level*. That meant they were buried deep, not even logged into the regular military transportation system. Ghost custody. But the charge left him puzzled—Article 134, UCMJ, Unauthorized Detention. Who did they detain? And when? Was this part of the play-acting Dorsey mentioned? Or was this simply a reason for their detention, a spacer, while waiting for larger, more serious charges?

The vehicle rolled forward, leaving the hospital behind in the foggy morning. No one saluted. No one looked back.

Within the hour, they would be wheels up. A medevac C-141 staged at Tan Son Nhut would take them to Clark Air Force Base in the Philippines, then a hop to Hawaii, and finally into North Carolina under the cover of darkness. Unlike everyone else, that plane was a ticket to lockup, not a "freedom bird." But at least it wasn't the CIA-run Air America, or he might have been dropped out of the rear loading ramp over the Pacific Ocean.

The war was over for them now. But the real fight—the one that wore no uniform, issued no orders, and erased its own trail—was just beginning.

CHAPTER 31

0545 Hours
July 1, 1972
Pope Air Force Base
North Carolina

The C-141 Starlifter touched down under a hazy, pre-dawn slate gray sky. Rain fell in heavy bursts, soaking the tarmac as the aircraft taxied to a remote section of Pope Air Force Base. No reporters with their live news trucks were present. No generals stood under umbrellas to sneer and gloat at their capture—only a waiting convoy of military police vehicles and a canvas-covered deuce-and-a-half six-wheeled truck. The atmosphere didn't feel like a celebration or a homecoming. It felt like a funeral.

Teddy winced with every step as he hobbled down the lowered rear cargo ramp on his cane. Luckily, the MPs showed enough pity for him—or maybe it was the order to remove the handcuffs for any movement on foot. His leg, still stiff and weak, was braced beneath his fatigues. The infection had cleared, but the lingering ache from the debridement surgery and jungle rot made every move a silent battle of painful attrition. Any illusion of strength was gone.

Jack Stratton and Eli Red Horse emerged from the dark interior behind him, each handcuffed in front but still walking under their own power. Their jungle uniforms were new, but their expressions remained the same—wary, silent, scrutinizing every detail as if they'd just landed behind enemy lines.

One MP approached with a wheelchair. "Protocol, sir," he said, avoiding eye contact with Teddy. "I have to follow the medical directive issued by your doctor. You're not cleared for full weight-bearing."

Teddy gritted his teeth but accepted the indignity. His leg really hurt, feeling like a red-hot poker being driven through it with a sledgehammer. Why not take advantage of the wheelchair now? Once he was in the stockade, he'd have to gut out the pain on two feet.

Jack and Eli were loaded into the truck. Teddy was placed in the back of a separate ambulance with two MPs riding shotgun. No conversations about anything. Just the silent roar of rubber tires on wet asphalt. It made for a very lonely ride.

The stockade at Bragg loomed ahead like a forgotten relic of another war—concrete, steel, and the stench of institutional decay. Inside, fluorescent lights buzzed overhead as processing commenced. First came the issuance of prison fatigues and a strip search, which didn't amount to much since all they had were the dog tags around their necks, boots, and the clothes on their backs. Even the day-old bandage wrapped around Teddy's ankle was inspected then replaced with the same one, which seemed a bit odd and somewhat gross. Why not use a clean bandage?

The medical check was more thorough and painful, at least for Teddy, as the doctor manipulated his left ankle in directions it didn't want to go. Surely it would have been easier to read the discharge report from the 3rd Field Hospital in Saigon than to put him through all that pain. Maybe that was the point—Dorsey's way of showing him that he was in charge, even here. The doctor must have missed that directive or chose to ignore it. He cleaned the surgical site and replaced the dirty, half-tightened bandage with a sterile one.

The final stop was cell assignment. Paperwork was piled haphazardly all over the intake desk. The sergeant in charge picked up a single sheet of paper.

"No JAG lawyer assignment on file. No Article 32 hearing scheduled. No cellblock designation or assigned cell numbers," the intake sergeant said, but even he looked confused.

"That's not how it works," Jack said. "You process us properly, or you don't. But you can't keep us in limbo. Where are you going to put us? The latrine? A concrete room out back? Your mother's house? Where, exactly, are you putting us?"

"I'm sorry, sir, but I only follow what's written on the page. Those are the orders," the sergeant replied, shrugging. "The rest of your paperwork hasn't caught up yet."

They were temporarily placed in adjacent solitary cells in maximum security, sparsely furnished with only a cot, sink, steel toilet in the corner, and a drain embedded in the center of the floor.

The cot—if you could call it that—was a steel bench bolted to the wall with a thin, sheetless mattress, suspended by two chains. A small, stained pillow and a folded Army-issue green wool blanket sat at one end.

Jack pounded the wall twice—their prearranged signal to keep communications open without talking to each other. Teddy responded once as proof of life. Eli gave the same signal on the other end of the row.

The fluorescent light above his head flickered, casting an uneasy pall over the dingy concrete walls. Teddy rubbed his aching left wrist, sore from the strain caused by the cane. This was not how he imagined his U.S. Army career coming to an end. What now? Why had his entire world crumbled into ashes?

```
0040 Hours
July 2, 1972
Stockade Cell Block D
Fort Bragg, NC
```

The cell was cold—the concrete walls leeched the last bit of warmth from Teddy's skin despite the long-sleeved standard OD-green field fatigues he wore, marked with the large black P on the back of his shirt.

Teddy sat on the cot, the pain in his leg forgotten beneath the weight of the silence. Something was wrong. Deeply wrong. The absence of a lawyer with no Article 32 hearing scheduled— violating the regulation that requires a hearing within fourteen days—and, on top of that, the blank stares from guards who had no idea what charges they were being held on.

He reached for the only thing he had left—his memory. Names, dates, locations. He recited them in his mind, grounding himself in the truth. Then, when the lights dimmed for lockdown, he limped toward the far wall and gazed at the barred window high above his cell—his only link to the outside world. What in the hell was going on? Was this Dorsey's way of making sure he played along with the "arranged" story? He wasn't going to act his part in Dorsey's plan. There were other options.

He sat on the edge of the bunk, leaning on the cane they'd allowed him to keep because it was medically necessary. It was either that or push him to the showers in a wheelchair. Although there was a guard at each end of the cellblock, none hovered nearby. That seemed odd since they were supposed to be dangerous. Which they were, to the enemy, but not to American soldiers.

And that was the problem.

No Article 32 proceedings. No signed legal forms. No JAG lawyer assignment. Not even a cursory confinement hearing to confirm their location and list the charges. He'd been in the Army long enough to know what that meant—they were freezing him out. Buying time. Waiting for something—or someone—to act.

The real danger wasn't the confinement. It was the silence.

The overhead light had been flickering for hours. It cast everything in a dim, intermittent glow—never quite dark, never quite bright. This was unusual because it was past the lights-out time at midnight—0000 hours.

Across the hall, two MPs stood guard, silent and unreadable behind their rigid uniform discipline. They hadn't spoken to him except when issuing orders, and they made damn sure he knew they'd been told to follow procedure to the letter.

He didn't hold them responsible.

They were simply doing their job.

The security camera mounted in the upper corner of the cell tracked movement, rotating every thirty seconds with a soft mechanical tick. Teddy had already timed it out. Twelve seconds of static followed by a whirr. Seventeen seconds later, it rotated back again. Every loop felt like a slow heartbeat.

He leaned his head back and exhaled.

It was time.

The contact point had been established years ago—back during Teddy's first secret, off-the-books mission for the U.S. Army which became so deeply buried in the folds of the intelligence community that even the Pentagon didn't have a name for it. He left behind more than one failsafe. Only a fool or someone with a death wish would enter the world of covert operations without a backup plan for escaping the system, even if escape was purely hypothetical and considered highly unlikely.

Then he realized he'd known about the legacy protocol for years, just under a different name and a different life. And Lieutenant Colonel Desmond knew that information while briefing him—that one day he would put it all together.

The drain was key.

Every maximum security and isolation cell had one, designed for easy cleaning when dealing with unruly prisoners. This one—just like all the others in the older part of the Fort Bragg stockade—had a vertical waste pipe that drained into the runoff lines below the building. Those lines were old, buried during the construction of Camp Bragg in 1918. They weren't sealed. And a decade ago, when Teddy still walked these halls as a Special Forces captain placed in temporary command of the MPs as part of a leadership exercise, he'd mapped the old schematics and recorded a message meant for no one—unless everything went wrong.

Now everything had.

Teddy waited until the camera passed him again then reached under the steel bench. He moved carefully without panic, making sure not to raise suspicion, hoping it was still close to the bolts. A single standard-sized flat washer had been glued to the bottom—rusted around the edges but still intact. A detail only someone who had been here before would remember.

He slipped his fingers inside and felt the slit in the rubber. He popped it off with his thumbnail and held it in his palm for a moment.

It was a small, stamped metal piece from a standard bunk frame or locker hinge. Nothing unusual—ordinary for everyone else—except Teddy had placed one exactly like it in a dead drop outside Da Nang five years earlier. And that one had been coated in graphite and marked with a barely visible groove to authenticate its sender.

This was the same—having an identical groove—and two characters and a number—*EV5*—which represented the phonetic code phrase—*Echo-Victor–Five*—designating the location. Same weight. Same purpose. A backup plan. It was a silent message. A lifeline buried beneath bureaucracy. A trigger, waiting for the right moment.

He waited for the camera to pass his position again and made sure the guards weren't looking in his direction. Then he slipped off the bench, lowering himself to the floor to avoid any suspicion, suppressing a pained grunt as his ankle protested loudly about the excessive movement, sending a shockwave up his spine.

Carefully, he slid his fingernails under the edge of the drain cover. The screws had been stripped smooth a long time ago and left loose under the assumption no prisoner would ever have the leverage or tools to exploit an open access point only four inches in diameter.

Teddy pried it free, just enough to angle his mouth toward the opening.

The contact phrase had been agreed upon in a different lifetime—back when Theodore "Teddy" Roosevelt IV was still a rising star in the Special Forces community, before the shadows of darkness claimed him.

He spoke the words given to him by Desmond into the darkness of the pipe.

"Delta-one-niner-black. Echo–Victor–Five. This is Rough Rider, statutory clearance. Legacy network. Five-minute override." It sounded absurd. Insane. Talking to a floor drain in the middle of the night. At least, if spotted, that's what the guards would think—he was crazy, a victim of Vietnam Syndrome, or what they called shell shock during WWII. If they called for a psych eval, then he would know he'd been spotted. And that would give him more options to escape since the hospital's mental ward was less secure than maximum security.

But this wasn't meant for the guards. It was for the acoustic pickup hardwired into the plumbing—a handshake protocol—one-way. A back-channel route connected to an old signal chain from when this stockade housed intelligence operatives with nowhere else to go.

A call made this way through an encoded, passive relay system guaranteed that only the right ears would hear it. Once the signal was received, everything else would be set into motion.

That depended on whether the protocol still existed and if anyone was listening. Someone would record it in the logbook within the next twelve hours. He replaced the drain cover and lay back down, hoping the signal would reach its intended target and that he would receive confirmation of receipt. Time would tell. He had to hope and pray. If not, he was already marked for death. He wasn't going along with Dorsey's plan for him and his men.

0734 Hours
July 2, 1972
Stockade Cell Block D
Fort Bragg, NC

The clang of metal on metal echoed down the hallway—food trays sliding into place, boots scuffing on concrete—the dry shuffle of morning routines dressed up as institutional order. Teddy heard it before he saw them.

"Breakfast. Don't get too excited," the guard said outside his cell. "It's the same thing as yesterday."

The flap on the bottom door slot squeaked open, and a tray slid out on squealing, rusted metal rollers. Teddy remained on his bunk with his hands behind his head. Walking hurt, so why cause himself more pain?

"Come on, Colonel Roosevelt," the MP said, leaning just enough to look through the bars. "It ain't the Ritz, but if you don't eat this…food, the medical officer in the infirmary will get on our asses. Again."

Teddy stood, using his cane to push himself up into a standing position. Although healed externally, pain still burned deep in his muscles with every step. He hobbled forward, crouched down, and dragged the tray in with the toe of his boot.

The guard smirked. "Enjoy the fine cuisine the mess hall has prepared for you today. Rehydrated eggs, rubbery toast, and coffee that could clean a rifle barrel."

"Smells like the war crimes trial has already started," Teddy said, shaking his head. "And I got all the rotten leftovers."

The MP laughed and walked away without looking back.

Teddy placed the tray on the edge of his bunk and examined its contents without touching anything yet. The eggs were overcooked into a dry, spongy clump that resembled spray-on insulation foam. A half-burned

159

slice of white toast curled at one end like a dying leaf, and the thin smear of margarine hadn't melted, indicating it was ice cold. A single Styrofoam cup of watery black coffee sat next to a bruised, overripe banana. It was prison food—standard-issue and deliberately devoid of dignity—but he needed the calories to keep his strength up. He picked up the fork and forced himself to take a bite of the eggs.

Then he saw it.

The cup.

Not the contents—though the coffee smelled burnt—but the material of the cup—Styrofoam. This cup had been scored along the rim. At first glance, it looked like damage from shipping or exposure to heat. But Teddy turned it in the light and saw it clearly.

✓ = *1*

An out-of-service confirmation mark. Not Morse code. Not CIA codebook inscriptions. It was something older—an archaic black-world shorthand he'd seen only once in a handwritten ledger at a safehouse in Saigon.

One checkmark, one equal sign, and the number 1—*Signal received. One window authorized.*

Teddy said nothing and didn't even pause.

He took a sip of the bitter, lukewarm coffee, letting it settle into the pit of his stomach like gravel. He pushed the cup away from the tray, turning it so the mark faced away from the guards and the security camera, then started eating with mechanical precision. He didn't glance at the camera in the corner or lift his eyes to the hallway.

But in his mind, the clock had started.

The five minute window would come soon.

And when it did, he'd be ready.

CHAPTER 32

0900 Hours
July 4, 1972
Stockade
Fort Bragg, NC

The air inside the processing wing of the stockade smelled of bleach and rusted metal. Echoes bounced off the green-painted cinderblock walls, and low voices filtered through the bars, but the usual rhythm of Army protocol—morning briefings, paperwork, lawyer assignments—was noticeably absent.

Teddy leaned against the wall near the barred window, watching the trees sway in the breeze, each step a slow, deliberate negotiation with pain. Why had the guards brought them into this room on the 4th of July—Independence Day? Was it some sick joke? While everyone else across the country celebrated independence from England with fireworks, homemade ice cream, and a hot dog cookout, they were trapped inside four cold walls, unable to taste the freedom that they and other soldiers like them had sacrificed and died to protect.

Jack sat hunched on the metal bench inside the small holding room, arms crossed over his knees. Across from him, Eli paced in tight, measured steps, going back and forth, each step stiff with barely contained frustration.

"No assignment?" Jack asked again, louder this time, addressing the sergeant posted next to the door. "We've been here three goddamn days. Where's the JAG officer? And why today, of all days, are we in here? No one works on a holiday."

The guard avoided his eyes. "You'll be notified when your case is docketed. As for why today, don't ask me. I just follow orders. I'd rather be home eating ice cream and watching fireworks with my kids tonight than in here with three murderers."

Jack stood, careful not to appear aggressive or threatening. "Sergeant, we were pulled out of Vietnam and put in chains with no charges filed on any official paperwork. That's not how this works. As for being with your kids, you're a damn soldier. You took an oath just like us. Suck it up."

The sergeant threw his shoulders back in defiance, clearly disagreeing with Jack's dressing down. "I'm just following orders, sir."

"Whose?"

The man hesitated. "I don't know a name. Command level. High up. Somewhere in the Pentagon. Way above my pay grade and clearance level. That's all I was told…sir."

Eli stopped pacing. "This is a stall tactic. They're isolating us. There's no record trail, no movement. Just holding us here in limbo."

Teddy nodded. "They're running out the clock. Every day we sit here without legal representation, the more the story behind Operation Firelight gets rewritten, and we get buried under carefully crafted lies and rumors."

Jack turned toward him. "I agree, they're burying us."

"And also rewriting us—about what happened," Teddy said. "By the time the Article 32 hearing is even scheduled—if it ever is—we'll be ghosts on paper. The records won't match. The operation won't exist— we'll be convicted as war criminals who weren't even at the scene of the crime."

Eli crossed his arms. "Do you think they'll risk trying to erase us completely?"

Teddy's expression remained unchanged. "No. They want to use us. Parade us around in front of the press as war criminals, disavow the mission, then walk away clean with no blood on their hands. But we're inconveniently still alive without a voice."

Just then, a clipboard slid through the slot in the door.

The sergeant picked it up and handed it to Jack, too lazy to walk five more steps to give it to the highest-ranking officer in the room—Teddy.

Jack flipped through the attached forms. "There's nothing here. It's all blank. No JAG counsel listed. No assigned CID investigator. No scheduled Article 32 or confinement hearing. And at the bottom of this page, it says—*Status pending internal review. Do not proceed without additional authorization.* What does that mean?"

"They're locking us out of the system," Teddy replied, just as he expected.

Eli nodded. "Looks like we're on our own."

Teddy moved toward them slowly, the cane steadying his gait. "We won't be in here forever. I've arranged…something. Not much. But enough. Wait for my signal."

Jack narrowed his eyes. "Enough for what?"

"When the window opens, we move quickly. No hesitation. No questions. Just follow my lead and don't hesitate."

Eli studied him for a moment then nodded. "Understood."

Jack shook his head. "I really hope you know what you're doing, Colonel."

Teddy looked at the barred window again. "So do I."

0205 Hours
July 5, 1972
Stockade Cell Block D
Fort Bragg, NC

The metallic click was soft, barely audible.

Teddy lay awake on the thin, institutional mattress, eyes fixed on the ceiling. He had counted the men on every shift, memorized their routines, and listened to the guard patrols echo through the concrete halls night after night. He knew every sound, every movement. And this sound—the quiet, deliberate snick of a door latch disengaging—was different and intentional. That could only mean one thing.

The five-minute window had just opened.

He sat upright, careful not to make the cot squeak and alert the guards usually stationed a few feet away. Standing required effort. His leg still burned with each step, muscles tight around the embedded rod, but adrenaline dulled the sharp pain. Grabbing his cane, which he might need later for support or as a weapon, he crept down the hallway, checking every dark corner—his Special Forces training kicking in—toward the barred cell door.

The door slid open, unlocked by an unseen hand—not from inside the stockade but from somewhere outside the U.S. Army's and the federal government's sphere of influence. Maybe it was the Subnet Echo location Desmond briefed him on—a place where calls for help, like the one he made with the drain, were routed to the right location and undercover operatives.

Teddy pushed the door open wider. Luckily, the rails were well-lubricated. He looked left and right. No guards in sight. Something highly unusual. Where did they go? Computer error? Who ordered them to leave or take their lunch break without relief? Probably whoever remotely opened the door as part of the legacy protocol.

The usual blinking red lights on the security cameras were not working—nonfunctional.

The hallway outside was lit by red emergency lights, casting narrow pools of shadow between the cells. The power to the cell block had been shut off, leaving them fighting against time. Exactly five minutes.

Jack was already at his cell door, ready and waiting to leave. Teddy exchanged a glance with him and nodded once—an unspoken affirmation. Jack nodded back, prepared to follow him.

At the far end, Eli emerged from his cell, ghost-quiet, his broad frame moving from shadow to shadow with practiced ease. They converged near the center of the cell block. There was no need to speak. They had rehearsed this moment countless times in training, during dozens of different operations. The timing was instinctive, sharpened to a razor's edge.

Teddy pointed at the maintenance door built into the back wall of the cell block, which led to a utility access corridor connected to a maintenance tunnel beneath the stockade.

Jack moved forward, testing the door handle. It moved up and down. Unlocked. Someone had made sure the latch bolt and internal lock would fail tonight. Inside, the air smelled of dust, rust, and stale, moldy water— pipes dripped rhythmically somewhere below.

Eli closed the door behind them, paused to listen for any pursuers. Nothing. Not yet.

They descended a narrow concrete stairwell lined with rusted steel handrails into a cramped, damp service tunnel filled with steam pipes and electrical conduits.

Teddy's rubber-tipped cane tapped on the concrete, each step a cautious negotiation with his injured leg. His pulse pounded behind his temples, each beat a silent countdown to the end of their five-minute window.

At the midpoint of the tunnel, Eli reached up to a low-hanging pipe bracket and pulled out a rusted metal box hidden behind it. A dead drop— placed within the last few days—waited until needed. Inside, wrapped in an old mechanic's rag, were three sets of fake identification cards, a folded map, a car key, a watch set to the local time, a loaded M1911A1 Colt .45 caliber pistol, and fifty dollars in cash.

Teddy grabbed the watch and the pistol, tucking the weapon into his waistband while Eli pocketed the key. Jack handed out the rest, giving Teddy a North Carolina driver's license with his picture—*Anthony Richards*—and a P.O. Box in Spring Lake. Jack's new name was *Parker Stevenson,* and Eli's was *Takoda Running Bear.* Whoever set up the dead drop did their homework, providing accurate photos and physical details on the licenses. The addresses, of course, were fake, meant to lead law enforcement in the wrong direction.

They moved forward without hesitation. Ahead, the tunnel split into two. Teddy turned left, his memory guiding each step from the map he had seen of the layout years earlier. A cool night breeze drifted in from a side grate near the ceiling, moonlight shining through the opening. They were close.

At the end of the tunnel, Teddy climbed a pitted iron ladder to a rusted hatch—a maintenance access point sealed by a bent padlock, intentionally weakened by their unknown benefactor.

Teddy descended the ladder because holding onto his cane prevented him from exerting his full strength to open the lock.

Jack climbed up, using the crowbar from the fire emergency box to break the shackle off the lock. He lifted the hatch and slipped out into the darkness beneath the low-hanging pine branches, staying hidden from view. Teddy and Eli followed him, crouching to avoid detection by the guards manning the watchtowers and the floodlights surrounding the walls.

Cicadas buzzed, covering their breathing. Teddy checked the glowing dial on his new watch—three minutes gone. Two remaining.

He led them along the perimeter fence to a weathered side gate—forgotten, unsecured, and rarely used in years. With a gentle push, the gate swung open outward, revealing a dirt service road just beyond the main fence line.

Waiting there was a battered black Ford Torino sedan covered in dust. Eli pulled the key from the dead drop in his pocket and unlocked the doors in one smooth motion.

Jack slid into the driver's seat without a word. The engine turned over after the third turn of the key.

Teddy eased into the front passenger seat, his leg throbbing now but still manageable, the adrenaline from the escape keeping some of the pain at bay.

Eli sat in the back seat, scanning the empty road behind.

No search lights popped on. No cars sped up in pursuit. No alarms started ringing.

Jack drove the speed limit, heading toward the narrow dirt road that led to the distant highway, dust billowing up behind them. Teddy leaned back into the worn upholstery, breathing through gritted teeth to deal with the pain radiating from his leg. Eli kept watching their backtrail.

They had mentally prepared for chaos—sirens, pursuits, and running gun battles. But instead, silence followed them into the darkness—the silence of careful planning, precision, and the unseen hand that had opened doors and weakened locks without leaving any fingerprints behind.

The car's tires hummed over the black asphalt as Jack accelerated, merging onto a deserted back road heading west, away from Bragg, away from confinement, and away from the only life all three of them had known for years.

Teddy leaned back in the seat, granting himself a brief moment of relief.

Five minutes. Surgical precision.

They were ghosts now.

And the real war had just begun.

CHAPTER 33

0530 Hours
July 5, 1972
Backroads
North Carolina Foothills

The sun hadn't risen yet, but the sky was starting to brighten at the edges—fading from a muted indigo to gray then to reddish-orange as dawn spread across the eastern horizon of North Carolina.

Teddy sat in the passenger seat, one hand curled around the vinyl door handle, the other resting on his thigh, tracing the edge of the fake ID tucked in his pocket. The pain in his leg had intensified now that the adrenaline was starting to wear off—hot, steady pulses running from his hip to his ankle, each jolt a reminder that this was no longer a controlled operation. They weren't behind enemy lines—not officially. But they weren't free either. They were, as they say in the movies—flying by the seat of their pants—improvising everything along the way.

They were fugitives once more—homeless, without financial support, and unable to contact their families to explain what had happened or that they were still alive.

Jack drove with the focus of a man threading a needle in a thunderstorm. No headlight beams revealing their location, no sharp turns or high speeds to attract the police. Every movement was deliberate, every glance in the rearview mirror calculated. He didn't speak. None of them did—not since they'd cleared the side gate. That kind of silence didn't come from fear. It stemmed from long experience—from knowing exactly how fragile the moment was and how it could turn from good to bad in less than a second.

Eli leaned back in the passenger seat, one arm crossed over his chest, boots resting flat on the floorboards. He appeared calm, but Teddy knew better. Eli Red Horse didn't waste tension on appearances. He stored it deep inside, letting it smolder. When it ignited, it did so with purpose and the fury of a category five hurricane.

They were now twenty miles out, traveling along a gravel road that wound through dense pine forests and backwater farms. Behind them, only darkness and the faint echo of the life they'd just left behind. Fort Bragg. The stockade. The wreckage of everything they'd once been—Special

Forces soldiers—Green Berets. A title with a proud history stretching back to the Office of Strategic Services during World War II, a legacy that led to the formation of the 10th Special Forces Group in 1952—a legacy now lost, gone in the blink of an eye amid doctored reports and false charges.

Jack broke the silence. "We'll need to ditch the car soon."

Teddy nodded. "Burn it or leave it?"

"Burning draws too much attention," Eli said. "Better to wipe it clean and walk out of a dead end."

Teddy looked ahead through the bug-covered windshield. "There's a train yard near Raleigh. Cargo only. Unsecured and easy to hop onto an empty car. There should be food in the caboose."

Jack nodded. "I can get us close. Our unknown benefactor made sure we had a full tank of gas."

They let the silence stretch again.

Five minutes. That was all it took to disappear. Five minutes to cut the thread connecting them to everything official, everything explainable. And it had been waiting for them—hidden inside an institutional cot, a standard washer tucked between slats, an old code whispered down a drainpipe. That wasn't improvisation. It was insurance. Someone had buried a key years ago, and Teddy had been smart enough to remember where it was hidden.

But now came the part no one ever planned for or expected.

What's next?

Teddy clenched his jaw as he watched the road curve through stands of dense pine trees. They were out—for now. But for how long? There would be a response—a manhunt of biblical proportions. The brass would lose their minds. CID would be called in to investigate their disappearance under suspicious circumstances with no clues about what or who triggered it. Maybe the FBI would get involved with a broader network of informants. And the people who organized the escape—whoever was still pulling the strings—wouldn't do it again. This was their one chance. Their only window of opportunity.

They couldn't go underground. Not just yet.

Instead, they had to go loud.

"I want the truth out there," Teddy muttered, mostly to himself. "I want Operation Firelight exposed. The names. The funding. Everything."

Jack kept his eyes on the road. "Then we've got to make some noise. A whole lot of it."

"Controlled noise," Eli added. "Not panic. We need to put pressure on those involved—Dorsey, Kohrs, and Armstrong."

Teddy reached up and rubbed the corner of his eye, the memory of Kohrs' voice still fresh in his mind. One sentence. That was all the bastard had said.

If you vanish again, Colonel Roosevelt, someone you care about will be next.

It hadn't been a threat. It was a conclusion.

They had gotten out, but they were still in the game.

And the rules hadn't changed.

But that didn't mean they couldn't do it their way or change how the game was played. It only took one piece of information going public. It was just a question of when to release it.

CHAPTER 34

0145 Hours
July 8, 1972
Harrison's Auto Salvage Yard
Richmond, VA

The humid summer heat had cooled just enough to make the night tolerable. All around them, the strong smell of burnt motor oil, gasoline, and rusted metal filled the salvage yard. The full moon in the cloudless black sky cast an eerie pale glow over rows of twisted wrecks—Fords, Chevrolets, Pontiacs—all in various stages of mechanical decay, some stripped down to their frames, others more intact, waiting for rebirth thanks to some ambitious teenage mechanic in his high school shop class. Shadows danced ominously around them, silhouettes of discarded car parts resembling abstract sculptures in the darkness.

Teddy leaned against the trunk of a rusted gray Chevrolet Impala, one hand gripping a makeshift cane fashioned from a salvaged steel pipe, the other near the worn pistol grip of his Colt .45 tucked into his waistband. A faded red flannel shirt hung over his shoulders, and worn khaki pants covered scuffed, nearly black combat boots. He had lost at least twenty pounds since they escaped from Laos. The lingering pain in his leg came and went like a dull ember—manageable but never forgotten. Every sound—an owl's distant call, the breeze rustling dry leaves—made him tense, though outwardly he remained calm and focused.

Eli crouched next to a faded blue '68 Plymouth Road Runner, its paint bubbled and peeling in long strips, but the chassis remained solid, and the engine compartment housed a 426 Hemi V8. They'd need the extra horsepower if chased by the police.

He wore threadbare jeans and a faded green fatigue shirt, the sleeves rolled past his elbows. A thick smear of engine grease ran along his jawline, a testament to his careful and methodical work on fixing their new ride. With a quiet grunt, Eli ratcheted loose a rusted starter assembly, removing it from beneath the battered engine block. He wiped sweat from his forehead with the back of a grease-streaked hand and inspected the worn gears with his flashlight.

Jack stood nearby, alert and silent, his tall, slender silhouette blending into the pile of discarded chrome fenders and hood panels. He held a small flashlight, its narrow beam illuminating Eli's tools but barely reaching beyond a few feet. His clothes—an old denim jacket and work pants bought at a roadside flea market—were intentionally plain, practical, and unremarkable. He glanced toward the front gate, scanning for movement and listening for the sound of approaching engines or footsteps. His body remained perfectly still, every muscle coiled like a tightly wound spring, ready to burst.

"How much longer?" Teddy asked, his voice low and hoarse from exhaustion.

Eli didn't look up. "Twenty minutes, give or take. The carburetor's shot, but the one from that '69 Plymouth Satellite over there is good enough. The battery's hooked up, the alternator's working, and I filled up the tank with gas from the yard's pump. The engine should turn over, and it's got a four-speed Hurst shifter." He connected wires with steady fingers, focused on his task, ignoring the mosquitoes buzzing around his neck.

Jack shifted his weight, restless but disciplined. "And the plates?"

Eli pointed at a nearby vehicle, a wrecked 1965 Ford Falcon with bent axles and a shattered windshield. "Swapped them out already. They'll match long enough to get us clear of town. After that, we're ghosts, blending into the traffic on the highway."

Teddy shifted his weight, grimacing at the dull pain shooting through his left leg. "Any tools we should keep?"

"Just the wrench set, screwdriver, tire iron, and pry bar. Nothing that stands out or looks like a burglary kit," Eli responded, checking the coolant reservoir and oil levels one last time.

Jack turned to face both of them. "We're burning moonlight. Let's get that thing fired up and rolling. We don't want a security patrol to spot us here and call the cops."

Eli slammed the hood shut and hurried over to the driver's side. He yanked the door open with a rusty squeal. He eased into the driver's seat, turning the ignition key while Teddy prayed the heap would start on the first try.

The engine coughed, sputtered, then roared to life, belching thick smoke from the tailpipe before settling into a rough but steady idle. Relief washed over Eli's face.

Teddy lowered himself into the passenger seat, holding onto the door frame for support as he sat down, keeping his injured leg straight out. The interior reeked of mildew and old vinyl.

Jack slid into the back seat, scanning the yard once more.

Eli looked at both men, quietly confident. "It'll get us there."

Teddy nodded, preparing himself for the bumpy road ahead. "Then let's move out. Carefully. We don't want to attract the attention of the cops."

"Agreed. The two days at Bragg, eating that awful food and sleeping on a stinky, pee-stained, lumpy mattress, were enough for me."

The Plymouth pulled out of the yard, its headlights off until it reached the deserted road. The junkyard disappeared into the darkness behind them, swallowed up by the North Carolina night.

0615 Hours
July 10, 1972
Downtown Alexandria Post Office
Alexandria, VA

The early morning sun cast a pale orange glow over the damp, empty streets, highlighting the tired brick facade of Alexandria's main post office. Teddy stood near the street corner, his posture relaxed but his senses razor-sharp. The wooden cane felt heavy in his left hand, and underneath his loose-fitting denim jacket, the Colt .45 rested against his ribs, tucked into the waistband of his trousers. The street was quiet and deserted, aside from a paperboy on his bicycle and a woman unlocking a small diner down the block, the faint scent of freshly brewed coffee drifting through the crisp morning air.

Jack hurried up the concrete steps, keys jingling in his hand, wearing a tan windbreaker and faded jeans with a navy blue Alexandria Senators baseball cap shading his eyes.

Eli waited in the idling Plymouth, its engine rumbling across the street, watching for any signs of trouble, drumming his fingers on the steering wheel.

Teddy watched Jack through the windows lining the front of the building, knowing it took just one phone call to alert the police or MPs of their location in the city. Andrews Air Force Base, in Prince George's County, Maryland, was only twelve miles away, with Fort Belvoir, home of the U.S. Army's Office of Covert Operations (OCO), twenty miles away.

Inside the post office, Jack approached a row of tarnished brass PO boxes. He looked around once, making sure he was alone, then inserted his key into Box 452. The lock opened easily, revealing a narrow slot filled with mail—junk flyers and a few official-looking envelopes. Shoving his hand into the back of the slot, he pulled out a thicker package, heavily taped and wrapped in brown paper.

Jack slipped it inside his jacket before going through the remaining mail, tossing most of it into a nearby trash can. Moments later, he stepped back outside, walking down the steps toward Teddy. "We're good," he said, his voice just loud enough for Teddy to hear.

"What exactly was in there?" Teddy asked as they headed toward the waiting Plymouth, keeping an eye out for passing police cruisers or Army MPs.

"Everything important," Jack replied, his voice showing no emotion. "The original orders for Operation Firelight, the microfilm copies from that Black Lotus binder, and a few personal items. IDs, cash, and—"

"A safe deposit box key?" Teddy asked, never breaking his limping stride.

Jack nodded, his expression grim. "From a bank in Richmond. Burn IDs, passports, cash reserves—tradecraft material I've collected over the years. Stuff we'll need to disappear. Also, backup IDs, clean driver's licenses, credit cards under assumed names, and my old intel network contact list from my days working for the CIA. If things go really sideways, we'll need every resource available."

"Agreed. And I have a few personal contacts as well. Let's hope we never have to use them." Teddy looked up and down the street again, taking in the sleepy cityscape around them, aware that even tranquility could hide danger. "Does anyone else know about your stash?"

Jack shook his head. "Just me. Not even Dorsey would know about that box. I set it up years ago, during my first intel rotation—insurance for days like this."

"Let's hope that's true," Teddy said.

"Got this too," Jack held up a slip of paper, letting it flutter from his fingers in the breeze, "notifying me of overdue box rental fees. Who cares. This box is now compromised and worthless."

They reached the Plymouth, and Teddy opened the passenger door, sliding into the seat with a pained grimace. Jack climbed into the back, the package now secure on his lap, addressed to his alias, *Mr. Carter E. Stroud.*

Eli glanced back from the wheel, reading their expressions. "Clean?"

Jack nodded, his gaze steady. "We're good. Let's move before anyone realizes we're here."

The Plymouth rolled forward, merging onto the empty street, heading north toward Richmond and their next move.

Teddy checked the mirrors for any signs of pursuit, his fingers still wrapped around the reassuring grip of his Colt .45. His mind raced through plans, options, and contingencies.

For now, they were ghosts again—armed with enough proof to turn the tables on the black-world players hunting them. But ghosts had to keep moving, invisible, always one step ahead of the demons chasing them.

The road ahead stretched long and uncertain. But it was a start, and it was more than they had yesterday. With the money from the post office box, maybe tonight they could eat a hot meal instead of what they managed to scrounge out of the trash bin behind the local restaurants.

CHAPTER 35

2230 Hours
July 12, 1972
Fort C.F. Smith Park
Arlington, VA

The park was an ideal meeting place, located on the site of a Civil War fort built in 1863. It was almost deserted at this late hour, the benches wet with dew and the faint scent of freshly cut grass hanging in the summer air. Streetlights flickered along the main road two blocks away, but here, beneath the shadow of ancient oak trees over a century old, the only light came from the moonlight filtering through the leaves.

Teddy sat alone on a wrought-iron bench near the duck pond, the worn collar of his cheap Army surplus jacket turned up against the breeze. He still walked with a visible limp, worsened by too little time to heal properly. A wooden cane rested against his thigh, unused for now but close enough to grab if needed for mobility or as a weapon. Jack and Eli were stationed elsewhere, both armed with sidearms—questionable U.S. Army-marked M1911A1s they bought from a black market arms dealer. Their job was to watch the perimeter without drawing attention to themselves. They were soldiers, even now—ghosts wrapped in quiet tension.

Teddy checked his watch. Exactly on time—2230 hours.

The man who approached didn't hurry. His stride was steady and confident with a quiet presence that drew the eye. He wore a simple black trench coat and polished dress shoes, his tie neatly knotted, as though he'd come straight from Capitol Hill. His posture was ramrod-straight— military-influenced, yet refined and graceful. A scholar-warrior— someone who both fought and wrote about it.

When he reached the bench, he didn't speak right away. He sat beside Teddy, leaving a respectful gap between them. Then he removed his gloves and laid them across his knee.

"Still walking with that confident Roosevelt pride, I see," the man said.

Teddy offered a faint, pained smile. "Takes more than a broken leg and a court-martial to change my gait, Clay."

Clayton Monroe Harrison IV—a descendant of President William Henry Harrison. A former Army intelligence officer—now a mid-level State Department attaché who wore the anonymity of bureaucracy like armor. Years ago, he and Teddy served together on an early advisory mission in Vietnam. They spoke the same language—not just Khmer, but the unspoken one of legacy. Both men understood what it meant to carry a famous name in quiet places.

"You look like you've been through hell, Teddy," Clay said without judgment. "Which means it all must be true."

"It is," Teddy replied. "They're erasing us. Not just about Operation Firelight. For everything."

Clay watched the pond for a long moment. "You wouldn't have reached out if it wasn't serious. And if you used the code...*Forty-Nine Stones Fallen.*"

"I did." During the brief phone call, Clay gave the correct response to confirm his identity—*And one left standing.*

The coded phrase had been exchanged years earlier between them in a Hanoi safehouse after a failed extraction nearly cost both of their lives. A fallback intended only for when one of them needed to disappear forever—figuratively.

The phrase, *Forty-Nine*, referred to the 49 stars on the U.S. flag before Hawaii was added—a symbolic nod to something unfinished or left behind. *Stones Fallen* was a quiet reference to Arlington headstones or the loss of fellow operatives—men erased, forgotten, or buried under lies.

To an untrained ear or someone eavesdropping on a phone tap or public conversation, it sounded poetic or cryptic. To the right contact, it was a go-code, and coming from Teddy, it meant—*Roosevelt has fallen off the grid. He needs assets moved.*

"I don't need much," Teddy said. "Just enough to disappear for a while. Quietly. I have the men. I have a plan. But we're going to need money, extra IDs, and housing—both stateside and abroad. No questions asked. And no flag waving. We need to stay clear of all political influence, or none of this will mean a damn."

"You'll have it," Clay said. "But you need to understand something. This isn't charity. You're not just a name I grew up hearing about. You're a reminder that men like us don't get to choose the battles—we only decide how we fight them." He reached inside his coat and handed over a slim black envelope sealed with wax. "The bank account is in Zürich. Names aren't traceable. The keys are split between three deposit boxes in different states—Oklahoma, Missouri, and Nebraska. The safe house is located near Choteau, Montana—a quiet, isolated spot, far from any neighbors or prying eyes. No roads within a mile of it, so you'll need to go off-road in a four-wheel drive to get there along the fire trail. There's a Jeep inside the shed with Montana plates that don't match the VIN. New, clean IDs are with it, one for each of you. And two weapons—an M1911A1 and an AR-15, modified for automatic fire with ten boxes of ammo each. I couldn't get an off-the-books M16 on short notice. Besides, if you live off the land, you'll need something to hunt deer and defend yourselves—remember that's bear, wolf, and mountain lion country."

Teddy turned to him and smiled. "I will. Why are you doing this?"

Clay stood and looked down at him. "Because I've seen what happens when the government forgets who it serves—the people. And because if they're trying to silence you, it means you're still a threat to the shadow government we all know exists but no one talks about in the D.C. political circles. Which means you still matter and can provide the evidence to bring it down. And I don't let family legacies like ours die because of lies."

"I know. Families like ours have ingrained that into us since birth."

"Yes. And because one day I might need the same favor," Clay whispered.

Teddy nodded once. "You'll get it."

They didn't shake hands—only a quick glance, a silent shared understanding of their purpose and family history. Then Clay turned and walked away, his footsteps fading into the night.

Jack emerged from the trees a few moments later, his pistol tucked into his waistband, Eli a silent shadow behind him. Neither of them spoke.

Teddy pushed himself to his feet, pain shooting through his left leg with every shift of his weight. "We've got what we need. Time to go dark." And get off his feet for a few weeks to allow his leg time to heal, eat a few decent meals instead of restaurant garbage and surplus WWII C-rations, and a proper bed, rather than sleeping upright in their current mode of transportation.

And with that, the men who no longer officially existed stepped off the path—and back into the shadow war.

CHAPTER 36

0400 Hours
August 14, 1972
Abandoned Farm near Spring Lake
Moore County, NC

The predawn sky, filled with rolling, cloud-choked layers, hung low and colorless, the air damp with humidity and the sharp scent of wet pine needles. Teddy drove the truck himself this time—an old '59 Chevrolet Apache with a cracked windshield, faded green paint, and Virginia plates that didn't match the registration. It coughed smoke when idling and had a rattle somewhere in the front axle, but it got him where he needed to go. No one followed. No one could. He was that careful, using dirt roads and switchback trails to lose any possible tails.

The old fire road wound southeast through the North Carolina woods, so narrow it scraped against both sides of the truck. No lights or reflective trail markers—just instinct and an old topographic map folded into the glove box like contraband. The kind of road you didn't use unless you'd memorized its sharp curves in another life.

He pulled off the road into a clearing bordered by young pine trees and the gnarled, twisted, storm-damaged skeletons of older ones. Deadwood littered the area like bleached bones. Teddy turned off the engine, letting the ticking sound of cooling metal fade into the hushed tones of the forest. The silence out here wasn't peaceful—it was expectant—waiting for the right person to appear and grow into something more.

A hundred meters in, beneath a pine tree split down the middle and blackened by a lightning strike, he found the right spot.

Three stones—roughly fist-sized—arranged in a triangle in the way his father and grandfather had once shown him when burying personal effects of long-gone comrades in arms at a battlefield marker in the Ardennes during a family vacation. The sacred site marked the location of the Battle of the Bulge during World War II where his father earned the Distinguished Service Cross for his bravery and lost most of his platoon, being the only man to walk out alive.

The three stones depicted the Valknut from Norse mythology, featuring three interlocking triangles connected to the god Odin, which symbolized the transition between life and death and the bond between the living and the dead.

Teddy knelt on his right knee, placing his cane beside him.

His breath came in shallow inhales and exhales—the leg still throbbed from the infection, the bone surgery, the long run through Laos, and the escape from the Bragg stockade—but he could move. Barely. And tonight, movement mattered more than comfort.

The ground had already been broken once weeks earlier. He chose the spot even before Operation Firelight started, during a week-long emergency leave in the States to bury his father at Arlington and accept the burial flag with his mother, when the last envelope from Langley arrived and he realized the full extent of what was being planned. Not just a black operation, but a purge. And he trusted his gut, his ingrained intuition from years of combat training, not the CIA's promises.

He dug in silence using a military surplus WWII folding entrenching tool, uncovering a steel 155mm shell casing wrapped in canvas and a rubber liner. It had no metal tags or identifying marks, only the old brass rim and the headstamp on the baseplate—*LOT 59-MC-7842*—a relic left behind after a failed training operation in Vietnam. It made the perfect dead man's safe.

He cracked it open and placed inside—

A stack of carbon copy orders bound with a rubber band—Operation Firelight, dated 4 June 1972, initialed and unredacted. The ones he kept instead of destroying, as per protocol, and Jack sent back from Vietnam for him.

A microfilm cartridge wrapped in a waterproof sleeve, encoded with photographic captures of the CIA's covert operations briefings by Lieutenant Commander Nathan Kaufman, and a hand-drawn organizational chart—lines sketched in pencil and more. All of it came from the binder they discovered during Operation Silent Arrow—Grid Sector Whiskey-Nine in southern Laos. The one labeled Black Lotus.

A sealed letter addressed to one person, someone he trusted with his life and legacy—*Jack Stratton—Open if I Don't Come Back.*

He paused, his hand hovering over the envelope before tucking it beneath the other items.

Teddy pulled a small object from his front pants pocket—a half-inch graphite-coated steel washer he'd hidden in his boot during their last night in the Fort Bragg cellblock. He rolled it between his fingers, scraped it along the edge of his casing, and dropped it inside. It served as a confirmation code for someone who might someday come looking and recognize what they had just found.

He sealed the tube, buried it, and arranged the stones in the same triangle.

And then he stood, leaning on his cane and staring down at the battered pine tree that marked the spot. Blackened by lightning, split almost to the ground, but still standing.

And so was he.

Now he could wait for the day when the truth finally came out. And it would—someday.

Until then, he would find a way to carry on his family's legacy by charging into battle like his great-uncle did at the Battle of San Juan Hill on July 1, 1898, while leading the 1st United States Volunteer Cavalry Regiment known as the Rough Riders.

His great-uncle relinquished his role as Assistant Secretary of the Navy to lead men into battle. Teddy sacrificed his U.S. Army career for honor and truth in much the same way. He would keep his men alive, and the truth would eventually shine through, like a beacon in the daylight, showing others that staying true to your beliefs doesn't mean losing your morality.

Just as President Theodore Roosevelt refused to shoot a bear in captivity, considering it unsportsmanlike, Teddy also refused to kill innocent civilians. One of his favorite childhood toys was a teddy bear dressed like his great-uncle at San Juan Hill.

A few of his great-uncle's quotes, learned from his father while standing in front of Mount Rushmore, came to mind.

"In any moment of decision, the best thing you can do is the right thing. The worst thing you can do is nothing," and "Nothing worth having comes easy."

Teddy's other favorite quote was, "Complaining about a problem without posing a solution is called whining." Theodore Roosevelt IV was not a whiner. A solution would present itself in due time. And when it did, it would roll down the plains like a thunderstorm with him charging from the front of the line to show that honesty, integrity, and honor beat corruption and betrayal every time. But sometimes, it wasn't a quick and easy path. Timing was everything when rooting out traitors.

Like his namesake, both presidential and paternal, he was prepared to face any and all challenges that lay ahead, ready to stand up for what was right and just. His father taught him that true strength of character comes not only from taking action but also from having the courage to lead and, sometimes, to admit defeat. But he wasn't defeated…yet. And that would never happen as long as he was still breathing.

Like his father told him on his twelfth birthday when he gave him the 30-40 Krag brass shell casing fired by his great-uncle at San Juan Hill, *"Remember, Theodore—every Roosevelt must carry his own hill. Don't let the name carry you. You carry it."* He would continue to carry that hill and make his father and the original Rough Rider, the Colonel, proud of him.

At that moment, he realized something—he was standing at a crossroads, facing his great-uncle's legacy and his father's. It wasn't just about the battles they fought but also the principles both men upheld throughout their lives. Theodore Roosevelt IV was ready to carry that torch forward, lighting the way for others to follow, wherever it might lead him.

Glossary

Military and Intelligence Acronyms and Terms:

1. AK-47:
It is officially called the Avtomat Kalashnikova Model 1947 and is a widely used assault rifle around the world. Designed by Mikhail Kalashnikov, it is chambered for the 7.62x39mm cartridge. The rifle features a gas-operated, rotating bolt mechanism and can fire in both semi-automatic and fully automatic modes, with a cyclic rate of roughly 600 rounds per minute.

2. AO (Area of Operations):
An AO is a specified geographic area where military forces conduct active missions. It determines where units are permitted to move, engage, and coordinate their operations.

3. Article 32 Hearing:
A preliminary hearing under the Uniform Code of Military Justice (UCMJ) to determine if there is sufficient evidence to move forward with a court-martial.

4. Army JAG (Judge Advocate General's Corps):
The legal branch of the U.S. Army that provides legal services to soldiers, including advice on military law, criminal defense, and legal assistance. JAG officers serve as attorneys and manage various legal matters, such as court-martial proceedings and administrative law.

5. C-4 or Composition C-4:
A type of plastic explosive containing 91% RDX, a powerful explosive, combined with plasticizers and binders to give it a moldable, clay-like texture. It is commonly used in military operations for demolition and tactical purposes because of its effectiveness and flexibility. The explosive remains stable under normal conditions, does not easily detonate, and requires a detonator to trigger an explosion. It can burn and was used in Vietnam as a means to heat C-rations.

6. CAR-15:
It is a lightweight, air-cooled, gas-operated, magazine-fed assault rifle developed in the 1960s as a variant of the M16 rifle. It features a shorter barrel and a collapsible stock, making it more compact and easier to handle in close-quarters situations. This design benefits special operations and urban warfare. It typically fires the 5.56x45mm NATO cartridge, known for its low recoil and high velocity.

7. CIA (Central Intelligence Agency):
A U.S. government agency responsible for collecting and analyzing foreign intelligence to support the national security of the United States. Established in 1947, it conducts intelligence operations, including covert actions, and provides policymakers with vital information.

8. CID (Criminal Investigation Division):
The branch of the U.S. Army responsible for investigating felony crimes, war crimes, and intelligence-related offenses within Army jurisdiction.

9. Claymore Mine:
Directional anti-personnel mine (M18A1) used by U.S. forces. When triggered, it releases steel balls in a fan-shaped spray, causing severe damage within its 60-degree arc.

10. COLT M1911A1:
A .45 caliber semi-automatic pistol that was widely used by the United States Armed Forces. It is an updated version of the original M1911, designed by John Browning and adopted by the U.S. military in 1911.

11. CONUS (Continental United States):
A military abbreviation for the 48 contiguous states of the U.S., excluding Alaska and Hawaii.

12. Cutout:
An intermediary or third party is used to transmit information or orders between two parties. The purpose of using cutouts is to maintain secrecy and prevent direct contact among those involved in sensitive operations. By relaying information through cutouts, identities are protected, and information remains separate, ensuring no single person has access to all aspects of a sensitive operation. This method improves security and reduces exposure.

13. Danger Close:
A term used when requesting fire support—such as artillery, airstrikes, or mortars—that indicates friendly forces are very close to the target and require extreme caution.

14. Det Cord (Detonation Cord):
A flexible explosive tubing used to connect charges for simultaneous detonation. Burns at approximately 7,000–8,000 meters per second and is highly reliable in combat demolitions.

15. DIA (Defense Intelligence Agency):
A combat support agency within the U.S. Department of Defense that provides military intelligence for strategic and operational purposes.

16. Drop Signal:
A covert signal placed at a specific location to verify contact, show a safe route, or indicate the delivery or collection of information. In black-ops activities, drop signals are often improvised and cryptic to avoid detection.

17. DSCS (Defense Satellite Communications System):
The military satellite communication system was employed to provide secure voice and data links for military operations in the 1970s.

18. Freedom Bird:
A colloquial phrase used by U.S. military personnel during the Vietnam War to describe the aircraft that transported soldiers back to the United States after their tours of duty.

19. G-2:
The military intelligence staff in the United States Army at the divisional level and above is usually led by a Lieutenant General. It is distinct from roles such as G–1 (personnel), G–3 (operations), G–4 (logistics), G-5 (planning), G-6 (network), G-7 (training), G-8 (finance), and G-9 (civil-military operations). G-2, responsible for intelligence gathering and analysis, has roots dating back to the American Revolution. The Military Intelligence Service was established during World War II and later evolved into the Military Intelligence Corps, one of the primary branches of the United States Army.

20. Hooah:
A U.S. Army phrase used to show high morale, spirit, or affirmation. It can mean anything from "understood" to "hell, yes." Common in military culture, it's often shouted during physical training, operations, or speeches to unify teams.

21. Joint Personnel Recovery Center (JPRC):
A task force within the Military Assistance Command, Vietnam (MACV), active from 1966 to 1973, focused on locating and recovering U.S. and allied personnel listed as Prisoners of War (POWs) or Missing in Action (MIA) during the Vietnam War.

22. KA-BAR:
A fixed-blade combat knife with a 7-inch high-carbon steel blade and a handle made of Kraton or leather. It was adopted by the U.S. Marine Corps during World War II and is used by the Special Forces due to its reliability and performance in the field.

23. Khmer Rouge:
A brutal communist movement that ruled Cambodia from 1975 to 1979 under Pol Pot. Known for genocide and forced labor, they were an active threat in the region throughout the Vietnam War era.

24. M16:
This is a military rifle that has been the standard issue firearm for the United States Armed Forces since the 1960s. It is chambered for the 5.56x45mm NATO cartridge, known for its high velocity and low recoil, and features a gas-operated, rotating bolt mechanism. The rifle can operate in semi-automatic and fully automatic modes, depending on the specific variant. The M16A2, for example, offers a three-round burst mode instead of fully automatic.

25. M72 LAW:
A lightweight, portable, single-use rocket launcher designed for anti-tank and anti-armor purposes, suitable for infantry units. The M72 LAW had a range of about 200 meters (656 feet) and was effective against lightly armored vehicles.

26. MACV-SOG (Military Assistance Command, Vietnam – Studies and Observations Group):
A highly classified, multi-service special operations unit during the Vietnam War that conducted reconnaissance, sabotage, and psychological warfare missions in Vietnam, Laos, and Cambodia. It carried out covert operations in Laos, Cambodia, and North Vietnam from 1964 to 1972.

27. MP (Military Police):
The enforcement division of military law within the armed forces. In the manuscript, MPs at Firebase Buttons and later at Fort Bragg are responsible for arresting, detaining, and transporting Colonel Roosevelt's team.

28. NOFORN (Not Releasable to Foreign Nationals):
It is a marking used on classified documents to show that the information inside should not be shared with foreign nationals or entities, regardless of their security clearance level.

29. NVA (North Vietnamese Army):
The regular army of North Vietnam, separate from the Viet Cong insurgents operating in the south, is known for its well-trained, uniformed units and involvement in large-scale battles.

30. Pathet Lao:
A communist political and military group in Laos allied with the NVA. Played a key role in the Laotian Civil War and collaborated on operations along the Ho Chi Minh Trail.

31. Penetrator:
A rescue device lowered from helicopters to extract personnel in confined or hazardous areas.

32. Phonetic Alphabet:
The NATO phonetic alphabet is used to clearly spell out letters during radio communications.

A   Alpha
B   Bravo
C   Charlie
D   Delta
E   Echo
F   Foxtrot
G   Golf
H   Hotel
I   India
J   Juliet
K   Kilo
L   Lima
M   Mike
N   November
O   Oscar
P   Papa
Q   Quebec
R   Romeo
S   Sierra
T   Tango
U   Uniform
V   Victor
W   Whiskey
X   X-Ray
Y   Yankee
Z   Zulu

33. PLAAF (People's Liberation Army Air Force):
The air warfare branch of China's military. Referenced in operations involving Chinese equipment, surveillance, or indirect support during regional conflicts.

34. PRC-25 / PRC-77:
Man-portable field radios used during the Vietnam War for secure voice communication between Allied forces. The PRC-77 is an improved version of the PRC-25 with better electronics and greater compatibility with encryption equipment.

35. PRC-6 Radio Receiver Transmitter:
A portable, battery-powered two-way radio transceiver used by the U.S. military, mainly during the Vietnam War. It operates in the VHF band and is designed for short-range communication, providing durable reliability for field use.

36. SIGINT (Signals Intelligence):
Intelligence gathered from intercepting communications, radar, or other electronic signals. Crucial for locating enemies or verifying covert operations.

37. Signal for Extraction:
A specific signal or code used to indicate that troops or equipment should be evacuated or that an air drop is about to happen. This could involve visual signals, radio communication, or pre-arranged codes.

38. Sitrep (Situation Report):
A short summary of a unit's current status or tactical update.

39. Special Forces (Green Berets):
An elite unit of the U.S. Army specializing in unconventional warfare, foreign internal defense, counterterrorism, direct action, and special reconnaissance. Officially called the U.S. Army Special Forces, these units are highly trained for operations behind enemy lines, often working in small teams to train and support indigenous forces or execute high-risk missions. Their distinctive green beret, authorized by President John F. Kennedy in 1961, symbolizes their independence, adaptability, and expertise in asymmetrical warfare.

40. Tango:
The military phonetic code for the letter "T" is often used to identify enemy combatants or hostiles during radio transmissions. Example: "Two tangos spotted at grid 441."

41. Tiger-striped Fatigues:
A camouflage pattern created for jungle combat, first used by the South Vietnamese Armed Forces and later adopted by U.S. Special Forces during the Vietnam War. The design features thin green and brown stripes resembling a tiger's stripes, helping soldiers blend into dense jungle environments.

42. TOC (Tactical Operations Center):
A forward command post used to coordinate missions, track movements, and manage tactical decisions during live operations.

43. UCMJ (Uniform Code of Military Justice):
A federal law enacted in 1950 that establishes the legal framework for the United States military justice system. It governs the conduct of Armed Forces members, defining offenses, procedures, and penalties for violating military law. The UCMJ applies to all active-duty personnel, reservists, and National Guard members when in federal service, ensuring discipline and order within the military.

44. UH-1 Iroquois (Huey):
A utility military helicopter built and manufactured by the American aerospace company Bell Helicopter. It is the first turbine-powered helicopter to serve with the United States military. Originally designated HU-1, it earned the nickname Huey, which remained in everyday use even after the official redesignation to UH-1 in 1962.

45. Viet Cong (VC):
Guerrilla insurgents operating in South Vietnam, aligned with the North Vietnamese government, are known for ambushes, sabotage, and blending in with civilian populations.

46. Wet Boy:
Black-world slang for a covert agent who specializes in wet work—such as assassinations, sabotage, or secret eliminations. Operates with plausible deniability under deep-cover protocols.

Key Characters and their Callsigns/Names:

1. Colonel Theodore "Teddy" Roosevelt IV ("Bull" or "Bull Moose"):
Main protagonist, a decorated Special Forces officer and distant relative of President Theodore Roosevelt. Known for leadership, strategic thinking, and loyalty. Family legacy in the military dating back to the Rough Riders. Graduate of West Point, class of 1955. Former Green Beret turned covert operations specialist. He earned the nickname Bull for his ability to charge through bureaucratic red tape and battlefield chaos alike. Involved in a classified reconnaissance advisory group operating along the Ho Chi Minh Trail. Additional call sign for covert operations—" Rough Rider."

2. Captain Jack Stratton ("Ghost"):
Former Army intelligence officer and linguist—fluent in multiple languages, master of disguise and covert infiltration. Silver-tongued former Army Intelligence officer. Grew up bouncing between foster homes in Southern California. Brilliant at infiltration, language, and psychological operations. Called "Ghost" for his ability to vanish into civilian populations near enemy lines, flawlessly assume roles, and then reappear with actionable intelligence. He served alongside Roosevelt in Laos.

3. Master Sergeant Eli Red Horse ("Stone"):
Oglala Lakota Sioux, demolition expert and close combat specialist, remains calm and composed under fire. Born on the Pine Ridge Reservation in South Dakota, he served with distinction as a heavy weapons and engineering specialist, as well as a hand-to-hand combat instructor. He has a towering build, is soft-spoken, and deeply loyal. Known as "Stone" for his calm, unyielding presence in combat.

4. Colonel Vincent Cross ("Iron Vince"):
Former CID investigator turned Military Intelligence officer, friend of Colonel Roosevelt. A career military officer who takes pride in duty and order. Stoic, skeptical, but ultimately loyal to justice. Known as "Iron Vince," a nickname he earned for his strict discipline in combat zones.

5. Major General Franklin A. Dorsey:

A high-ranking officer who authorized Operation Firelight. As a senior figure in the shadow world of intelligence, Dorsey operates beyond agency limits, managing covert missions through hidden funding and unofficial chains of command. He speaks in veiled threats wrapped in politeness and is rarely seen without Kohrs nearby. Dorsey's methods appear bureaucratic on the surface but are deadly underneath—covering paper trails, burying missions, and choosing scapegoats. He embodies the true face of American deniability: urbane, calculated, and ruthlessly patriotic. Working under Dorsey means realizing too late that compliance isn't safety, and silence is survival.

6. Colonel Martin Kohrs (The Cleaner):

A covert CIA operative operating undercover, Kohrs is known in black-world circles as a "wet boy"—an agent who specializes in deniable killings, asset neutralization, and psychological intimidation. Cold, precise, and always quiet, Kohrs never raises his voice or repeats himself. He's Dorsey's trusted assistant, often sent in when fear alone must do the talking. His presence serves as a warning: someone in the room is already dead—they just don't know it yet. Kohrs moves like an assassin, lean and still, with movements that never waste energy. Officially, he doesn't exist. Unofficially, his name is whispered by those who understand the high cost of crossing the line.

7. Lt. Commander Nathan Kaufman (The Ghost Handler):

A Naval Intelligence officer, Kaufman, worked undercover as a liaison between Roosevelt's team and Langley during the planning and execution of Operation Firelight. Although he was never officially part of the CIA, his clearance and conduct indicated strong ties to the clandestine world. He operated in the shadows—never issuing direct commands, only passing sealed packets and verbal summaries to Roosevelt as part of interagency coordination. He provided the initial intelligence for Firelight, including vague satellite images, unauthenticated SIGINT, and a broken target profile. His involvement suggested that the mission was unusual. When Roosevelt refused to carry out the final phase, Kaufman disappeared. His disappearance confirmed the extent of the cover-up and how essential Shadow Lance had become. Some believe he was a fall guy. Others think he was the mastermind. Roosevelt still isn't sure which would be worse.

8. Christopher Armstrong:

Official CIA liaison for Operation Firelight and other covert missions in Southeast Asia, Armstrong handles orders that no one else wants to be traced. He specializes in ambiguous directives, verbal-only mission briefings, and "ghost protocols" designed to keep operations hidden at all levels. Calm, precise, and dressed like an aid worker or journalist depending on the day, Armstrong appears cooperative and professional—but he is fully Langley underneath. When Teddy refused to carry out the final phase of Firelight, it was Armstrong who cut the team loose. He didn't need to threaten them. His silence was enough.

9. Shadow Lance:

An off-the-books Special Forces team formed under MACV-SOG with covert CIA support during the Vietnam War. Composed of elite operators from Special Forces, Intelligence, and Indigenous Warfare units, Shadow Lance was never officially activated or disbanded. Their primary mission—Operation Firelight—was to monitor Chinese weapons trafficking through Laos and Cambodia, but it was later exposed as a false-flag operation to justify U.S. intervention. Betrayed and left behind, Shadow Lance was framed for atrocities they didn't commit.

Operation Names and Terms:

1. Operation Firelight:

A fictional covert Vietnam-era operation involving MACV-SOG with CIA support was officially created to monitor Chinese arms-smuggling routes supplying the Khmer Rouge through secret Laotian villagers. Unbeknownst to Colonel Roosevelt and his team, it was actually a CIA-backed false-flag operation intended to justify future U.S. military intervention in Laos by planting evidence of Chinese atrocities to eliminate the Pathet Lao. When Roosevelt discovered this deception and attempted to stop the false-flag scheme, his team was cut off, blamed for a massacre they didn't commit, and arrested upon returning to Vietnam. The team was codenamed Shadow Lance.

2. Operation Midnight Echo:

A covert cross-border demolition mission called Operation Midnight Echo was carried out by Shadow Lance early on November 24, 1970. It was officially ordered to destroy a Viet Cong supply cache in southern Laos based on secret intelligence. The orders arrived by courier with no information about their source, and the map overlays seemed overly detailed—an early warning sign that was ignored due to the team's busy schedule. Once they infiltrated, Roosevelt's team discovered the structure was actually a civilian hut, not a military staging area. Although they saw noncombatants, the demolition charges had already been set, and the hut was destroyed, injuring a local teenage boy and leaving the team shaken. This event marked a turning point in Roosevelt's disillusionment with black-world orders, confirming that civilian targets were being camouflaged as enemy assets for strategic deception. Midnight Echo was never documented, reported, or acknowledged—but it remained etched in the conscience of every man who escaped the flames.

3. Operation Shatterhorn:

A covert 1971 mission under MACV-SOG targeted rogue CIA activities near the Bolaven Plateau. Its goal was to map unauthorized operations and recover stolen SIGINT equipment, but it fell apart when their extraction point was ambushed. Most of the team was killed. Roosevelt survived with serious injuries after days in the jungle. Shatterhorn was buried, and Roosevelt was quietly transitioned into black-ops activities.

4. Operation Silent Arrow:

A covert reconnaissance and sabotage mission conducted by Shadow Lance in southern Laos on November 14, 1970. The objective was to infiltrate a suspected enemy weapons depot, verify its contents, and disrupt the supply chain. The team discovered U.S.-issued weapons, ammunition, and medical supplies—brand new and officially requisitioned—being directly funneled to enemy forces. Among the cache was a manifest signed by DIA planner MG F. A. Dorsey, revealing a sanctioned black-world operation called "Black Lotus." The discovery confirmed corruption at the highest levels of strategic command. Shadow Lance destroyed the camp and escaped with the evidence, marking Silent Arrow as the first direct proof that U.S. intelligence assets were supplying enemy camps in Laos.

5. Operation Wild Lantern:

A false flag operation within Operation Firelight was staged as a raid on a Chinese-backed weapons depot in Laos. Shadow Lance was sent with vague orders and false intelligence, only to find a civilian village already slaughtered. There were no weapons—just fake evidence and corpses. The team realized they had been set up to justify the massacre and take the blame.

Related Operational Terms:

1. Beaucoup dinky dau:

Derived from the French-Vietnamese phrase beaucoup dien cai dau, which means very crazy. It was commonly used by American soldiers during the Vietnam War to describe people or situations that seemed absurd or irrational.

2. Black-World Asset:

A covert operative used in highly classified missions so secret that their existence can be denied. Often employed for tasks that are not acknowledged in any official record.

3. Black-World Operation (Black Ops):

Covert or clandestine operations carried out with extreme secrecy, often without official acknowledgment, plausible deniability, and minimal oversight. Fully deniable, undocumented government activities. Frequently kept off budgets and hidden from congressional oversight.

4. Bolaven Plateau:

A rugged area in southern Laos that was a secret strategic zone during the Vietnam War. In this novel, it serves as part of the team's escape route after being burned during Operation Firelight.

5. Burn Folder/Burn Notice/Burn Vault:

A classified folder or communication used in covert operations that can be quickly destroyed or disavowed if compromised.
  a. Burn notice: An official order that disavows a field agent or operation, ending all support.
  b. Burn vault: a secure chamber used to permanently destroy or seal classified materials.

6. CONEX Box:
Shipping containers used for transporting goods.

7. Dead Drop:
A secret method of communication or transferring materials, usually in a pre-arranged location without direct contact. Roosevelt uses one to activate an old contact and facilitate their escape.

8. Dead Man's Hand:
A famous poker hand associated with the death of Wild Bill Hickok, a well-known figure of the American Old West. The hand symbolizes both luck and misfortune, with some players viewing it as unlucky because of its connection to Hickok's tragic end. It is commonly recognized as a two-pair hand consisting of black aces and black eights (A♠ A♣ 8♠ 8♣). An unknown fifth card, often speculated to be a queen (Q♣ or Q♥), is considered a kicker.

9. Delta-One-Niner-Black:
A covert, legacy activation phrase used to trigger interference protocols embedded in deep black-world networks. Unlike formal extraction codes or support requests, this phrase does not summon help—it initiates limited disruptions designed to delay, confuse, or stall adversarial actions long enough for an asset to respond. Often linked to buried contacts, dead-drop systems, or old signal paths, it was reserved for extreme circumstances when a black-world operative was marked for elimination or erasure. Considered a last resort.

10. Directive Seven-Two:
A classified fail-safe overseen by the Joint Chiefs and Operation Subnet Echo activates only when a trusted asset faces elimination by rogue internal command elements. Once triggered via the Legacy Protocol, Directive Seven-Two enables controlled exposure of compromised networks through intelligence leaks, financial triggers, and disruption of covert infrastructure. It is not designed to save the asset. It aims to destroy the system attempting to erase them. Originally rooted in the dismantled Mongoose List (a post-Bay of Pigs CIA/Phoenix offshoot targeting politically protected assets), Directive Seven-Two targets those who abuse black-world authority to silence dissent. It has only been activated twice in recorded history. The consequences are irreversible—and usually permanent.

11. False-Flag Operation:
A covert operation designed to appear as if it was conducted by someone else, intended to deceive or influence perception for political or strategic advantage.

12. Ghost Protocol:
A verbal-only command system used by the CIA in covert operations. Orders are kept secret to protect the personnel issuing them. Used during Operation Firelight.

13. Legacy Protocol:
A secret black-world contingency within Operation Subnet Echo's structure. Triggered by a hidden phrase—Delta-One-Niner-Black—spoken over a secure, legacy-monitored line, the Legacy Protocol acts as a last-resort signal from a presumed-dead or compromised asset. Once activated, it quietly alerts dormant counterintelligence units that the asset remains active, alive, and under threat from hostile internal forces. Unlike overt rescue efforts, the Legacy Protocol does not send reinforcements or establish direct contact. Instead, it awakens silent allies, initiates automated countermeasures, and redirects surveillance—giving the asset time to vanish or prepare for fallout. The Legacy Protocol isn't an extraction. It's a covert signal buried deep within the intelligence community's archives, meant only for those who know how to find it.

14. Medevac:
Short for "medical evacuation," this term generally refers to helicopter transport, known as "dust off," used to move injured personnel from the field to medical facilities.

15. PRC (People's Republic of China):
The official name of the country commonly known as China, established on October 1, 1949, after the Chinese Civil War. It is a unitary Marxist-Leninist one-party socialist republic led by the Chinese Communist Party (CCP) and the Nationalist Party (Kuomintang, KMT). China supported communist forces in North Vietnam and Laos by providing military aid, logistical support, and political backing.

16. Rượu cần:
A fermented rice wine in Vietnam made from fermented glutinous rice (nếp), chewed by the women of the Montagnards, and mixed with various herbs (including leaves and roots) from local forests. The mixture is then poured into a large earthenware jug, covered, and allowed to ferment for at least one month. Its alcohol content typically ranges from 15 to 25 percent by volume.

17. Safehouse:
A secure location used for refuge, planning, or fallback after missions. The fallback safe house outside Paksé has been cleared out, indicating betrayal.

18. Signal Received:
A confirmation of contact through black-world channels. In this novel, this is delivered via a subtle message on Roosevelt's breakfast tray while he is held in the Ft. Bragg stockade.

19. Stockade:
A military prison facility. At Fort Bragg, this is where the team is detained and held while awaiting nonexistent legal proceedings.

20. Wet Work / Cleaner:
A term for the assassination or covert elimination of threats. Kohrs is described as a CIA "cleaner"—lethal, precise, and employed when plausible deniability is necessary.

United States Military Academy (West Point) Terms:

1. Area Tour:
One hour of full-dress punishment, under arms, marching in front of the barracks while in uniform. Not open to the general public. Area—the large quad bordered by Old South Barracks, Nininger Hall, Old Cadet Barracks, and Central Barracks. Formations and tours take place here.

2. Brace or Grab Some Wrinkles:
Craning your neck back until your chin was level with your neck, causing wrinkles. Punitive neck retraction and painful. A form of hazing.

3. Dumb Squat, Beanhead, Beaner, Smackhead
All derogatory terms used by upperclassmen cadets to refer to Plebes (first-year cadets).

4. Firstie:
A senior upperclass cadet, First Classman, in their fourth year at West Point, holds the highest rank among cadets. They are often seen as leaders and role models for younger cadets, taking on various responsibilities, including mentoring underclassmen, leading training exercises, and assuming leadership roles within the cadet organization. They play a vital role in upholding the academy's standards and traditions. Their position is signified by a red sash worn around the waist, hanging behind the hip, and the cadet officers carry swords under arms instead of rifles.

5. Ghost:
A cadet who avoids his responsibilities.

6. Plebe:
Freshman cadet, fourth-classman, and the newest members of the cadet corps in their first year are beginning their military education and training while holding the lowest rank in the Corps of Cadets. The Plebe year is a significant transition period where cadets adapt to a demanding academic and military environment. They undergo intense training, including physical fitness, military drills, and leadership development. (The lowest of the low.) From Bugle Notes: What do plebes rank?—" Sir, the Superintendent's dog, the Commandant's cat, the waiters in the Mess Hall, the Hell Cats, the Generals in the Air Force, and all the Admirals in the whole damned Navy."

7. Quill:
USMA Form 2-1 is used to record cadets' poor performance and document deficiencies that lead to demerits, often called being "gigged." For Plebes, the 4-C, 4th class deficiency report was used. To add to the humiliation, the Plebe had to deliver it to the upperclassman.

8. Swim to Newburg:
A type of hazing where a Plebe climbs onto the alcove rail, lies across it, and "swims" until told to stop.

9. Tool:
A cadet who believes he knows everything or acts like he does.

10. White Tornado:
A type of hazing where a Plebe is made to eat all the condiments on the table in Washington Hall.

Medical Terms:

1. Antipyretics:
Substances that lower fever help the body reduce its temperature. They work by signaling the hypothalamus in the brain to lower the body's temperature. This process helps relieve the discomfort caused by fever.

2. Broad-Spectrum Antibiotics:
A class of antibiotics that targets a wide range of bacteria. These were commonly used in Vietnam to prevent or treat infections from battlefield wounds, including those caused by Staph aureus or Pseudomonas. Examples of this include gentamicin and cephalothin.

3. Dorsalis Pedis:
An important artery in the foot, originating from the anterior tibial artery, is vital for supplying blood to the dorsal (top) part of the foot. It branches into several arteries, including the medial and lateral tarsal arteries, which deliver blood to the tarsal bones and surrounding tissues. The pulse can be felt to assess blood flow to the foot and is often checked in clinical settings to evaluate peripheral circulation.

4. Drainage Tube:
A medical device used to extract fluids such as blood, pus, or other bodily fluids from a wound, abscess, or body cavity. These tubes are usually made of flexible materials and can differ in size and design depending on their specific use.

5. Evacuation Hospital:
A fully equipped Army hospital located in-theater but behind combat zones, such as the 85th Evacuation Hospital at Phu Bai or the 95th Evacuation Hospital at China Beach near Saigon. These facilities handled serious injuries requiring surgery, intensive care, or extended recovery before transfer to CONUS hospitals.

6. Fever Spike:
A sudden, sharp rise in body temperature, often indicating infection or sepsis in a post-operative patient. Monitoring fever spikes was crucial in Vietnam-era military medicine to detect early signs of complications.

7. Gangrene:
Gangrene is a serious medical condition in which body tissue dies due to lack of blood flow, infection, or injury. It can occur in any part of the body but is most common in the extremities, such as fingers, toes, and limbs. There are two main types of gangrene.

1. Dry Gangrene happens when blood flow to a specific area decreases, often due to conditions such as diabetes or atherosclerosis. The affected tissue becomes dry, shriveled, and discolored.
2. Wet Gangrene: This type is associated with bacterial infection and can develop rapidly. It is characterized by swelling, blisters, and a foul odor, and it can quickly spread to surrounding tissues.

8. ICU (Intensive Care Unit):
A specialized hospital unit dedicated to close monitoring and life-saving treatment for critically ill or postoperative patients. Roosevelt spends time in the ICU during his most vulnerable recovery phase.

9. Intramedullary Nail (or rod):
A medical device used in orthopedic surgery to stabilize fractured long bones, such as the femur or tibia. Inserted into the medullary canal, it provides internal support, keeps the bones aligned during healing, and allows early movement. This procedure offers a faster recovery than traditional methods like casting. However, it also carries risks, including potential infection and the need for later removal. Intramedullary fixation was a common orthopedic procedure by the 1970s, especially in military hospitals.

10. Intravenous Fluids (IV):
Sterile fluids administered directly into a vein to maintain hydration, deliver medications, or support blood pressure in trauma patients. In the manuscript, IV drips are part of Teddy's post-op stabilization and infection treatment.

11. Ketamine:
Developed in the 1960s and used as a battlefield anesthetic during the Vietnam War because of its unique properties, including rapid onset and safety for unstable patients, it provided effective anesthesia with quick recovery, making it suitable for emergencies. Ketamine offers rapid anesthesia, enabling immediate surgical intervention. Its use does not require extensive monitoring equipment, making it ideal for field conditions.

12. Narrow-Spectrum Antibiotics:
A class of antibiotics that target a limited range of bacteria, typically Gram-positive or Gram-negative organisms. They are intended to treat infections caused by specific pathogens while minimizing effects on the body's normal flora and reducing the risk of antibiotic resistance. Examples of narrow-spectrum antibiotics include penicillin, cefazolin, and vancomycin.

13. ORIF (Open Reduction and Internal Fixation):
A surgical procedure to realign and stabilize a broken bone using hardware such as plates, screws, or rods. "Open reduction" involves surgically exposing the fracture, while "internal fixation" refers to placing hardware inside the body to hold the bones in place. It is often used for complex or compound fractures.

14. Percussion Tenderness:
A diagnostic sign where gentle tapping on an area causes pain, suggesting possible internal inflammation or infection. In the novel, early signs of Teddy's infection are identified through clinical indicators like these.

15. Purulent Drainage:
A thick, yellow, green, or brown fluid produced by the body in response to infection. It mainly consists of pus, a mixture of dead white blood cells, bacteria, and tissue debris. Purulent drainage is often found in wounds, abscesses, or infections and can indicate an ongoing infection that may need medical evaluation and treatment. (Example: Abscess Drainage—a minor surgical procedure to relieve pressure and remove pus from a localized infection beneath the skin or in deeper tissues. It is a common complication in battlefield wounds or surgical cases, especially in tropical environments.)

16. Rongeur:

A heavy-duty surgical instrument with a sharp-edged, scoop-shaped tip used for gouging out bone. Rongeur is a French word meaning rodent or "gnawer." It can be used to open a window in bone to access tissue underneath. They are used in neurosurgery, podiatric surgery, maxillofacial surgery, and orthopedic surgery to expose areas for operation.

17. Sepsis:

A life-threatening condition caused by the body's severe reaction to an infection, leading to widespread inflammation, tissue damage, and possible organ failure. It requires urgent medical attention to prevent serious complications or death.

18. Soft Tissue Trauma:

Damage to muscles, ligaments, or skin that does not involve the bone is common in blast injuries, falls, or crushing trauma. In Roosevelt's case, soft tissue injuries add to the complexity of his fracture and increase the risk of infection.

19. Staph Infection:

Short for *Staphylococcus aureus*, this bacterial infection frequently affects surgical wounds, especially in hot, humid climates like those in Southeast Asia. In the manuscript, Roosevelt develops a serious staph infection after surgery, which delays his discharge and significantly risks his recovery.

20. Wound Debridement:

The medical removal of dead, damaged, or infected tissue from a wound to promote healing and prevent infection. Field surgeons and evac hospitals often performed manual debridement using scalpels, forceps, or irrigation under sterile conditions—sometimes urgently during post-combat triage.

Maps

Vietnam

Cambodia

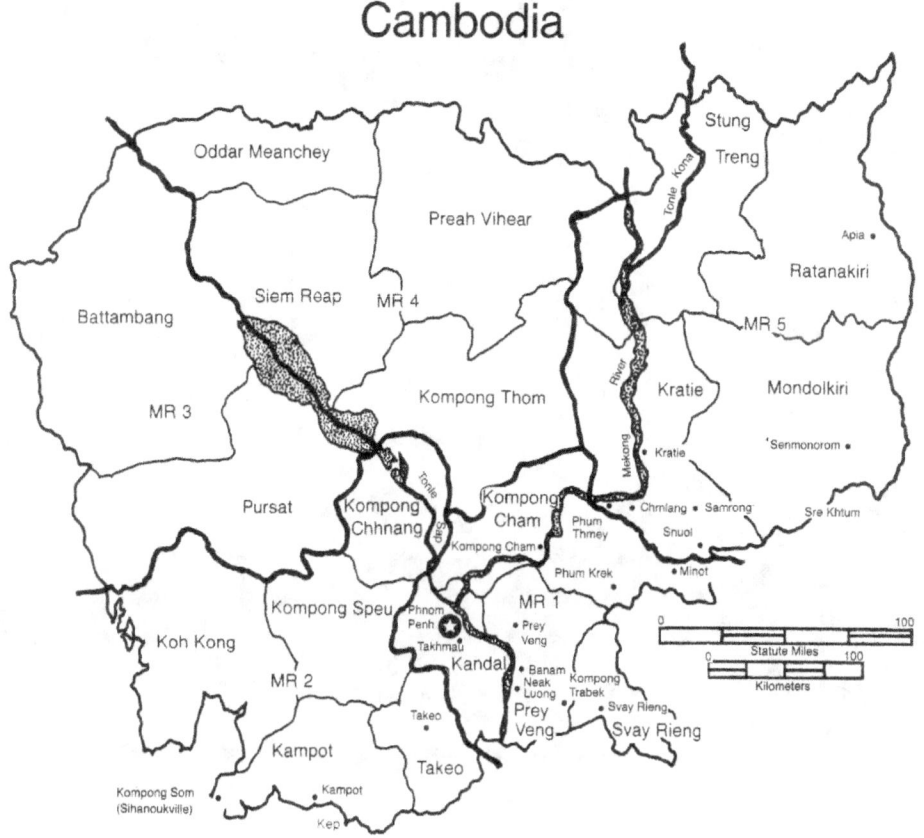